MODERN PHILIPPINE SHORT STORIES

FRANCISCO ARCELLANA

MANUEL ARGUILLA

AMADOR DAGUIO

RONY V. DIAZ

N. V. M. GONZALEZ

NICK JOAQUIN

HERMEL A. NUYDA

BIENVENIDO N. SANTOS

EDITH L. TIEMPO

EDITED BY

LEONARD CASPER

THE UNIVERSITY OF NEW MEXICO PRESS

MODERN
PHILIPPINE
SHORT STORIES

The bird-shaped design on the title page is called *sari-manok,*
a festive symbol, derived from photograph of a brass rouge container
exhibited at the Mindanao Folk Arts Village, Davao.
Drawing by Richard Kurman.

© *THE UNIVERSITY OF NEW MEXICO PRESS* 1962

Composed, printed and bound at the University of New Mexico
Printing Plant, Albuquerque, New Mexico, U. S. A.
Library of Congress Catalog Card No. 61-10048. First edition.

For Linda and Pipit
green circuits of the sun

CONTENTS

ACKNOWLEDGMENTS

1. "Wedding Dance" by Amador Daguio. Copyright 1953 by the Board of Trustees of the Leland Stanford Junior University and reprinted from *Stanford Short Stories 1953* by Wallace Stegner and Richard Scowcroft, editors, with the permission of the Stanford University Press and of the author.

2. "The Dead" by Amador Daguio. Copyright 1931 by the *Sunday Tribune Magazine* (Manila); copyright 1952 by the U. P. Writers Club (Quezon City) and reprinted by their permission and by permission of the author.

3. "Summer Solstice" by Nick Joaquin. Copyright 1951 by the Philippines Free Press and reprinted by their permission and by permission of the author.

4. "Three Generations" by Nick Joaquin. Copyright 1949 by Wake Editions; copyright 1952 by Graphic House (Manila). Reprinted by permission of Wake Editions and of the author.

5. "How My Brother Leon Brought Home a Wife" by Manuel Arguilla. Copyright 1936 by Story Magazine Inc.; copyright 1940 by the Philippine Book Guild, and reprinted by their permission and by permission of Lydia Arguilla.

6. "Epilogue to Revolt" by Manuel Arguilla. Copyright 1936 by the Philippines Free Press; copyright 1940 by the Philippine Book Guild, and reprinted by their permission and by permission of Lydia Arguilla.

7. "The Common Theme" by Bienvenido N. Santos. Copyright 1952 by the Manila Chronicle, *This Week Magazine,* and reprinted by their permission and by permission of the author.

8. "Scent of Apples" by Bienvenido N. Santos. Copyright 1948 by the Manila Chronicle, *This Week Magazine,* and reprinted by their permission and by permission of the author.

9. "Where's My Baby Now?" by N. V. M. Gonzalez. Copyright 1951 by the *Hopkins Review,* and reprinted by their permission and by permission of the author.

10. "Lupo and the River" by N. V. M. Gonzalez, Copyright 1953 by the *Diliman Review* (Quezon City), and reprinted by their permission and by permission of the author.

11. "A Warm Hand" by N. V. M. Gonzalez. Copyright 1950 by the *Sewanee Review,* and reprinted by their permission and by permission of the author.

12. "Death in a Sawmill" by Rony V. Diaz. Copyright 1954 by the U.P. Writers Club, and reprinted by their permission and by permission of the author.

13. "Two Brothers" by Rony V. Diaz. Copyright 1955 by the *Diliman Review;* copyright 1956 by *Panorama* and reprinted by their permission and by permission of the author.

14. "Chambers of the Sea" by Edith L. Tiempo. Copyright 1955 by the Philippines Free Press, and reprinted by their permission and by permission of the author. The epigraph to Edith L. Tiempo's Story is from *Collected Poems 1909-1935* by T. S. Eliot, copyright 1936 by Harcourt, Brace and World Inc., and reprinted with their permission.

15. "Divide by Two" by Francisco Arcellana. Copyright 1954 by the Manila Chronicle, *This Week Magazine,* and reprinted by their permission and by permission of the author.

16. "Pulse of the Land" by Hermel A. Nuyda. Copyright 1952 by Philippines Free Press, and reprinted by their permission and by permission of the author.

INTRODUCTION

THE SHORT STORIES which Jose Garcia Villa wrote as a
student at the University of New Mexico and, later, in a
walk-up Greenwich Village apartment cannot withstand the
increasingly professional inspection of Philippine critics.
Nevertheless, no Filipino writer wholly or willingly relin-
quishes his recollection of Edward J. O'Brien's high enthusi-
asm for Villa's prose. *The Best Short Stories of 1932* was
dedicated by O'Brien to Villa, one of whose stories was included in that year's collection while eleven others were
indexed among the distinctive. In addition, *Clay,* the mimeographed magazine migrant with Villa from New Mexico to
New York, was declared a prospective rival to *Story,* itself
otherwise unequaled, according to O'Brien, anywhere in the
world. Villa was in self-imposed exile less than three years
when Charles Scribner's Sons published *Footnote to Youth,*
a collection of his short fiction. This substantial achievement,
O'Brien declared in his introduction, placed Villa "among
the half-dozen short story writers in America who count." Just
as Filipinos cannot forget Villa's nomination for the 1943
Pulitzer Prize in poetry, they are obliged to remember how
O'Brien compared him with an earlier "discovery," Sherwood
Anderson.

Rarely are stories from *Footnote to Youth* anthologized
now, nearly thirty years later. Almost none are re-readable.
What O'Brien described in them as the "classical reticence of
form" is, more accurately, segregation of routine incident in

enumerated paragraphs resembling stanzas. To nearly all the stories a judge's comment, on the 1929 occasion of Villa's having won a *Philippines Free Press* literary award with a semi-allegorical fable, is appropriate: ". . . in spots there are traces of actual characterization. . . ." Although O'Brien prophesied a career for Villa as novelist, the writer himself found his sense of symbol and of cycle, his embarrassment when required to sustain narration, the sometimes bizarre wrenching of his words more appropriate to experiments with compact lyric poetry.

Yet Villa continues to be celebrated, not as one of the earliest Filipino writers of short stories in English nor as one of the best of the forerunners for all his faults: but as the envied *arrivé*. Those very countrymen from whom he disassociated himself so long, in so many ways, share his apotheosis abroad. While the Philippine nation, still on probation, slowly proved its right to political independence, significant writers were choosing English—a minority language—for their fiction, again and again, to test their equality among those whom they admired in America. How else, except by such motives of friendly comparison, can one explain the remarkable development of short fiction represented in this collection, after only sixty years of English in the islands? Lesser writers have been satisfied with imitation. The more mature have been rewarded with self-discovery, as surely as Teodor Josef Konrad Korzeniowski was, by the stringencies of public meditation in a foreign mode.

In 1900, it would have been impossible to predict such progress. American administrators, attempting to propagate general education for the first time, adopted English temporarily as the language of instruction in the absence of any native national language or textbooks. Characteristic of a crossroads culture, the Philippine national anthem was written in Spanish, under American rule, by a Filipino. After partial self-government was established in the 1930's, Quezon as the Commonwealth's first President encouraged the gradual transformation of Tagalog into a medium for inter-island communication and commerce. Nevertheless, in 1940 he offered generous national awards to literary works in English or Spanish, as well as in Tagalog.

Twenty years later the contest of languages and literatures still continues, in schoolhouse and press room. Although only the Commonwealth prize winners in English were ever published, this fact alone is no guarantee that a replacement will never be found for English, now that nationalism is at high pitch in Asia and Africa.[1] One can only say, reading the stories of Gonzalez, Joaquin, Daguio and Santos and realizing the folkways and historical accidents which might have been expected to prevent their appearance, that the unlikely has happened before and may happen again.

Because Spain's colonial administrators withheld education from impoverished *indios*, depriving them of any secure share in the Spanish renaissance, Spanish exists today largely as loan words, visibly modified, in Tagalog. Courses in the language are compulsory at the college level, but these have been protested by mass student rallies. The modern Filipino is likely to argue that the only literature of importance to him since Pigafetta's journal of Magellan's death, is the work of the Propaganda and Revolutionary periods, the nineteenth century's last two decades. The novels and essays of men like Rizal were written in Spanish and published in Madrid, in hope of changing colonial policy at the summit, and later were smuggled into the Philippines. As a result, Rizal, in spite of never having counseled armed revolt, was executed publicly as a traitor. His countrymen consider it ironic, under such cir-

---

1. See the author's discussion in "The Great Accommodation: Filipino-English," *South Atlantic Quarterly*, LIX (Spring 1690), 184-91; as well as "Reconnaissance in Manila," *Antioch Review*, XVII (Autumn 1957), 316-26.

cumstances, not to complete that historic rebellion by reading Rizal, del Pilar, Lopez-Jaena and others in Filipino vernaculars. Consequently, Spain's contributions to Philippine religion, its civil code, courtship, family folkways, the arts of jai-alai, food and dance will undoubtedly survive linguistic and literary legacies far less engrained.

When American generalship failed to clarify its intention as liberator of a Philippine people already in open, organized revolt against Spain since 1896, it too found hostile critics and endured a two-year "Fil-American War." The Malolos Constitution (drafted in Spanish and advocating adoption of the Spanish civil code) declared the country an independent republic under Aguinaldo, in 1899. All the vernaculars and Spanish itself—in the skilled accusations of Claro Recto and Teodoro Kalaw—were used to denounce as treachery America's decision to "civilize and Christianize" Filipinos who had been Catholics for centuries and whose culture was ancient! Only the Democratic Party's immediate proposal of Philippine independence as a campaign issue and Taft's remarkable civil rule could ameliorate the initial ill-feelings. Occupation troops in the *barrio* often served as teachers until mass public education could be systematized. By the time that most modern Filipino writers were born, the good will of America was clear (however errant, occasionally, its implementation); so there was no longer widespread resentment that English, rather than one of nine major native languages, had become the language of instruction.

Despite absence of a compulsory attendance law, the number of public school children rose from two hundred thousand in the last days of Spanish rule (indicative of last-minute increases in admissions because of public discontent) to two million under the Commonwealth.[2] Partly these statistics are

---

2. Robert Aura Smith, *Philippine Freedom, 1946-1958* (New York: Columbia University Press, 1958), p. 44.

accounted for by improvement in public health as well as in education. Infant mortality dropped from 80% to 5.4% by 1933. Americans found tuberculosis, malaria, and dysentery endemic, beriberi prevalent, leprosy widespread, cholera and smallpox killers: gradually Philippine sanitation became an example to the Orient. Writers who reached manhood in the midst of a fearful depression were consoled by the knowledge that their life-expectancy had increased from eighteen years to forty-six.[3] At the same time, participation in civil service and self-government gave this survival pattern more than statistical significance.

Although the convention which in 1934 drafted the Commonwealth's Constitution (adopted by the Republic, as well, in 1946) was multilingual, the Constitution itself was couched in English. The choice was dictated in part by the necessity of submitting the Constitution to the President of the United States; in part, by a people's gratitude for having been permitted exercise of their right to self-respect. The exceptional bravery of Filipinos which, during World War II, restricted movement of Japanese garrisons mainly to principal port areas was, similarly, an act of loyalty not only to their American allies but equally to their own proud aspirations.

Meanwhile, the importance which Philippine vernaculars had first assumed under the Commonwealth when an Institute of National Language was established with American approval, was augmented by their use as the language of underground conspiracy and, later, by the fact of the Republic's official independence. President Ramon Magsaysay's contribution to the movement was a practical one, a demonstration of personal fluency in several vernaculars while he tried to redeem democracy from disrepute by literally bringing government to the people. No world capital except Warsaw had been

---

3. *Sociology in the Philippine Setting,* ed. Chester Hunt, Richard Coller, *et al.* (Manila: Alemar's, 1954), p. 303.

more devastated than Manila during World War II. Moral damage done thousands of displaced persons multiplied in the presence of black markets and war surplus goods. President Roxas' sudden death in office and Quirino's weakness in the face of his party's corruption fed the nation's cynicism, abetting the Hukbalahaps' agrarian revolt against absentee landlords. Magsaysay, dedicated to restoration of domestic order, went daily among the *provincianos* and even held Cabinet meetings in the field, until his personal example of moral severity rallied the people.

Nevertheless, for a portion of the new generation the prospering of Tagalog was less inspirational than was the confidence coined by national recovery. These few individuals, while appreciative of the need for domestic solidarity, refused to let their country become wholly insular again. They used English so that their voices would carry overseas, just as the Philippines herself honored foreign commitments and assumed full international character in the U.N., the Korean War, SEATO and the Pacific Charter, as well as at the Bandung Conference.

The divisions between Philippine writers due to indecisions about the role of languages has been difficult for literature to endure. Increasingly the language of instruction for elementary grades is not English but the National Language, based on Tagalog, indigenous to roughly one-third of the population. In a typical provincial school, English is allotted thirty minutes daily throughout the first two elementary grades—with classes averaging between fifty and eighty children, often present on half-time basis.[4] Nearly half these students are

4. From Clifford H. Prator's mimeographed First Annual Report: Philippine-UCLA Language Program, August 1958, Appendix A-7; and confirmed in the Third Annual Report, June 1960. An initial stage in this ICA-Rockefeller-supported program has been the arrangement of elaborate field consultations, so that contrastive analyses can be made, for the first time, between English and Philippine languages. The exploratory procedures employed are the most prac-

forced, by economic necessity, to leave school before their fourth year and return to non-English-speaking communities. Even for the rest, English is actually a second (or third) language, despite the fact that lectures and textbooks are in English.

The circulation of Manila's daily newspapers in English (65 per cent of which are sent to the provinces) outnumbers, six to one, combined Chinese, Spanish, and Tagalog sales; but this ratio is reversed, one to four, among weekly magazines in which fiction appears, and some 300,000 comic books published fortnightly in Manila are all in the vernacular. So are all movies produced locally, although foreign films enjoy equal popularity. Where is the audience for the imaginative writer in English? What incentive drives him to write as well as he does even though publication of his book is delayed for months, to be squeezed in quickly by the press between runoffs of comic books and political broadsides? His book may win awards for beauty of type and binding, only to lie in warehouses afterwards, unpromoted except by the author's personal attention. Why does he bother? What persuasion urges him to give his best to Sunday supplements which, by Wednesday, may become torches for burning out nests of termites?

Partly the compulsion originates in the irresistible call of the white collar. In Spanish times knowledge of the language of the elite was required in a clerk, the highest position to which any *indio* might presume. (Intermarriage and especially distribution of power was encouraged only between the Spanish and former princes, or *datus,* who had become major landholders—*caciques.* The lot of the *mestiza* was enviable.)

---

tical ever applied to the Philippine language situation. The resultant descriptive grammars should be valuable to the Institute of National Language, whatever the ultimate disposition of English itself, as the normal schools and Philippine government bureaus assume full responsibility for the program beyond its initial phases.

Such a motive goes far to explain parallel phenomena: why today there are four teachers for every teaching position; or why, in a primarily rural country, there are four law students for every college agricultural student (in the U.S. the numbers are nearly even).[5] English has become identified with the educated classes—and office opportunities; while education, often an end in itself, is chiefly regarded as a status-symbol . . . nevertheless, no explanation will be complete which ignores the writer's faith, his capacity for dreams, his pride in achievement.

For pay and popularity the formula writer generally turns to Tagalog or Cebuano. With some notable exceptions, whose numbers have grown since the Palanca memorial awards for literature in the vernacular as well as in English were inaugurated in 1950, the more outstanding Filipino writers have chosen English for entrance to their insights. If they have accepted a limited readership, it is because they have felt their truths would be distorted by present traditions in the vernaculars. Artificial elegance, a Victorian sensibility, grand melodrama and elaborate plot contrivance (to compensate for skin-thin characterization)—these are "literary" conventions which do not respect experience. The writer's dilemma long has been that to be widely read, he cannot be profound, he dare not disturb false images. To write honestly *about* his people he must risk not writing *for* them. The quality of so much of English fiction in the Philippines depends on the difficult decision to put craft and art first, and to let readers founder if need be. Lately, however, serious attempts at bilingualism have been made by men of reputation in English. And should the time come when all major Filipino workers have to be read in translation, such men, far from having surrendered their integrity, will have improved literature in the vernacular

---

5. *Sociology in the Philippine Setting,* p. 397.

through their own encounters with Western concepts of organic form and fidelity to character. Far from being a pious hope, this recognizes the past salvage of their integrity from those privative human circumstances which have surrounded and informed the Philippine writer-as-citizen.

The impulse towards conservatism in the Philippines owes less perhaps to centuries of colonialism than to the rural nature of her society. Her estimated coal reserves are of such low grade that at best they could support only a small steel mill.[6] Most of her iron ore, therefore, has been sold to Japan for manufacturing. In the absence of oil deposits of her own, her claim to oil fields in North Borneo (within the jurisdiction of the Sultan of Sulu, a Philippine citizen) may prove crucial but shows little promise of prospering in international courts.[7] Meanwhile, the Philippines only now is beginning to enjoy fractional compensation through hydroelectric power.

Consequently, 40 per cent of the gross national product is still agricultural; 80 per cent of her population lives in small fishing *barrios* or on farms. Much of the rice land traditionally has been cultivated by tenant sharecroppers who, far from earning subsistence, annually have increased family indebtedness to grand *hacenderos*. The birthright of the young has been stark poverty in provinces such as Pampanga, once 70 per cent tenant-tilled, whose Candaba swamps used to be called Huklandia during the postwar revolts. Although Spanish rule ended slavery, it strengthened previous class distinctions by accepting former *datus* as *cabezas de barangays* (heads of subdivisions of a *pueblo* or municipality) or as *caciques*—large landholders and tax collectors. As a result of such special privileges for the few, many former freeholders

6. Warren S. Thompson, *Population and Progress in the Far East* (Chicago: University of Chicago Press, 1959), pp. 341-45.

7. Conrado Villafuente, "Disputed North Borneo," *Panorama*, X (April 1958), 15-20 *passim*.

were reduced to tenancy. So firm was this control system that American rule had difficulty reshaping it. Consequently the Philippine middle class—estimated at 10 per cent of the population—is especially rare in rural areas.[8]

Poverty and the unchanging practice of wet-rice agriculture are, in turn, as responsible as Chinese ancestor worship or Spanish patriarchal customs for the Philippine family's authoritarianism. All Souls' Day becomes a gathering of clans in every candle-lit cemetery, marked more by celebration than by mourning. Among the living even the most distant cousin is considered close kin and, wherever practicable, is domiciled communally with the rest. The greatest virtue is obedience, elders of each rank bearing special titles of respect. The individual often seems to exist for the family. This principle of seniority is so strictly enforced because the eldest brother, for example, inherits great family responsibility should the father die. Similarly absolute unity is required because for years the poor have had recourse, in adversity, to no one but their own kin. Nepotism is natural to such a system of group survival. So is strict chaperonage throughout courtship. Although introduced by Spaniards, it was readily accepted as an apparatus for parental supervision of the young man about to be absorbed into the family structure. Consequently, loyalty is often considered more enduring than love, after marriage.

Without drastic changes in economy, the Philippine family and society can hardly become less ingrown; but the *will* to change is often restricted by the arrested rise in literacy. In the first twenty years of this century the literacy level advanced from 20-40 per cent; however, the next forty years have not been able to increase the level far beyond 60 per cent. Even

---

8. One of the most informative descriptions of tenancy conditions occurs in F. Sionil Jose's "The Philippine Agrarian Problem," *Comment* 9 (Third quarter, 1959), pp. 85-143. In report form, this article won the 1958 National Press Club-Stanvac Journalism Award.

though this is high for the Orient, it hardly reflects extensive Philippine effort and expenditure. Are such dilemmas to be explained by heavy wartime tolls; the law of marginal returns; or the attrition of poverty? At present half the children cannot afford to study beyond fourth grade (although education is free); only one-fourth finish sixth grade.

In this otherwise oppressively circular labyrinth, the responsible writer's open mind and trained imagination act like a skylight and occasionally a portal. He suffers its effects, as man, with others; and is penalized for every reader disabled by it: but his own existence, almost in defiance of conditions, is persuasive of hidden possibility for the rest. By what grace does he care; does he not conform? The culture around him generates such irrational sentiment and quick oversensitiveness that courtesy expects truth to be shaped to the listener's requirements. The writer who is escapist accedes; romanticizes. Only the consecrated writer rebels; he has too much faith in what can be, to accept permanently whatever is; he reveals. He seems to sense, if not actually remember, the provocative historic interplay of foreign ways which have produced this native complex; and especially that time of ferment which has never really stopped, since its first stir during Propaganda and Revolutionary periods. In a society designed to be static, he is a force of transition, a sign of life. And fortunately he is not alone.

Earlier generations took heart—in the midst of revolt, depression, total war, corruption, and privation—from the exuberance of American administrations which were already prototypes of self-rule. An inner animation as important as prolonged life-expectancy was born in men of imagination. That same spirit was aloft again during the settlement of crises in Magsaysay's presidency. While Communist leaders were imprisoned, Huks with legitimate grievance were offered amnesty (a precedent set by Quezon in the bloody Sakdal uprising of 1935) if they would resettle on pioneer lands in Mindanao. The government passed new laws to restrain usury, tenancy abuses, accumulation of giant *haciendas*. Where lands held by small owners could not support private ownership of machinery, co-ops were organized. Communication improvements were planned so that word of law would not be sidetracked in some *población,* fifteen miles from the *barrios.* Processing of local products came into Filipino hands. The Chinese who, though constituting only 2 per cent of the population have controlled over 75 per cent of the retail trade, were given a deadline for change in ownership. People were encouraged to place savings in banks, to provide investment capital for promised industries, strengthened in turn by strict import control to protect dollar resources. Consequently, initiative which had been dissipated by penury and the claims of familism, was in the process of restoration. Democracy found prepolitical practice.

Other changes have occurred less consciously. During the war years the population of Manila increased more than 50 per cent, to over a million, as refugees fled the confiscated plains. Urbanism brought its own problems but, in the meantime, it modified traditional *damay* (face to face) culture and its customs. Whatever was lost in hospitality was gained in freedom of movement and moderation of temperaments through less constant personal relations. Similarly, after the toll of war, once more the Philippines has enjoyed a low Western death rate and high Eastern birth rate. The continued predominance of young people (by 1948 over half the population was under twenty) is certain to modify the distribution of family authority.

The maker of literature is part of this awakening. He has taken comfort from Palanca equivalents of Pulitzer prizes, since 1950; from Republic Awards offered the fine arts during President Magsaysay's administration; from the more recent

Stonehill fellowships and Cultural Heritage awards. He has repaid those honors, those hopes for a renaissance, by not being a mere observer of custom. Sometimes he has criticized, sometimes commemorated; but always he has aspired to understanding. Consequently, there is a sense of search in his fiction, a careful attending to the patterned evolution of events, rather than to their clamor or color. Often there is a slowness of motion which owes something to timeless folkways' sacred, seasonal mysteries but as much, again, to the questing spirit for quietly profound consequence. The function of literature is not to take for granted, but to recalculate; to validate one mode of experience by another.

The most representative stories, although written in English and therefore accessible chiefly to urban cadres or the imagined reader abroad, remember rural people—but rarely with contempt or nostalgia. The Filipino experience, to these writers, is apparently that of being unborn, in a world itself not wholly created yet. Often a sense of personal incompleteness is conveyed by the author's choice of uninitiated narrators. Pisco in Gonzalez' "Lupo and the River," is thunderstruck with sudden manhood, with wonder at how woman's carelessness kills. In Arguilla's "How My Brother Leon Brought Home a Wife," because the eyes of a half-knowing, yet all-caring child are borrowed, the hazards of courted joy can go unmentioned without remaining untold. The same respect for the personal locus of human circumstance prevents Arguilla's Sakdal stories from becoming doctrinaire protest for mass ideals at individual expense. Restraint of sentimental tendencies, in Daguio, shapes suffering into assertions of worth: sympathy becomes irrelevant to the tribal outcast or fleshless leper. Similarly, in treating the anguished privacy of her characters, Edith Tiempo endures their experience without extraneous commentary; and so creates, in those who become untouchables against the sweat of their will credible images of cosmic rather than local insularity. And Bienvenido Santos goes even farther in understatement; is gentle with the Filipino Dream of his "Pinoy" exiles because it was true to their need, if not to fact.

The more controversial the author's convictions, the greater the poise of caution; the greater the dependence on the evidence of event fulfilled. Joaquin's elegiac recall of Spanish times and their now-lost virtues is clear only in his play, *Portrait of the Artist as Filipino,* and his novella, *The Woman Who Had Two Navels.* Otherwise it is a pagan world of unsublimated sensuality which he explores with Lawrencean intensity. His legends reflect vestigial superstitions among the not-quite converted; and he tempers his inclination to romanticize the past by recording the constancy of everyday's subtle moral trials. The ambiguities of "Summer Solstice," as uncompromising as Euripides' *Bacchae,* are proof that he is no indiscriminate apologist for the past.

Even the most violent of these writers, Rony Diaz, depends on craft and control, not on sensationalism. "Death in a Sawmill" deliberately undercuts suspense by revealing the fact of murder at once, in order to track instead the spoor of human motive—in the true victim, the accomplice-spectator, the boy admirer for whom flowing event condenses into terrible, tangible images. The sudden summoning of guilt, despoiling pleasure, in "Two Brothers" is like the burst of conscience in Arcellana's "Divide by Two" which admits that marriage has become an accident of ceremony. Man and wife speak in one another's presence; but are separated by a barrier more real than their neighbor's spite fence.

Yet, because only the conscience-stricken can care, incompleteness itself provides the quest for an identity beyond differences. In many of these stories, however spring-green or defective, however mutilated their protagonists, the same mature realization is reached which is implicit in Nuyda's final scene: that one begins to measure closeness by estimating distances.

Each writer has found his own way of speaking the unspeakable: his personal annunciation. Earlier, Philippine tales tended to be narrative essays, oratorical pieces for propaganda's occasions, chronicles of blood-lust passing as heroic deed, sentimental valentines. Now there is greater attendance on the tremulous; the nearly intangible, the exquisite pain of the unwrapping of bandages. The cause for this new *delicadeza* could be assigned to the Filipino's customary self-effacement, were it not so rare in the vernacular. More likely it springs from fuller realization of what independence means in a shaken age; from perception of other sides to aspiration's slogans and habits too soon rejected; from cautious enjoyment of self-discovery, self-determination in spite of the inauspicious; from the struggle for poise in the very act of seizing experience. Its subtleties of insight and regard for craft show affinity, too, with contemporary American critical theories in revolt against Romantic and Victorian sensibilities. The English language and the western concept of the short story as more than parable or entertaining tale were introduced together in the Philippines. It is neither coincidence nor condescension that five of the authors in this present collection have quickened their vision on Rockefeller grants (and one on a Guggenheim) in the States; that their stories have appeared in the *Hopkins Review,* the *Pacific Spectator, Prairie Schooner, Sewanee Review, Story, Wake,* and the special Philippine issue of Fairleigh Dickinson University's *Literary Review* (Summer 1960), as well as in O'Brien and Martha Foley's lists of distinction; that the Swallow Press published Gonzalez' first book of stories, *Seven Hills Away* (1947), and *Partisan Review* devoted a complete issue to Joaquin's "The Woman Who Had Two Navels."

Paradoxically, those writers who have paid allegiance to literary standards unmeasured by latitude or longitude have advanced Philippine literature much farther than have its most ardently narrow nationalists. They would seem to accept as spokesman Frank Arcellana who once said, "The writer commits himself in an act—not necessarily just in something written but in joining a group or attending a conference—to be useful to people and not to programs. It is well enough for those who delight in being used . . . . The only political action for the writer is to remember . . . . He must remember that he is first a human being before he is a national . . . . He should not relinquish the primacy of his mind . . . ."[9]

For such men the primary question has never been: Which language is the best medium for Philippine writers? but: Which writers are the best medium for the urgencies of language? Because of them, what began originally as a demonstration of cultural equality has become now proof of a greater value: the gift of being unforgettable.

---

9. Quoted in editorial, *Comment* 8 (First quarter, 1959), p. 11. The entire issue, entitled "The Filipino Writer and National Growth," is a report on the National Writers Conference held in Baguio late in 1958, under the auspices of P. E. N.

MODERN PHILIPPINE SHORT STORIES

AMADOR DAGUIO [1912–]

Amador Daguio grew up in the malarial regions of Mountain Province, in northern Luzon, where his *constabulario* father helped bring order to the non-Christian Kalinga tribes. However, his own love was for adventure of a different kind, and at the age of four he "ran away to school," to dream the youthful idylls later included in his unpublished novel, *The Cradle of Summer*.

In 1924, when his father moved to Makati, Rizal, his lyric free verse made him class poet in high school. Later, to earn tuition for the University of the Philippines, Daguio worked as caddy, houseboy, and street-car ticket seller. Nevertheless, he completed his Ph.B. in four years and still found time to win every important literary contest and the encouragement of his professor from Australia, T. Inglis Moore. When the seventeen-year-old boy had an offer from *Poet Lore* in America to publish a chapbook of his verses, it was Moore who advised him to work for perfection instead—but sponsored his appearance in the *Sydney Bulletin*.

During the early depression years, tubercular lesions forced Daguio to return to the Mountain Province, to heal. Then from the elementary schools of Lubuagan and Banko he was sent on assignment to the southernmost part of the archipelago, to Bukidnon Agricultural high school. Briefly he returned to Manila, as a textbook writer with the Bureau of Education; but in 1937 went south again to Zamboanga Normal School. There his first book of poetry was completed and he married a fellow teacher, descendant from Moslem royalty.

Just three months before the outbreak of the war, in 1941, Daguio moved to Leyte Normal School. Not only did he serve as intelligence officer under Colonel Juan Causing, but he also organized the Tacloban Theatre Guild which produced his plays *Prodigal Son* and *Filipinas*. The latter actually displayed the Philippine flag at a time when to do so was criminal. After the Japanese threatened execution unless certain patriotic lines were deleted, he merely put them into the mouth of a soldier suffering from combat fatigue who immediately was knocked down by another soldier. The show went on; the flag went up.

Out of the war years also came Daguio's second volume of poetry, *Bataan Harvest,* and a novel, *The House of My Spirit,* which recounts in terms quite different from his *Cradle of Summer* the struggle of his parents to rear thirteen children.

Even while he taught at the Normal School, he helped to establish two private colleges in Leyte. Then, in 1951, aware that most Filipinos thought he had died during the war, he accepted a *pensionadoship,* in order to translate the epic harvest songs of the Kalingas, for his master's thesis at Stanford, and to develop his craft as writer under Wallace Stegner. On his return, he deserted the outer provinces where he had spent his youth and settled in Manila. In quick succession Daguio served as chief of the editorial board of the Public Affairs Office, in the Department of National Defense; as Public Relations Officer for Magsaysay's Huk resettlement commission, after passing the bar in 1954; and as assistant to the director of the Bureau of the Budget. Between bureaucratic assignments he lectures at the state university; but ghost-writing political speeches has prevented him from publishing more than a single book of poetry, *The Flaming Lyre* (1959), since the war. Most of his works are still unpublished and some, unwritten, although one small group of poems appeared in *Six Filipino Poets* and others in the *Pacific Spectator* and the *Beloit Poetry Journal.* "Wedding Dance" was included in *Stanford Short Stories 1953.* But there are other childhood plans apparently just as pressing: to represent Mountain Province in Congress; to restore his father's family farm (his main purpose in becoming a lawyer); and to record still-current tribal songs that retain the sound and dream of centuries ago. Meanwhile, since 1958, he has served as Chief Editor for the Philippine House of Representatives.

WEDDING DANCE

AWIYAO reached for the upper horizontal log which served as the edge of the headhigh threshold. Clinging to the log, he lifted himself with one bound that carried him across to the narrow door. He slid back the cover, stepped inside, then pushed the cover back in place. After some moments during which he seemed to wait, he talked to the listening darkness.

"I'm sorry this had to be done. I am really sorry. But neither of us can help it."

The sound of the *gangsas* beat through the walls of the dark house, like muffled roars of falling waters. The woman who had moved with a start when the sliding door opened had been hearing the *gangsas* for she did not know how long. The sudden rush of the rich sounds when the door opened was like a sharp gush of fire in her. She gave no sign that she heard Awiyao, but continued to sit unmoving in the darkness.

But Awiyao knew that she heard him and his heart pitied her. He crawled on all fours to the middle of the room; he knew exactly where the stove was. With bare fingers he stirred the covered smouldering embers, and blew into them. When the coals began to glow, Awiyao put pieces of pine on them, then full round logs as big as his arms. The room brightened.

"Why don't you go out," he said, "and join the dancing women?" He felt a pang inside him, because what he said was really not the right thing to say and because the woman did not stir. "You should join the dancers," he said, "as if—as if nothing has happened." He looked at the woman huddled in a corner of the room, leaning against the wall. The stove fire played with strange moving shadows and lights upon her face. She was partly sullen, but her sullenness was not because of anger or hate.

"Go out—go out and dance. If you really don't hate me for this separation, go out and dance. One of the men will see you dance well; he will like your dancing; he will marry you. Who knows but that, with him, you will be luckier than you were with me."

"I don't want any man," she said sharply. "I don't want any other man."

He felt relieved that at least she talked: "You know very well that I don't want any other woman, either. You know that, don't you? Lumnay, you know it, don't you?"

She did not answer him.

"You know it Lumnay, don't you?" he repeated.

"Yes, I know," she said weakly.

"It is not my fault," he said, feeling relieved. "You cannot blame me; I have been a good husband to you."

"Neither can you blame me," she said. She seemed about to cry.

"No, you have been very good to me. You have been a good wife. I have nothing to say against you." He set some of the burning wood in place. "It's only that a man must have a child. Seven harvests is just too long to wait. Yes, we have waited too long. We should have another chance before it is too late for both of us."

This time the woman stirred, stretched her right leg out and bent her left leg in. She wound the blanket more snugly around herself.

"You know that I have done my best," she said. "I have prayed to Kabunyan much. I have sacrificed many chickens in my prayers."

"Yes, I know."

"You remember how angry you were once when you came home from your work in the terrace because I butchered one of our pigs without your permission? I did it to appease Kabunyan, because, like you, I wanted to have a child. But what could I do?"

"Kabunyan does not see fit for us to have a child," he said. He stirred the fire. The sparks rose through the crackles of the flames. The smoke and soot went up to the ceiling.

Lumnay looked down and unconsciously started to pull at the rattan that kept the split bamboo flooring in place. She tugged at the rattan flooring. Each time she did this the split bamboo went up and came down with a slight rattle. The gongs of the dancers clamorously called in her ears through the walls.

Awiyao went to the corner where Lumnay sat, paused before her, looked at her bronzed and sturdy face, then turned to where the jars of water stood piled one over the other. Awiyao took a coconut cup and dipped it in the top jar and drank. Lumnay had filled the jars from the mountain creek early that evening.

"I came home," he said, "because I did not find you among the dancers. Of course, I am not forcing you to come, if you don't want to join my wedding ceremony. I came to tell you that Madulimay, although I am marrying her, can never become as good as you are. She is not as strong in planting beans, not as fast in cleaning water jars, not as good in keeping a house clean. You are one of the best wives in the whole village."

"That has not done me any good, has it?" she said. She looked at him lovingly. She almost seemed to smile.

He put the coconut cup aside on the floor and came closer to her. He held her face between his hands, and looked longingly at her beauty. But her eyes looked away. Never again would he hold her face. The next day she would not be his any more. She would go back to her parents. He let go of her face, and she bent to the floor again and looked at her fingers as they tugged softly at the split bamboo floor.

"This house is yours," he said, "I built it for you. Make it your own, live in it as long as you wish. I will build another house for Madulimay."

"I have no need for a house," she said slowly. "I'll go to my own house. My parents are old. They will need help in the planting of the beans, in the pounding of the rice."

"I will give you the field that I dug out of the mountain during the first year of our marriage," he said. "You know I did it for you. You helped me to make it for the two of us."

"I have no use for any field," she said.

He looked at her, then turned away, and became silent. They were silent for a time.

"Go back to the dance," she said finally. "It is not right for you to be here. They will wonder where you are, and Madulimay will not feel good. Go back to the dance."

"I would feel better if you could come, and dance—for the last time. The *gangsas* are playing."

"You know that I cannot."

"Lumnay," he said tenderly. "Lumnay, if I did this it is because of my need for a child. You know that life is not worth living without a child. The men have mocked me behind my back. You know that."

"I know it," she said. "I will pray that Kabunyan will bless you and Madulimay."

She bit her lips now, then shook her head wildly, and sobbed.

She thought of the seven harvests that had passed, the high hopes they had in the beginning of their new life, the day he took her away from her parents across the roaring river, on the other side of the mountain, the trip up the trail which they had to climb, the steep canyon which they had to cross—the waters boiled in her mind in foams of white and jade and roaring silver; the waters rolled and growled, resounded in thunderous echoes through the walls of the stiff cliffs; they were far away now but loud still and receding; the waters violently smashed down from somewhere on the tops of the other ranges, and they had looked carefully at the buttresses of rocks they had to step on—a slip would have meant death.

They both drank of the water then rested on the other bank before they made the final climb to the other side of the mountain.

She looked at his face with the fire playing upon his features—hard and strong, and kind. He had a sense of lightness in his way of saying things, which often made her and the village people laugh. How proud she had been of his humor. The muscles were taut and firm, bronze and compact in their hold upon his skull—how frank his bright eyes were. She looked at his body that carved out of the mountains five fields for her; his wide and supple torso heaved as if a slab of shining lumber were heaving; his arms and legs flowed down in fluent muscles—he was strong and for that she had lost him.

She flung herself upon his knees and clung to them. "Awiyao, Awiyao, my husband," she cried. "I did everything to have a child," she said passionately in a hoarse whisper. "Look at me," she cried. "Look at my body. Then it was full of promise. It could dance; it could work fast in the fields; it could climb the mountains fast. Even now it is firm, full. But, Awiyao, Kabunyan never blessed me. Awiyao, Kabunyan is cruel to me. Awiyao, I am useless. I must die."

"It will not be right to die," he said, gathering her in his arms. Her whole warm naked breast quivered against his own; she clung now to his neck, and her head lay upon his right shoulder; her hair flowed down in cascades of gleaming darkness.

"I don't care about the fields," she said. "I don't care about the house. I don't care for anything but you. I'll have no other man."

"Then you'll always be fruitless."

"I'll go back to my father. I'll die."

"Then you hate me," he said. "If you die it means you hate me. You do not want me to have a child. You do not want my name to live on in our tribe."

She was silent.

"If I do not try a second time," he explained, "it means I'll die. Nobody will get the fields I have carved out of the mountains; nobody will come after me."

"If you fail—if you fail this second time—" she said thoughtfully. Then her voice was a shudder. "No—no, I don't want you to fail."

"If I fail," he said, "I'll come back to you. Then both of us will die together. Both of us will vanish from the life of our tribe."

The gongs thundered through the walls of their house, sonorous and far away.

"I'll keep my beads," she said. "Awiyao, let me keep my beads," she half-whispered.

"You will keep the beads. They come from far-off times. My grandmother said they came from way up North, from the slant-eyed people across the sea. You keep them, Lumnay. They are worth twenty fields."

"I'll keep them because they stand for the love you have for me," she said. "I love you. I love you and have nothing to give."

She took herself away from him, for a voice was calling out to him from outside. "Awiyao! Awiyao! O Awiyao! They are looking for you at the dance!"

"I am not in a hurry."

"The elders will scold you. You had better go."

"Not until you tell me that it is all right with you."

"It is all right with me."

He clasped her hands. "I do this for the sake of the tribe," he said.

"I know," she said.

He went to the door.

"Awiyao!"

He stopped as if suddenly hit by a spear. In pain he turned to her. Her face was agony. It pained him to leave. She had been wonderful to him. What was it that made a man wish for a child? What was it in life, in the work in the fields, in the planting and harvest, in the silence of the night, in the communings with husband and wife, in the whole life of the tribe itself that made man wish for the laughter and speech of a child? Suppose he changed his mind? Why did the unwritten law demand, anyway, that a man, to be a man, must have a child to come after him? And if he was fruitless—but he loved Lumnay. It was like taking away half of his life to leave her like this.

"Awiyao," she said, and her eyes seemed to smile in the light. "The beads!"

He turned back and walked to the farthest corner of their room, to the trunk where they kept their worldly possession—his battle-axe and his spear points, her betel nut box and her beads. He dug out from the darkness the beads which had been given to him by his grandmother to give to Lumnay on the day of his marriage. He went to her, lifted her head, put the beads on, and tied them in place. The white and jade and deep orange obsidians shone in the firelight. She suddenly clung to him, clung to his neck, as if she would never let him go.

"Awiyao! Awiyao, it is hard!" She gasped, and she closed her eyes and buried her face in his neck.

The call for him from the outside repeated; her grip loosened, and he hurried out into the night.

Lumnay sat for some time in the darkness. Then she went to the door and opened it. The moonlight struck her face; the moonlight spilled itself upon the whole village.

She could hear the throbbing of the *gangsas* coming to her through the caverns of the other houses. She knew that all the houses were empty; that the whole tribe was at the dance. Only she was absent. And yet was she not the best dancer of the village? Did she not have the most lightness and grace? Could she not, alone among all the women, dance like a bird tripping for grains on the ground, beautifully timed to the beat of the *gangsas*? Did not the men praise her supple body, and the women envy the way she stretched her hands like the wings of the mountain eagle now and then as she danced? How long ago did she dance at her own wedding? Tonight, all the women who counted, who once danced in her honor, were dancing now in honor of another whose only claim was that perhaps she could give her husband a child.

"It is not right. It is not right!" she cried. "How does she know? How can anybody know? It is not right," she said.

Suddenly she found courage. She would go to the dance. She would go to the chief of the village, to the elders, to tell them it was not right. Awiyao was hers; nobody could take him away from her. Let her be the first woman to complain, to denounce the unwritten rule that a man may take another woman. She would break the dancing of the men and women. She would tell Awiyao to come back to her. He surely would relent. Was not their love as strong as the river?

She made for the other side of the village where the dancing was. There was a flaming glow over the whole place; a great bonfire was burning. The *gangsas* clamored more loudly now, and it seemed they were calling to her. She was near at last. She could see the dancers clearly now. The men leaped lightly with their *gangsas* as they circled the dancing women decked in feast garments and beads, tripping on the ground like graceful birds, following their men. Her heart warmed to the flaming call of the dance; strange heat in her blood welled up, and she started to run.

But the flaming brightness of the bonfire commanded her to stop. Did anybody see her approach? She stopped. What if somebody had seen her coming? The flames of the bonfire leaped in countless sparks which spread and rose like yellow points and died out in the night. The blaze reached out to her like a spreading radiance. She did not have the courage to break into the wedding feast.

Lumnay walked away from the dancing ground, away from the village. She thought of the new clearing of beans which Awiyao and she had started to make only four moons before. She followed the trail above the village.

When she came to the mountain stream she crossed it carefully. Nobody held her hands, and the stream water was very cold. The trail went up again, and she was in the moonlight shadows among the trees and shrubs. Slowly she climbed the mountain.

When Lumnay reached the clearing, she could see from where she stood the blazing bonfire at the edge of the village, where the dancing was. She could hear the far-off clamor of the gongs, still rich in their sonorousness, echoing from mountain to mountain. The sound did not mock her; they seemed to call far to her; speak to her in the language of unspeaking love. She felt the pull of their clamor, almost the feeling that they were telling to her their gratitude for her sacrifice. Her heartbeat began to sound to her like many *gangsas*.

Lumnay thought of Awiyao as the Awiyao she had known long ago—a strong, muscular boy carrying his heavy loads of fuel logs down the mountains to his home. She had met him one day as she was on her way to fill her clay jars with water. He had stopped at the spring to drink and rest; and she had made him drink the cool mountain water from her coconut shell. After that it did not take him long to decide to throw his spear on the stairs of her father's house in token of his desire to marry her.

The mountain clearing was cold in the freezing moonlight. The wind began to sough and stir the leaves of the bean plants. Lumnay looked for a big rock on which to to sit down. The bean plants now surrounded her, and she was lost among them.

A few more weeks, a few more months, a few more harvests—what did it matter? She would be holding the bean flowers, soft in the texture, silken almost, but moist where the dew got into them, silver to look at, silver on the light blue, blooming whiteness, when the morning comes. The stretching of the bean pods full length from the hearts of the wilting petals would go on.

Lumnay's fingers moved a long, long time among the growing bean pods.

THE DEAD

THE SOLDIERS and the sanitary inspector climbed the last winding of the trail and soon entered the village. They stopped to smoke under some trees.

"Not that I hate to do this job," said the sanitary inspector, "but human elements here are involved. This is what the government often overlooks."

"This is the first case in this place, isn't it?" inquired the corporal.

"Yes. Two brothers and a sister. Almost eaten up." This the sanitary inspector said as if only to himself.

"I have never seen lepers," said one of the privates. "Culion must be a dreadful place."

"It is not as it used to be any longer. Culion is a complete village, with many conveniences. The inhabitants even intermarry and have children." The sanitary inspector paused.

"A leper is always a leper," commented the corporal.

"I tell you they are not a pleasant sight," said the sanitary inspector.

"Did you say they should have been in Culion long ago? What happened?" asked one of the privates.

"Escaped. They were in the hospital then. Four or five years ago. Nobody knew at first that they were sick except the doctor and the hospital personnel. The night before the day they were to be transported away, they escaped, somehow having heard of the news of their fate. Nobody knew where they had fled. Subsequent investigations did not reveal their hiding place. The natives of this village knew where they had gone but nobody betrayed them. Sympathy. It was only last month that we found out, but then the disease had already progressed, beyond recovery."

From somewhere in the villages came the *teniente del barrio*. Like the rest of the male villagers, he wore G-strings. Only a cane topped with nickel showed that he was a representative of the government. He greeted the sanitary inspector and soldiers, then added, "I think they suspect what is coming to them. But we must get them by persuasion, not by force. They are ready to fight, you see."

The soldiers looked at each other. "I told you this was going to happen," mumbled the sanitary inspector.

"They have sharpened spears," continued the *teniente del barrio*. "And battle-axes. They are determined to stay their ground."

"Well, then, let us go," said the sanitary inspector. "Let's see what we can do."

"We cannot shoot if they fight," said the soldiers. "We have no orders."

"But if you must?" asked the sanitary inspector.

"I hate to get into this sort of thing," said the corporal in a strange voice.

The group passed through the village climbing the terraces upon which octagonally-shaped brown houses had been built. There was silence in the air; even the children and women standing by their doors to watch the government men as they passed were silent and speechless. A dog barked but was stoned immediately by its master. The house of the lepers was way out of the village.

"Even the villagers had to isolate them afterwards," said the sanitary inspector, "in that little hut."

"How do they eat then?" asked one of the privates.

"The relatives throw them food," answered the *teniente*

del barrio. "As if they were pigs. Nobody cares to go near them. You see, their faces are almost eaten up, full of sores and pus. Their fingers and toes are no more. They look like thin, bony, hairless ghosts. Our children are scared of them."

The soldiers climbed the last terrace outside of the village, then stopped as planned. The sanitary inspector and the *teniente del barrio* proceeded a little farther. Suddenly they also stopped. From a little hut only a little larger than a pig pen came a twanging, vicious sound.

"Arrows!" exclaimed the sanitary inspector, jumping with shocked surprise as an arrow whisked by.

"They have made bows and arrows!" said the *teniente del barrio.*

From the hut three almost naked bodies, ugly, weird, ghostly, suddenly moved out, huddled together in battle formation, each holding a bow and arrows, a spear and a battle-ax. A pair of arrows followed the first shaft.

"They can shoot!" exclaimed the sanitary inspector. "Comrades!" he shouted, holding up his arms. "We are not going to harm you. Look, I come alone near you. Soldiers are with me, it is true but they are behind and wouldn't do anything to you. I come to help you. Understand me?"

The three weird figures of living death held their places suspiciously. "I know what you want to do," said their spokesman, the eldest undoubtedly, his voice a ringing hollow of anger. "You want to bring us once more to the hospital. We don't want any hospital."

"We want to cure you. The governor ordered us to get you. You must come with us peacefully," said the sanitary inspector.

"We will die here," said the spokesman. "We don't want to go away. They wanted to take us away to a far place long ago."

To this the sanitary inspector had no answer. What

could he say? The realization came—I will not be able to get them, my mission is useless. Can I tell a lie?

"We shall not do that sort of thing," said he. "When the governor came last month, he heard of you. He even saw you. It is his kindness that moved him to send us that you may be cured of your disease."

The spokesman of the three raised his spear wildly in defiance. "We shall not go with you. You think you can cure us. Do you think you can cure us?"

"We shall cure you," said the sanitary inspector, almost choking.

"You cannot cure us," the three said.

Then the woman painfully lumbered a little forward as if to show her whole being before all men. Her face was almost a hole, her fingers nothing but stumps. And yet the wonder of it was that she could still hold a spear and a battle-ax, ready to fight.

"We are entirely helpless," cried the other brother. "You see how we are. You cannot take us away. It is painful to move as it is, to live and know we cannot be cured any more. Please leave us in peace."

"Leave us to die in peace," cried the woman, her voice one nasal tone going out of the eaten-up hollow of her face.

The sanitary inspector looked at the *teniente del barrio*, then at the soldiers. He thought of his duty. What would the doctor say? The governor? Money had already been procured by the government for the transport of these living-dead, doomed ghosts of men whose bodies rotted. Here he was trying to cajole them, invite them, entreat them in the name of kindness and charity. For what? That the law of exiles be obeyed. What must I say?

"We have lived here during all our lives," said the spokesman, and now there was a new, almost tender ring in his voice. "You, too, have homes. All of you. You, too, have been born in the soil you love. We were born here, we grew up here. We lived all these long years here. This is our land, our home. We don't want any other."

That struck into the heart of the sanitary inspector. He was young again. He was going to school. He was singing, " 'Mid pleasures and palaces though we may roam . . . ."

And as if to carry on his point further, like a lawyer pleading his case before a stern, unsmiling judge, the spokesman suddenly flung his weapons away from himself, bared his breast in one wild, dramatic gesture, raised his hands in open pleading.

"Shoot us," **he** said. "It is better for us to die here. We know we shall not live long. Every day we bear the pain, the smell of our bodies poisons us, we await death that does not come. This is our fate, and we can die without complaint, but we don't want to go away from here. If we had wanted to go away we could have gone long ago. What did we do? We escaped. Please tell the governor our wish. We want to be left here. Let him be kind to us."

The leper then looked at the heavens, clear in the morning sunlight. The sanitary inspector unconsciously followed his gaze. Above the clouds an eagle was soaring, calm and majestic. Where was its home? The smell of blooming rice filled the air with sweet, floating peace. Even a leper must have a home in which to die.

Suddenly the sanitary inspector moved to the group of soldiers. There was a ring of exasperation in his voice. "Let's go," he said. "Let's go home." He felt sick. The three lepers stood in front of their huts looking at the men who suddenly had gone away, wondering what had happened, yet wordless in their surprise.

It was like the passing of a heavy cloud that promised rain—rain that would either flood over the earth and destroy living things, or lend unto creation the sweet, swift bountiful

sap of life. This coming of the soldiers and the sanitary inspector, strong-bodied symbols of health and life, had filled them
with a sense of foreboding and desolation. And yet they had
gone leaving behind them the skeletons that waited for death,
like the heavy cloud sweeping into space with all the promise
of hope it once held. There was a sudden loneliness come upon
the lepers. They wondered but did not know. They only felt
the desolation of the earth, the helpless striving of puny creation against the power and promise of life gone into the pus
and sores of inescapable annihilation. To the three of them the
sadness came and they stood speechless and forsaken.

Looking back once more, the sanitary inspector felt himself more sick. He thought of his own home. He hastened his
steps, feeling the charm of the skies.

"We'll say they are not here," he said to no one in par-
ticular. "We were told that they are dead. Yes, who would like
to transport them away in his truck seeing their sores, and what
passengers would ride in that truck again?"

NICK JOAQUIN [1917–]

As a child, Nick Joaquin used to roam the walls of Intramuros, the Walled City that Spain filled with churches and bazaars, on Manila Bay. Although his father had served bravely as a rebel colonel during the Revolution, no Philippine writer has paid such tributes as Nick Joaquin to the country's Spanish heritage. "To accuse the Spanish," he has said, "over and over again, of having brought us all sorts of things, mostly evil, among which we can usually remember nothing very valuable 'except, perhaps,' religion and national unity, is equivalent to saying of a not very model mother that she has given her child nothing except life."

After his father's death, Nick lived for years with his sister-in-law, whose children were put to bed with his improvised stories. He became so steeped in the romance of books that inadequate teachers in high school distressed him, and in his junior year he refused to return to class. He decided, flatly, to become a writer. In the meantime he read widely in his father's substantial library. Although his mother, a former schoolteacher, was dismayed, his sister-in-law convinced Nick that he should submit one of his stories to the *Herald Mid-Week Magazine*. It was accepted.

By the time of the Japanese Occupation, Nick Joaquin had found his theme: the modern Filipino's betrayal of his past: and narrated it forcefully in his story, "It Was Later Than We Thought." Throughout the war he was a daily communicant, walking all the way to Intramuros each day at dawn and making the rounds of churches until ten o'clock. His younger brothers, by then, were making a living by driving *calesas* which had replaced gas-driven vehicles. But Nick was satisfied to feed and water their horses (one of which he called Rosary); or to husk the floor with coconut shells until it shone; or to help in the kitchen.

After liberation he worked as stage manager for his sister-in-law's acting troupe until an essay, "La naval de Manila," won a contest sponsored by the Dominicans. They were impressed by his account of the miraculous defeat of a Dutch invasion fleet. Learning that Nick had secretly aspired to ordination, the Dominicans offered him a scholarship to Albert College in Hong Kong, in 1947 (and the University of Sto. Tomas gave him an honorary A.A., to make him eligible). Nevertheless, by 1950, regretfully he asked to leave the cloistered life of the seminary and was released.

The position that he chose on the weekly *Philippines Free Press*—proofreader—was as humble as a seminarian's; but for all its tedium it stationed him close to the written, creative word. Later he advanced to rewrite man, and then was allowed to contribute pieces of his own, about Old Manila. These he signed "Quijano de Manila," a fortunate anagram of his family name and a sign of his most lasting allegiance.

A limited edition of *The Prose and Poems of Nick Joaquin* was published in 1952, in Manila. Included were a novelette, "The Woman Who Had Two Navels," which subsequently filled an issue of the *Partisan Review;* and the distinguished play, *A Portrait of the Artist as Filipino,* which later was produced appropriately in the bombed-out ruins of Intramuros by the Barangay Theatre Guild. One story, "Summer Solstice," appeared in *Wake* and was read by Lionel Trilling to his classes in writing. Taken all together, his work indicates that, consciously or otherwise, the past which Joaquin actually courts is not always Christian or cosmic, but pagan and primordial. Constantly there is an urge for physical regeneration, renewal of youth, which rarely seeks sublimation or spiritual consummation. Such works are at least accurate records of contradictions within Philippine culture. Furthermore, in his most successful stories Joaquin seems repelled by his own fascination with this brute world and its cults; or seems convinced that to embrace a religious view of the world is to accept the implications of sin as well.

In 1953, Nick Joaquin left for Spain, the United States and Mexico on a two-year Rockefeller grant, so that he could start his first novel. True to his earliest inclination, he preferred Madrid to New York. Intermittently he has also translated the works of Jose Rizal, who also wrote best of the threat to his homeland while abroad.

In 1960, Joaquin was awarded the first Stonehill Fellowship for publication of his novel-in-progress.

THE SUMMER SOLSTICE

THE MORETAS were spending St. John's day with the children's grandfather, whose feast-day it was. Doña Lupeng awoke feeling faint with the heat, a sound of screaming in her ears. In the dining room the three boys, already attired in their holiday suits, were at breakfast, and came crowding around her, talking all at once.

"How long you have slept, Mama!"

"We thought you were never getting up!"

"Do we leave at once, huh? Are we going now?"

"Hush, hush, I implore you! Now look: your father has a headache, and so have I. So be quiet this instant—or no one goes to Grandfather."

Though it was only seven by the clock the house was already a furnace, the windows dilating with the harsh light and the air already burning with the immense, intense fever of noon.

She found the children's nurse working in the kitchen. "And why is it you who are preparing breakfast? Where is Amada?" But without waiting for an answer she went to the backdoor and opened it, and the screaming in her ears became a wild screaming in the stables across the yard. "Oh, my God!" she groaned and, grasping her skirts, hurried across the yard.

In the stables Entoy, the driver, apparently deaf to the screams, was hitching the pair of piebald ponies to the coach.

"Not the closed coach, Entoy! The open carriage!" shouted Doña Lupeng as she came up.

"But the dust, señora—"

"I know, but better to be dirty than to be boiled alive. And what ails your wife, eh? Have you been beating her again?"

"Oh no, señora: I have not touched her."

"Then why is she screaming? Is she ill?"

"I do not think so. But how do I know? You can go and see for yourself, señora. She is up there."

When Doña Lupeng entered the room, the big half-naked woman sprawled across the bamboo bed stopped screaming. Doña Lupeng was shocked.

"What is this, Amada? Why are you still in bed at this hour? And in such a posture! Come, get up at once. You should be ashamed!"

But the woman on the bed merely stared. Her sweat-beaded brows contracted, as if in an effort to understand. Then her face relaxed, her mouth sagged open humorously and, rolling over on her back and spreading out her big soft arms and legs, she began noiselessly quaking with laughter—the mute mirth jerking in her throat; the moist pile of her flesh quivering like brown jelly. Saliva dribbled from the corners of her mouth.

Doña Lupeng blushed, looking around helplessly; and seeing that Entoy had followed and was leaning in the doorway, watching stolidly, she blushed again. The room reeked hotly of intimate odors. She averted her eyes from the laughing woman on the bed, in whose nakedness she seemed so to participate that she was ashamed to look directly at the man in the doorway.

"Tell me, Entoy: has she been to the Tadtarin?"

"Yes, señora. Last night."

"But I forbade her to go! And I forbade you to let her go!"

"I could do nothing."

"Why, you beat her at the least pretext!"

"But now I do not dare touch her."

"Oh, and why not?"

"It is the day of St. John: the spirit is in her."

"But, man—"

"It is true, señora. The spirit is in her. She is the Tadtarin. She must do as she pleases. Otherwise, the grain would not grow, the trees would bear no fruit, the rivers would give no fish, and the animals would die."

"*Naku,* I did not know your wife was so powerful, Entoy."

"At such times she is not my wife: she is the wife of the river, she is the wife of the crocodile, she is the wife of the moon."

"But how can they still believe such things?" demanded Doña Lupeng of her husband as they drove in the open carriage through the pastoral countryside that was the *arrabal* of Paco in the eighteen-fifties.

Don Paeng, drowsily stroking his mustaches, his eyes closed against the hot light, merely shrugged.

"And you should have seen that Entoy," continued his wife. "You know how the brute treats her: she cannot say a word but he thrashes her. But this morning he stood as meek as a lamb while she screamed and screamed. He seemed actually in awe of her, do you know—actually *afraid* of her!"

Don Paeng darted a sidelong glance at his wife, by which he intimated that the subject was not a proper one for the children, who were sitting opposite, facing their parents.

"Oh, look, boys—here comes the St. John!" cried Doña Lupeng, and she sprang up in the swaying carriage, propping one hand on her husband's shoulder while with the other she held up her silk parasol.

And "Here come the men with their St. John!" cried voices up and down the countryside. People in wet clothes dripping with well-water, ditch-water and river-water came running across the hot woods and fields and meadows, brandishing cans of water, wetting each other uproariously, and shouting "San Juan! San Juan!" as they ran to meet the procession.

Up the road, stirring a cloud of dust, and gaily bedrenched by the crowds gathered along the wayside, a concourse of young men clad only in soggy trousers were carrying aloft an image of the Precursor. Their teeth flashed white in their laughing faces and their hot bodies glowed crimson as they pranced fast, shrouded in fiery dust, singing and shouting and waving their arms: the St. John riding swiftly above the sea of dark heads and glittering in the noon sun—a fine, blonde, heroic St. John: very male, very arrogant: the Lord of Summer indeed; the Lord of Light and Heat—erect and goldly virile above the prone and female earth—while his worshippers danced and the dust thickened and the animals reared and roared and the merciless fires came raining down from the skies—the vast outpouring of light that marks this climax of the solar year—raining relentlessly upon field and river and town and winding road, and upon the joyous throng of young men against whose uproar a couple of seminarians in muddy cassocks vainly intoned the hymn of the noon god:

> That we, thy servants, in chorus
> May praise thee, our tongues restore us . . .

But Doña Lupeng, standing in the stopped carriage, looking very young and elegant in her white frock, under the twirling parasol, stared down on the passing male horde with increasing annoyance. The insolent man-smell of their bodies rose all about her—wave upon wave of it—enveloping her, assaulting her senses, till she felt faint with it and pressed a handkerchief to her nose. And as she glanced at her husband and saw with what a smug smile he was watching the revelers, her annoyance deepened. When he bade her sit down because all eyes were turned on her, she pretended not to hear; stood up even straighter, as if to defy those rude creatures flaunting their manhood in the sun.

And she wondered peevishly what the braggarts were being so cocky about? For this arrogance, this pride, this bluff male health of theirs was (she told herself) founded on the impregnable virtue of generations of good women. The boobies were so sure of themselves because they had always been sure of their wives. *"All the sisters being virtuous, all the brothers are brave,"* thought Doña Lupeng, with a bitterness that rather surprised her. Women had built it up: this poise of the male. Ah, and women could destroy it, too! She recalled, vindictively, this morning's scene at the stables: Amada naked and screaming in bed while from the doorway her lord and master looked on in meek silence. And was it not the mystery of a woman in her flowers that had restored the tongue of that old Hebrew prophet?

"Look, Lupeng, they have all passed now," Don Paeng was saying. "Do you mean to stand all the way?"

She looked around in surprise and hastily sat down. The children tittered, and the carriage started.

"Has the heat gone to your head, woman?" asked Don Paeng, smiling.

The children burst frankly into laughter.

Their mother colored and hung her head. She was beginning to feel ashamed of the thoughts that had filled her mind. They seemed improper—almost obscene—and the discovery of such depths of wickedness in herself appalled her. She moved closer to her husband, to share the parasol with him.

"And did you see our young cousin Guido?" he asked.

"Oh, was he in that crowd?"

"A European education does not seem to have spoiled his taste for country pleasures."

"I did not see him."

"He waved and waved."

"The poor boy. He will feel hurt. But truly, Paeng, I did not see him."

"Well, that is always a woman's privilege."

But when that afternoon, at the grandfather's, the young Guido presented himself, properly attired and brushed and scented, Doña Lupeng was so charming and gracious with him that he was enchanted and gazed after her all afternoon with enamoured eyes.

This was the time when our young men were all going to Europe and bringing back with them, not the Age of Victoria, but the Age of Byron. The young Guido knew nothing of Darwin and evolution; he knew everything about Napoleon and the Revolution. When Doña Lupeng expressed surprise at his presence that morning in the St. John's crowd, he laughed in her face.

"But I *adore* these old fiestas of ours! They are so *romantic!* Last night, do you know, we walked all the way through the woods, I and some boys, to see the procession of the Tadtarin."

"And was that romantic too?" asked Doña Lupeng.

"It was *weird*. It made my flesh *crawl*. All those women in such a mystic frenzy! And she who was the Tadtarin last night—she was a figure right out of a flamenco!"

"I fear to disenchant you, Guido—but that woman happens to be our cook."

"She is beautiful."

"Our Amada beautiful? But she is old and fat!"

"She is beautiful—as that old tree you are leaning on is beautiful," calmly insisted the young man, mocking her with his eyes.

They were out in the buzzing orchard, among the ripe mangoes; Doña Lupeng seated on the grass, her legs tucked beneath her, and the young man sprawled flat on his belly, gazing up at her, his face moist with sweat. The children were chasing dragon-flies. The sun stood still in the west. The long day refused to end. From the house came the sudden roaring laughter of the men playing cards.

"Beautiful! Romantic! Adorable! Are those the only words you learned in Europe?" cried Doña Lupeng, feeling very annoyed with this young man whose eyes adored her one moment and mocked her the next.

"Ah, I also learned to open my eyes over there—to see the holiness and the mystery of what is vulgar."

"And what is so holy and mysterious about—about the Tadtarin, for instance?"

"I do not know. I can only *feel* it. And it *frightens* me. Those rituals come to us from the earliest dawn of the world. And the dominant figure is not the male but the female."

"But they are in honor of St. John."

"What has your St. John to do with them? Those women worship a more ancient lord. Why, do you know that no man may join in those rites unless he first puts on some article of women's apparel and—"

"And what did *you* put on, Guido?"

"How *sharp* you are! Oh, I made such love to a toothless old hag there that she pulled off her stocking for me. And I pulled it on, over my arm, like a glove. How your husband would have *despised* me!"

"But what on earth does it mean?"

"I think it is to remind us men that once upon a time you women were supreme and we men were the slaves."

"But surely there have always been kings?"

"Oh, no. The queen came before the king, and the priestess before the priest, and the moon before the sun."

"The moon?"

"—who is the Lord of the women."

"Why?"

"Because the tides of women, like the tides of the sea, are tides of the moon. Because the first blood—but what is the matter, Lupe? Oh, have I offended you?"

"Is this how they talk to decent women in Europe?"

"They do not talk to women, they pray to them—as men did in the dawn of the world."

"Oh, you are mad! mad!"

"Why are you so afraid, Lupe?"

"I, afraid? And of whom? My dear boy, you still have your mother's milk in your mouth. I only wish you to remember that I am a married woman."

"I remember that you are a woman, yes. A beautiful woman. And why not? Did you turn into some dreadful monster when you married? Did you stop being a woman? Did you stop being beautiful? Then why should my eyes not tell you what you are—just because you are married?"

"Ah, this is too much now!" cried Doña Lupeng, and she rose to her feet.

"Do not go, I implore you! Have pity on me!"

"No more of your comedy, Guido! And besides—where have those children gone to? I must go after them."

As she lifted her skirts to walk away, the young man, propping up his elbows, dragged himself forward on the ground and solemnly kissed the tips of her shoes. She stared down in sudden horror, transfixed—and he felt her violent shudder. She backed away slowly, still staring; then turned and fled toward the house.

On the way home that evening Don Paeng noticed that his wife was in a mood. They were alone in the carriage: the children were staying overnight at their grandfather's. The heat had not subsided. It was heat without gradation: that knew no twilights and no dawns; that was still there, after the sun had set; that would be there already, before the sun had risen.

"Has young Guido been annoying you?" asked Don Paeng.

"Yes! All afternoon."

"These young men today—what a disgrace they are! I felt embarrassed as a man to see him following you about with those eyes of a whipped dog."

She glanced at him coldly. "And was that all you felt, Paeng? Embarrassed—as a man?"

"A good husband has constant confidence in the good sense of his wife," he pronounced grandly, and smiled at her.

But she drew away; huddled herself in the other corner. "He kissed my feet," she told him disdainfully, her eyes on his face.

He frowned and made a gesture of distaste. "Do you see? They have the instincts, the style of the canalla! To kiss a woman's feet, to follow her like a dog, to adore her like a slave—"

"Is it so shameful for a man to adore women?"

"A gentleman loves and respects Woman. The cads and the lunatics—they 'adore' the women."

"But maybe we do not want to be loved and respected—but to be adored."

"Ah, he has converted you then?"

"Who knows? But must we talk about it? My head is bursting with the heat."

But when they reached home she did not lie down but wandered listlessly through the empty house. When Don Paeng, having bathed and changed, came down from the bedroom, he found her in the dark parlor seated at the harp and plucking out a tune, still in her white frock and shoes.

"How can you bear those hot clothes, Lupeng? And why the darkness? Order someone to bring a light in here."

"There is no one, they have all gone to see the Tadtarin."

"A pack of loafers we are feeding."

She had risen and gone to the window. He approached and stood behind her, grasping her elbows and, stooping, kissed the nape of her neck. But she stood still, not responding, and he released her sulkily. She turned around to face him.

"Listen, Paeng. I want to see it, too. The Tadtarin, I mean. I have not seen it since I was a little girl. And tonight is the last night."

"You must be crazy! Only low people go there. And I thought you had a headache?" He was still sulking.

"But I want to go! My head aches worse in the house. For a favor, Paeng."

"I told you: no! Go and take those clothes off. But, woman, whatever has got into you!" He strode off to the table, opened the box of cigars, took one, banged the lid shut, bit off an end of the cigar, and glared about for a light.

She was still standing by the window and her chin was up. "Very well, if you do not want to come, do not come—but I am going."

"I warn you, Lupe; do not provoke me!"

"I will go with Amada. Entoy can take us. You cannot forbid me, Paeng. There is nothing wrong with it. I am not a child."

But standing very straight in her white frock, her eyes shining in the dark and her chin thrust up, she looked so young, so fragile, that his heart was touched. He sighed, smiled ruefully, and shrugged his shoulders.

"Yes, the heat has touched you in the head, Lupeng. And since you are so set on it—very well, let us go. Come, have the coach ordered!"

The cult of the Tadtarin is celebrated on three days: the feast of St. John and the two preceding days. On the first night, a young girl heads the procession; on the second, a mature woman; and on the third, a very old woman who dies and comes to life again. In these processions, as in those of Pakil and Obando, everyone dances.

Around the tiny plaza in front of the barrio chapel, quite a stream of carriages was flowing leisurely. The Moretas were constantly being hailed from the other vehicles. The plaza itself and the sidewalks were filled with chattering, strolling, profusely sweating people. More people crowded on the balconies and windows of the houses. The moon had not yet risen; the black night smoldered; in the windless sky the lightning's abruptly branching fire seemed the nerves of the tortured air made visible.

"Here they come now!" cried the people on the balconies.

And "Here come the women with their St. John!" cried the people on the sidewalks, surging forth on the street. The carriages halted and their occupants descended. The plaza rang with the shouts of people and the neighing of horses— and with another keener sound: a sound as of sea waves steadily rolling nearer.

The crowd parted, and up the street came the prancing, screaming, writhing women, their eyes wild, black shawls flying around their shoulders, and their long hair streaming and covered with leaves and flowers. But the Tadtarin, a small old woman with white hair, walked with calm dignity in the midst of the female tumult, a wand in one hand, a bunch of seedlings in the other. Behind her, a group of girls bore aloft a little black image of the Baptist—a crude, primitive, grotesque image, its big-eyed head too big for its puny naked torso, bobbing and swaying above the hysterical female horde and looking at once so comical and pathetic that Don Paeng, watching with his wife on the sidewalk, was outraged. The image seemed to be crying for help, to be struggling to escape—a St. John indeed in the hands of the Herodiads; a doomed captive these witches were subjecting first to their derision; a gross and brutal caricature of his sex.

Don Paeng flushed hotly: he felt that all those women had personally insulted him. He turned to his wife, to take her away—but she was watching greedily, taut and breathless, her head thrust forward and her eyes bulging, the teeth bared in the slack mouth, and the sweat gleaming in her face. Don Paeng was horrified. He grasped her arm—but just then a flash of lightning blazed and the screaming women fell silent: the Tadtarin was about to die.

The old woman closed her eyes and bowed her head and sank slowly to her knees. A pallet was brought and set on the ground and she was laid in it and her face covered with a shroud. Her hands still clutched the wand and the seedlings. The women drew away, leaving her in a cleared space. They covered their heads with their black shawls and began wailing softly, unhumanly—a hushed, animal keening.

Overhead the sky was brightening; silver light defined the rooftops. When the moon rose and flooded with hot brilliance the moveless crowded square, the black-shawled women stopped wailing and the girl approached and unshrouded the Tadtarin, who opened her eyes and sat up, her face lifted to the moonlight. She rose to her feet and extended the wand and the seedlings and the women joined in a mighty shout. They pulled off and waved their shawls and whirled and began dancing again—laughing and dancing with such joyous exciting abandon that the people in the square and on the sidewalks and even those on the balconies, were soon laughing and dancing, too. Girls broke away from their parents and wives from their husbands to join in the orgy.

"Come, let us go now," said Don Paeng to his wife. She was shaking with fascination; tears trembled on her lashes; but she nodded meekly and allowed herself to be led away. But suddenly she pulled free from his grasp, darted off, and ran into the crowd of dancing women.

She flung her hands to her hair and whirled and her hair came undone. Then, planting her arms akimbo, she began to trip a nimble measure, an instinctive folk movement. She tossed her head back and her arched throat bloomed whitely. Her eyes brimmed with moonlight, and her mouth with laughter.

Don Paeng ran after her, shouting her name, but she laughed and shook her head and darted deeper into the dense maze of the procession, which was moving again, towards the chapel. He followed her, shouting; she eluded him, laughing —and through the thick of the female horde they lost and found and lost each other again—she, dancing, and he, pursuing—till, carried along by the tide, they were both swallowed up into the hot, packed, turbulent darkness of the chapel. Inside poured the entire procession, and Don Paeng, finding himself trapped tight among milling female bodies, struggled with sudden panic to fight his way out. Angry voices rose all about him in the stifling darkness.

"*Hoy*, you are crushing my feet!"

"And let go of my shawl, my shawl!"

"Let me pass, let me pass, you harlots!" cried Don Paeng.

"*Abah*, it is a man!"

"How dare he come in here?"

"Break his head!"

"Throw the animal out!"

"Throw him out! Throw him out!" shrieked the voices, and Don Paeng found himself surrounded by a swarm of gleaming eyes.

Terror possessed him and he struck out savagely with both fists, with all his strength—but they closed in as savagely: solid walls of flesh that crushed upon him and pinned his arms helpless, while unseen hands struck and struck his face, and ravaged his hair and clothes, and clawed at his flesh, as— kicked and buffeted, his eyes blind and his torn mouth salty with blood—he was pushed down, down to his knees, and half-shoved, half-dragged to the doorway and rolled out to the street. He picked himself up at once and walked away with a dignity that forbade the crowd gathered outside to laugh or to pity. Entoy came running to meet him.

"But what has happened to you, Don Paeng?"

"Nothing. Where is the coach?"

"Just over there, sir. But you are wounded in the face!"

"No, these are only scratches. Go and get the señora. We are going home."

When she entered the coach and saw his bruised face and torn clothing, she smiled coolly.

"What a sight you are, man! What have you done with yourself?" And when he did not answer: "Why, have they pulled out his tongue too?" she wondered aloud.

And when they were home and stood facing each other in the bedroom, she was still as light-hearted.

"What are you going to do, Rafael?"

"I am going to give you a whipping."

"But why?"

"Because you have behaved tonight like a lewd woman."

"How I behaved tonight is what I am. If you call that lewd, then I was always a lewd woman and a whipping will not change me—though you whipped me till I died."

"I want this madness to die in you."

"No, you want me to pay for your bruises."

He flushed darkly. "How can you say that, Lupe?"

"Because it is true. You have been whipped by the women and now you think to avenge yourself by whipping me."

His shoulders sagged and his face dulled. "If you can think that of me—"

"You could think me a lewd woman."

"Oh, how do I know what to think of you? I was sure I knew you as I knew myself. But now you are as distant and strange to me as a female Turk in Africa!"

"Yet you would dare whip me—"

"Because I love you, because I respect you—"

"And because if you ceased to respect me you could cease to respect yourself?"

"Ah, I did not say that!"

"Then why not say it? It is true. And you want to say it, you want to say it!"

But he struggled against her power. "Why should I want to?" he demanded peevishly.

"Because, either you must say it—or you must whip me," she taunted.

Her eyes were upon him and the shameful fear that had unmanned him in the dark chapel possessed him again. His legs had turned to water; it was a monstrous agony to remain standing. But she was waiting for him to speak, forcing him to speak.

"No, I cannot whip you!" he confessed miserably.

"Then say it! Say it!" she cried, pounding her clenched fists together. "Why suffer and suffer? And in the end you would only submit."

But he still struggled stubbornly. "Is it not enough that you have me helpless? Is it not enough that I feel what you want me to feel?"

But she shook her head furiously. "Until you have said it to me there can be no peace between us."

He was exhausted at last: he sank heavily to his knees, breathing hard and streaming with sweat, his fine body curiously diminished now in its ravaged apparel.

"I adore you, Lupe," he said tonelessly.

She strained forward avidly. *"What?* What did you say?" she screamed.

And he, in his dead voice: "That I adore you. That I worship you. That the air you breathe and the ground you tread is holy to me. That I am your dog, your slave. . . ."

But it was still not enough. Her fists were still clenched, and she cried: *"Then come, crawl on the floor, and kiss my feet!"*

Without a moment's hesitation, he sprawled down flat, and, working his arms and legs, gaspingly clawed his way across the floor, like a great agonized lizard, the woman steadily backing away as he approached, her eyes watching him avidly, her nostrils dilating, till behind her loomed the open window, the huge glittering moon, the rapid flashes of lightning. She stopped, panting, and leaned against the sill. He lay exhausted at her feet, his face flat on the floor.

She raised her skirts and contemptuously thrust out a naked foot. He lifted his dripping face and touched his bruised lips to her toes; lifted his hands and grasped the white foot and kissed it savagely—kissed the step, the sole, the frail ankle—while she bit her lips and clutched in pain at the window-sill; her body distended and wracked by horrible shivers, her head flung back and her loose hair streaming out the window—streaming fluid and black in the white night where the huge moon glowed like a sun and the dry air flamed into lightning and the pure heat burned with the immense intense fever of noon.

THREE GENERATIONS

THE ELDER MONZON was waiting for his wife to speak. He had finished breakfast and had just laid down the news-paper through which he had been glancing. Across the table, his wife played absently with a spoon. Her brows were knitted, but a half-smile kept twitching on her lips. She was a hand-some, well-preserved woman and, her husband was thinking, a great deal more clever than she allowed herself to appear.

"It is about Chitong," she said at last. "He does not want to continue the law-course he is taking. The boy has a vocation, Celo. He wants to study for the priesthood."

"When did he speak to you?"

"About a month ago, the first time. But I told him to make sure. Last night, he said he was sure. Of course, you have noticed how devout he has been lately?"

Monzon rose. "Well, I would never have expected it of him," he said, but his wife shook her head.

"Has he not always been quiet and reserved, even as a boy?"

"Yes, but not noticeably of a religious temper."

"Only because he did not understand then. He has taken a long time maturing, Celo, but I think it is for the best. Now he knows what really calls him, and he is really very sincere. Are you glad?"

"It is a career, like all the others. Did he say what seminary?"

"We can talk that over later. He feared you would refuse."

"What does he take me for? A heretic?"

The servant-girl came in to clear the table, and the señora rose and followed her husband to the *sala*. "Cleo, when are you going to see your father? Nena called up last night. She was crying. She says she can do nothing with the old man. Your cousin Paulo is not there anymore to help her. It seems the old man broke a plate on his head. . . ."

Monzon paused, his hand on the door-knob. He had put on his hat already. Suddenly, he looked very old and tired. His wife came nearer and placed a hand on his shoulder. "Why will you not let him have his woman again, Celo? He does not have very long to live."

He stared at her fiercely. "Please do not be vulgar, Sofia," he growled, but his wife only smiled.

For all the years they had lived together, he was still startled by a certain nakedness in his wife's mind; in the mind of all women, for that matter. You took them for what they appeared: shy, reticent, bred by nuns, but after marriage, though they continued to look demure, there was always in their attitude toward sex, an amused irony, even a deliberate coarseness; such as he could never allow himself, even in his own mind, or with other men.

"Well," said Doña Sofia, withdrawing her hand, "he has certainly become wild since you drove that woman away. Nena says he refuses to eat. He takes what is served to him and throws it to the floor, plates and everything. He lies awake the whole night roaring like a lion. Yesterday, Nena said, he tried to get up. She was outside and did not hear him. When she came in, there he lay on the floor, all tangled up in his blankets, out of breath, and crying to the heavens. She called in Paulo to get him in bed again, and he grabbed a plate and broke it on poor Paulo's head."

Monzon did not look at his wife's face: he knew very well what he would see. He stared instead at his hands, huge, calloused, and ugly, and suddenly they were his father's hands he was seeing, and he was a little boy that cowered beneath them and the whip they held: "Lie down, you little beast! Lie down, beast!" "Not in the face, father! Do not hit me in the face, father!" "I will hit you where the thunder I want to. I will teach my sons to answer back. Lie down, you beast!"

"Your father never could live without women," Doña Sofia was saying. "And now you have driven that one away. It is death by torture."

"You certainly can choose your words," Monzon retorted. "You know very well what the doctor said."

"But what does it matter since he is going to die anyway? Why not let him have what he wants?"

"You do not sound like a decent woman, Sofia." He turned his back on her and opened the door. "Tell Chitong to have the car ready this afternoon. He and I will go there together."

It was still early, only half-past seven; and when he came to the Dominican church, he went in. He knew he would find Chitong there. He did not know why he wanted to. But he went in and there were few people inside. From the high windows a many-colored light filtered in, drenching the floor violet, but in the side-chapel of the Virgin it was dark, with only the gold glow of candles: he saw his son kneeling there, near the altar, saying his rosary.

Monzon knelt down himself, and tried to compose his mind to prayer, but there was suddenly, painfully, out of his very heart, a sharp, hot, rushing, jealous bitterness towards that devout young man praying so earnestly over there.

He did not understand the feeling. He did not want to understand it. Enough that this thing was clear: that he hated his son for being able to kneel there, submitted utterly to his God. Yet why should he resent that so bitterly?

His own youth had been very unhappy, yes; but whose

fault was it that he had suffered so much? The old man had really been no more heavy of hand and temper than most fathers of that time. He knew that. Those times gave to the head of a family absolute dominion over his women and children. He could not remember that any of his brothers had found the system particularly oppressive. They bowed to the paternal whip as long as they had to; then broke away to marry and breed and establish families over whom they had in turn set themselves up as lords almighty.

As for the women, he had suspected that they even took a certain delight in the barbaric cruelties of their lords. His father was never without two or three concubines whom he had whipped as regularly as he did his sons; but none of them, once fallen into his power, had bothered to strive for a more honorable status. If they went away, it was because the old man wearied of them; though at his bidding, they would return as meekly, to work in his house or in his fields, to cook his food, to wash his clothes, to attend to his children, and to bare their flesh to the blows of his anger or to the blows of his love.

Monzon had wept as a boy for his mother; but later on he had found out that she was only too thankful, worn out as she was with toil and child-bearing, for the company and assistance of these other women. If she fought the old man at all, it was in defense of her children, and especially of himself (for she had been quick to notice that he would not be so easy to break).

She had singled him out from among all her sons to bear and fulfill her few childish dreams and ambitions; and in her last, long, lingering illness, this faith in him had shone in her eyes and trembled in her hands whenever he came near her, and it had frightened and terrified him. For, even then, he was beginning to realize that, though he might set himself against all those things for which his father stood as symbol, he, himself, would never quite completely escape them. Go where he might, he would still be carrying the old man's flesh along; and that flesh smouldered darkly with fires that all a lifetime was too short to quench.

Monzon buried his face in his hands. He felt strangely exhausted. Peace, he thought, peace of mind, of body: he had been praying for that all his life. Just a little peace. It was not possible that he was to go on forever and ever, divided against himself. But there was that little voice, as usual, that voice at his ears, mocking him: Your father could find peace in the simple delights of the body; but you thought yourself too good for that.

His bitterness leapt into active anger: Is this then what I get for having tried to be clean? But the voice laughed at him: When were you ever a lover of purity? All that solemn virtuousness of yours began as a gesture of rebellion against your father. And so it still is. If he had been a chaste man, your defiance would have taken a more perverse form.

And suppose I give up now, stop fighting, submit; would I be at peace? No, said the voice. You would be as miserable in your surrender to your body as you have been in your struggle against it. Besides, it is too late. Men like your father find their brief escapes in the whip, the table, and the bed. That rapt young man over there—your son!—is now groping for a more complete release. For him also there shall be peace. But for you. . . .

Monzon rose. And just then his son looked around. Their eyes met. The young man stood up and came towards his father. He was still holding his beads, and his hands began to tremble. Why does the old man look so fierce? Has mother told him? He looks as if he hated me. As if he would do me a violence.

But as the boy approached, the older Monzon turned away and walked rapidly out of the church.

"He was not angry at all," Doña Sofia said. "He was very pleased. You do not understand your father, Chitong. He does not speak much, but he is really concerned over what you are going to make of your life."

"But the way he looked at me . . ." Chitong began. He was having his breakfast and Doña Sofia sat across the table watching him.

"That, you probably imagined only."

"Oh, no," insisted her son. "And suddenly, he turned away, without even speaking to me." He pushed the plates away and propped his elbows on the table. "I could not pray anymore afterwards. I felt empty and ridiculous. Mother, I said last night I was sure about this thing, and I still am. But have I any right . . . I mean . . . But how shall I say it!" He paused and considered for a moment, drumming with his fingers on the table. "You know, mother, he did have a hard time of it. It shows in his face. I often feel sorry for him. He has made it possible that I should not go through whatever he had to go through. But is such a thing right? And anyway, is it good for me?"

"Whatever are you talking about, Chitong?"

Her son sighed and shrugged his shoulders. "Nothing," he replied, and got up.

"You are to accompany him this afternoon to your grandfather. The old man is getting worse. You are to take the car."

Chitong was standing by the window. She had never seen his face look so grave. She was worried and, rising, approached him.

"Son," she said, "if you are going to dedicate yourself to God, then nothing else should matter to you."

"But that is it, that is it precisely!" cried the boy. "I do wish there was something else that did matter. Something big and fierce and powerful. That I would have to fight down because I loved God more. But there is nothing." He made a gesture with his hand. "Nothing. And father knows it. And that is why he despises me. And he is right."

"Your father does not despise you. How you talk."

Suddenly the boy crumpled up on his knees, his face in his hands.

"I am not sincere, mother! I am a coward! I try to run away! I am nothing! And father knows it! Father knows it! He knows everything!"

She stooped and gathered him to her breast. She was terribly frightened. She was suddenly only a woman. Men were entirely different and alien creatures. Yes, even this one, whom she had borne in her own body. This one, also.

It was a good afternoon for a drive. The wind that met their faces smelled of rain and earth, and in the twilight became vaguely fragrant. They were silent most of the way for, usually, when they were alone together, they felt embarrassed and shy, as though they were lovers.

Chitong was at the wheel. The elder Monzon sat beside him, smoking a cigar. From time to time, he found himself glancing at his son's profile. There was a difference there, he felt. The boy looked tense, tight-strung, even ill. When the darkness fell about them, they both felt easier and the older man began to talk.

"Your mother tells me that you want to give up law."

"Did she tell you why?"

"And I could hardly believe my ears."

"I know I am quite unworthy."

"Oh, as for that, I should say that no one can ever be worthy enough. I was merely wondering at the sudden conversion."

"It was not sudden, father. I had been coming to this for a long time without knowing it."

"Well, how *did* you know?"

"I simply woke up one night and said to myself: I belong *there*. And all at once, I knew why I had been finding
everything so unsatisfactory."

"We all have such moments—when everything clicks
into place."

"And becomes beautiful."

"It was through the appeal of beautiful things that you
found God?"

"With the senses, yes. Certainly not with the mind: I am
no thinker. Nor yet with the heart: I am not a saint. I guess
that's why it took me so long to realize where I was heading."

"You should have come to me for information. I could
have shared my experience with you."

"Your experience, father?"

"—of a vocation. I could have—But why do you look so
shocked? I was young once myself, you know."

"But what happened, father?"

"Nothing. My mother wanted me to be a priest. I was
quite willing. But when she died, I abandoned the idea."

"I never knew!"

"I never told anyone—not even your mother. Shall we
keep it a secret between us?"

For a moment, the wall that stood always between them
disappeared, and they could touch each other. I am an unclean
man, the elder Monzon was thinking, but what was depravity
in me and my fathers becomes, in my son, a way to God.

And the young man thought: I am something, after all,
I am this old man's desire that he has fleshed alive. It sprang
from him, began in him; that which now I will myself to
be . . . .

The evening flowed turgid with the fragrance of the
night-flowers and of their thoughts; but the moment passed and
they were suddenly cold and tired. They fell silent again, and
shy, as though they had loved.

The house stood at the edge of the town. Monzon always thought of it as something tremendous and eternal. Each time he went back to it, he was surprised afresh to find that it was not very big really and that it would not last much longer; the foundations were rotting, the roof leaked, white ants were disintegrating the whole structure.

Here, at the foot of the stairs, always, he must pause and gather himself together. A shrunken, rotting house. But here it was that he had been a little boy; and the roof seemed to expand above his head till it was as high and wide as the heavens.

At the sound of their coming up, a little harassed-looking woman came to the door to meet them. Monzon felt sorry for her. She was his youngest sister. All of them had managed to get away except this one. And she would never get away at all, he thought, as he took her fluttering hands in his. "How is he?" he asked. She merely shook her head and turned to Chitong, who bowed and kissed her hand.

It was dark in that *sala*; an oil-lamp on a table gave the only light. As they moved, the three of them cast huge, nervous shadows. The old man lay in the next room and they could hear his heavy, angry breathing, punctuated with coughs and oaths.

"He is like that all the time," Nena complained, wringing her thin hands. "He has not eaten for days. He shouts at me whenever I enter. He tries to get up all the time and he falls, of course, and I have to call in someone to put him back." There was a pathetic pleading in the eyes she turned shyly on her brother. "He keeps asking for the girl, Celo. Maybe it would be much better. . . ."

But Monzon refused to meet her eyes. "Go and prepare something, Nena. I am going to make him eat," he said. She sighed and went off to the kitchen.

The door of the old man's room stood open. When the

two of them entered, the sick man, sprawled in the big four-posted bed upon a mountain of pillows became silent. As in the *sala*, a single oil-lamp illuminated the room. The bed stood in the shadow but they were aware of the old man's eyes, watching them intently.

Before those eyes, Monzon felt himself stripped, one by one, of all his defenses: maturity, social position, wealth, success. He was a little boy again and he bent down and lifted his father's enormous, damp hand to his lips, and at the contact, a million pins seemed to prick his whole body.

But Chitong came forward and kissed the old man on the brow. The boy felt himself fascinated by those intensely hating eyes. He, also, was rather afraid of this old man; but with a difference. Even as a boy, he had felt the force of those eyes, lips, hands; but his grandfather had still been, then, in the plenitude of strength. But now, when he lay helpless, his legs paralyzed, the flesh gone loose about the bones, the face grown pale and shriveled, did he communicate all the more unbearably that pride, that exultation in simple brute power.

The boy felt himself becoming a single wave of obedience towards the old man. His lips lingered upon that moist brow as though they would drink in the old man's very brains. The feel of the wet flesh was an almost sensual delight, something new and terrifying to him and, at the same time, painful; almost as if the kiss were also a kind of death. It was a multitudinous moment for the boy. When he straightened up, he found himself trembling. And at the same time, he wanted to run away—to some quiet corner, to pray.

"Well, father, why have you sent Paulo away?" Monzon asked, speaking very loudly. The old man continued to stare at them in silence. He seemed to be checking even his breath. His thick lips were pressed tightly shut. Only his eyes spoke. His eyes hated them. His eyes sprang at their throats and wrung lifeless their voices. His eyes challenged this unafraid-pretending solid man that was his son; at that challenge, Monzon stepped nearer and abruptly stripped the blankets from the old man. For a moment they stared at each other.

Monzon had collected himself. Of you, I am not going to be afraid, his eyes told the old man. Not anymore . . . Often had he said that in his mind; now, he wanted to say it aloud because, almost, he believed it to be true. But he spoke to Chitong instead: "Your Tía Nena may want you to help her. If the food for your grandfather is ready, bring it in here."

When Chitong came back with the tray of food, he found that his father had taken off his coat and rolled up his shirtsleeves. He had propped the sick man up to a sitting position and had changed his clothes.

The sick man's face had altered. He sat among the pillows, his face turned away, the eyes closed, the beautiful lips parted, as if in anguish. His hands lay clenched on his lap. He would not look at his son. He would not look at the food.

"You are going to eat, father," Monzon told him. He had taken the tray from Chitong. He did not speak loudly now. He knew he had won. This old man of whom all his life he had been afraid: had he not just dressed him like any baby? And now, like a mere baby again, he would be fed. "You are going to eat, father," he said again in his quiet voice.

The old man turned around and opened his eyes. They were fierce no longer. They were full of tiredness and the desire for death.

Chitong felt the old man's agony as his own. He could not stand it. He had an impulse to approach his father and knock the tray from his hands. He could not trust himself to speak.

The elder Monzon must have sensed this fury, for suddenly he turned to his son. "Chitong, you must be hungry. Better go and find something to eat."

Chitong swallowed the words in his mouth and turned

away. At the door he paused and looked back. His father had laid a hand against the old man's breast; with the other he tried to push a spoonful of food into the tightly closed mouth. The old man tried to evade it, but now he could not turn his face away; his son had him pinned against the bed. At last he gave up, opened his mouth, and received the food. His eyes closed and tears ran down his cheeks.

Chitong glanced at his father. The elder Monzon was smiling. . . .

In the kitchen, he found his Tía Nena, sitting motionless in a corner. She looked as if she had been struck down. Her eyes were full of fear and suffering. Chitong realized that what he had felt for a moment when he kissed the old man's brow, this woman had known all her life. That was why she could not leave the old man; why, of all his children, she had remained faithful. She was in his power; and like himself, Chitong thought bitterly, she was the kind for whom life is possible only in the immolation of self to something mightier outside it.

"Did he eat?" she asked and, when he nodded, began to cry. He stooped and took her in his arms and tried to still her sobbing, but he remembered how, this morning, he, himself, had cried in his mother's arms and was not able to find, nor in her bosom, nor in her words, the answering strength he sought. . . .

Monzon, when he came out, found them sharing a scanty supper. For once, he looked quite happy. He kept rubbing his hands and smiling absently. He shook his head at Nena's offer of food.

"No, I am not hungry. And I have to go now." He took out his watch. "Is there still a bus I can take, Nena? Chitong, you are to remain with the car. Tomorrow I will come back with the doctor."

Chitong rose and accompanied his father to the door. The

single lamp in the *sala* had gone out and they walked in darkness.

"Your grandfather is sleeping. If he wakes up, you can tell him I have gone."

They had reached the stairs. The elder Monzon paused and laid a hand on his son's shoulder. "Your mother has told you I am willing that you should follow your vocation, no?"

"Yes, father." Chitong could feel how in the dark his father's face had changed again. Even his voice had lost its momentary confidence.

"Yes. That is a good life," Monzon went on, "and it is, perhaps, the best for you."

He descended the stairs, opened the street-door below, and stepped out into the night. Chitong remained for some time at the head of the stairs, wondering just what those last words had meant.

In his grandfather's room, he spread a mat on the floor, undressed, and lay down. He had placed the lamp on a chair beside him and, now, he took out his breviary and began to read. The words that opened out to him were like cool arms into which he surrendered his troubled body. That had been a strange day, full of unrest and uncertainties; but as he read, an earlier sureness and peace came back to him.

"*. . . my soul had relied on His word. My soul had hoped in the Lord. From the morning watch even until night, let Israel hope in the Lord. For with the Lord, there is mercy and with Him plentiful redemption. And he shall redeem Israel from all his iniquities . . .*"

In his bed, on the other side of the room, the old man was awake and restless. Chitong could hear him turning, now to one side, now to the other. His breath came in short gasps, as if in difficulty. He reached out with his hands. He clutched at the pillows. He tried to rise.

The boy rose from time to time to cover him up again or

to pick up the pillows. The old man's hands sought and clung to the boy's arms but his eyes, Chitong saw, were closed.

Names poured from the old man's lips. He called on every woman he had ever loved. He wanted his women. He became angry and shouted for them as in the days of his strength. He commanded them to come near. He cursed and shook his fists at them. No one came. He tried to rise and fell back, moaning and beating on the bed with his hands.

Afterwards, he became quiet. He must have realized that he was powerful no longer. Then he began to call on his women again, but softly, tenderly. He wooed them as a shy boy might; his lips shaped broken and beautiful phrases of adoration. But still no one came.

He fell into despair. He became furious again. He raged in his bed. He howled with all his might. He tore at the pillows. He tried to get up. The bed shook with his anger.

Chitong, lying on the floor, tried to deafen his ears to the old man's cries. He tried to read, but the words would not stand still. He closed the book and tried to sleep but, even in the intervals when the old man lay silent, he could feel him suffering, desiring, despairing, there in his bed in the darkness.

He got up and thought: I will pray for him. I will pray that he be delivered from temptation. I will pray that God quiet the fever of his flesh.

He approached and knelt beside the old man's bed, but a glance at that tortured face shot hollow all the prayers in his mouth. He felt again, as at Santo Domingo that morning, empty and ridiculous.

The sick man stared at him, yet did not see him. Those eyes saw only women and the bodies of women. Pain and desire had made him blind to all else. He stretched out his shriveled hands for the women that were not there. He had exhausted his voice; now he could only moan. Chitong could bear it no longer.

He rose and left the room. He was thinking of that woman—no, only a girl really—whom his grandfather had kept before his legs collapsed. The older Monzon had driven the girl away, but she might still be living somewhere in the town. His Tía Nena was still up, ironing clothes in the kitchen; he would ask her.

But she was frightened when she learned what he proposed to do. Yes, the girl was living in the town. "But your father will surely find out, Chitong, if she comes here. Oh, do not ask me how. He will. He knows everything."

The words cut through the boy. "Then, let him!" he cried. "But I am going to bring the girl back. The old man needs her. Now, tell me where she lives."

It took him almost an hour to find the house, but only a few words to make the girl come. Chitong had seen her many times before, but when she came running down the stairs and stood beside him in the moonlight, he knew that he was seeing her really for the first time.

She was not very pretty, and still very young; but her body, her eyes, the way she moved, hinted that attractive maturity which only physical love develops. She had wrapped an old shawl around her head and shoulders, and as they hurried through the empty streets, Chitong could feel her thoughts running ahead towards the old man. But his mind, sensitive in such things, was not repelled.

There was in her, he knew, as in his grandfather, that simple unity which he, himself, had been denied. It was not strange that two such people should desire each other, or that so young a girl, when she might have more youthful lovers, should prefer the sexagenarian in whose arms she had become a woman. They had had to drive her away when he fell sick.

Chitong had been there when it happened and he recalled his father's exquisite brutality and how this girl had seemed to him, at the time, incapable of either fear or shame.

She had refused to leave the house; had stood before the elder Monzon, thrusting her defiant face into his; and Chitong remembered how his father's hands had trembled, though not a nerve in his face had twitched.

Monzon had released his belt on the sly, pushed the girl away suddenly, and given her a full stroke across the shoulders with the belt. And with the belt, he had pursued her out of the room and down the stairs, slamming the door in her face. She had remained down there, screaming and kicking at the door till the police came and dragged her away.

But she was not thinking at all of those things, Chitong saw, as he hurried beside her, glancing into her passionate face. She was going to her first lover. He had called her. He needed her. Young men were only young men: they could offer nothing in love to make her wiser than she had been in such things from the very beginning. And her nervous fingers, clutching the shawl across her breasts, spoke almost aloud the violence of her need.

A few steps from the house, a woman abruptly emerged from shadow. Chitong recognized his Tía Nena. She had been running; she could hardly speak.

"Chitong," she gasped, "your father has come back. He could not find a bus." She turned to the girl: "You must not come. Go back at once!"

The girl stepped back, but Chitong grapsed her hand. "Do not be afraid," he said. "You are coming."

His aunt stared at him. "Chitong, you know how it is when your father gets angry. . . ."

"I am not afraid."

"I think he suspects where you went. . . ."

"So much the better then. Come on."

It was the first time in his life he had made a decision. He felt released.

The elder Monzon was standing in the *sala* when they

entered. He had lighted the lamp and now stood watching it thoughtfully, his hands locked behind him. He glanced up as they filed in. When he saw the girl, he flushed darkly and he felt again the multitude of pins pricking his flesh. He dropped his eyes at once, but the girl's image persisted before him: the fierce eyes, the small, round mouth, the long, thin, girlish neck. She had drawn her shawl away, and he had seen where her breasts began and how they rose and fell with her breath.

He had a sudden, delirious craving to unloose his belt and whip her again, to make her suffer, to tear her flesh into shreds, to mutilate that supple, defiant, sweet, animal body of hers. His hands shook and his desire became an anger towards his son who had brought this voluptuous being so near.

"Who told you to bring this woman here, Chitong?" He tried in vain to make his voice calm. He doubled his fists: the nails dug into his flesh.

Chitong stared, open-mouthed. He realized now that what he had done was an action for which his soul would later demand reasons. It was not his father before whom he stood. It was God.

The girl was standing beside him and he felt her moving away. He sprang to life. "No, no," he cried. "You are not to go! He needs you! You must not go!" He held her back.

"A fine priest you will make!" snapped the elder Monzon.

Chitong came nearer. His eyes entreated the older man to understand. He stretched out a hand; with the other, he detained the girl. He had never found it so hard to make himself articulate.

"Father," he said at last, "if it is a sin to allow him his woman, then I will take the sin on my shoulders. I will pray that it. . . ."

"Release that woman!" cried the older man. "Let her go away!"

The boy's face hardened. "No, father. She is not going."

They were standing almost face to face. Suddenly, the father lifted his clenched fist and struck the boy in the face.

"Not in the face, father!" the boy cried out, lifting his hands too late to shield himself; the blow had already fallen.

Monzon, horrified, heard the boy's cry through every inch of his body. He had never before laid hands on the boy. The impulse to strike had come so suddenly. He tortured his mind for an explanation. He had not wanted to hurt the boy, no. He had, the moment before, desired the girl evil, but it was not she, either, who had prompted his fist. Was it the old man, then? Was it his father he had struck?

No. No, it was himself: that self of his, inherited, long fought, which had the moment before, looked on the girl with strange fury. It was that self of his, which perpetuated the old man, against whom he had lifted his fist, but it was his son who had received the blow—and the blow was a confession of his whole life.

Now he stood silent, watching the boy's flesh darken where his fist had fallen, and the gradual blood defining the wound.

They stood staring at each other, as if petrified, and the girl, forgotten, slipped swiftly away from them and into the old man's room, locking the door behind her.

A clock somewhere began striking ten. Nena sat in a corner, crying. A late cock could be heard crowing. And from the next room came the voices of the lovers: the old man's voice, tired and broken; the girl's, sharp and taut and passionate.

"No," she was saying, "I shall never leave you again. I am not going away again. No one shall take me away from you again."

MANUEL ARGUILLA [1911-1944]

Of all his three birthdays—the one according to his mother, the one on his birth certificate, and the one in school records—Manuel Arguilla preferred the last, since it coincided with that of national hero, Jose Rizal. But just to be sure, Arguilla used to celebrate all three. So much of an endless celebration was his whole life, that his wartime death seems the act of an impostor. In Nagrebcan, wedged between the northern mountains and the sea, his father, muscular even in old age and still able to plant his field and do carpenter work and smoke homemade Ilocano cigars with his wife, long outlived the son who dared to become a public figure.

In Manuel's boyhood Nagrebcan had only fifteen houses and two hundred farmers. It has changed no more than has the distance, by *carretela,* from railroad station to *barrio.* Manuel's first stories were about the plowing of Nagrebcan farm lands, the feeding and watering of work animals, planting, harvesting, courtship. "Keats may write on skylarks," he said, "but Arguilla will write on *mayas.* . . . I can write truly and authentically only of people, places and things that I know." He wrote well also of San Fernando, the provincial capital with its hillside of *madre de cacao* trees; the lighthouse at Poro Point; the beaches of Carlatan: and when, later, he wrote of Manila, his sympathies were with the workers who had migrated hopefully from the *barrios* only to sell chewing gum and cigarettes in the alleyways, sitting hunched day after day over rotting lungs.

Like his father, Manuel loved to tinker; and he enjoyed his body. He practiced with barbells; became backstroke champion of the state university swimming team; won prizes tangoing. He delighted in simple, sensuous pleasures such as bathing; or dressing; or cooking. He always had time to visit a sick friend, his wife Lydia has said, ". . . . and bring him eggs, oranges and a new fund of anecdotes, but had no time for big, impersonal social affairs. . . . Once a psychoanalyst told him he had a therapeutic personality. . . . It was a fact that all kinds of people enjoyed talking to him because he enjoyed talking to them. . . . Once he picked up an interest, he concentrated on it with such intensity that it became an inalienable part of his personality."

His home on M. H. del Pilar, only blocks away from Manila Bay, was everyone's home, at any hour. On the mosaic-floored porch with its zinc roof jutting out among ferns and butterfly orchids growing in coconut husks, gathered the country's future writers— N. V. M. Gonzalez, Estrella Alfon, Jose Garcia Villa when he came home on rare visits—along with publisher A. V. H. Hartendorp. They drank beer together under the *macopa* tree or swam in the bay.

In 1940, Manuel Arguilla won the Commonwealth prize for his volume, *How My Brother Leon Brought Home a Wife and Other Stories*. Most of his stories are notable for their complex illusion of simplicity, their restraint of passion in the grace of form, their "objective intimacy," the realistic check on sentimental extravagance.

The Commonwealth prize was his last award. During the Japanese Occupation, he commanded the Porch, a supply, counter-propaganda and intelligence unit of Marking's Guerrillas in Manila. Meanwhile, he was employed by the unsuspecting Japanese in their own traveling propaganda unit and, later, as censor for stage shows. At last suspicious, the Kempeitai turned his house inside out; and in February 1944, arrested him. Although his wife escaped to the provinces, the Japanese imprisoned Manuel's mother and other relatives in Fort Santiago. Two months later these were released; but he himself was transferred to Old Bilibid on May 16, to be tortured and given a mock trial. As his thirty-third birthday approached, he and other prisoners were taken to Fort McKinley. There, as Rizal had been before him, Manuel Arguilla was executed.

HOW MY BROTHER LEON
BROUGHT HOME A WIFE

SHE STEPPED DOWN from the *carretela* of Ca Celin
with a quick, delicate grace. She was lovely. She was tall. She
looked up to my brother with a smile, and her forehead was
on a level with his mouth.

"You are Baldo," she said and placed her hand lightly on
my shoulder. Her nails were long, but they were not painted.
She was fragrant like a morning when papayas are in bloom.
And a small dimple appeared momently high up on her right
cheek.

"And this is Labang of whom I have heard so much." She
held the wrist of one hand with the other and looked at Labang, and Labang never stopped chewing his cud. He swallowed and brought up to his mouth more cud and the sound
of his insides was like a drum.

I laid a hand on Labang's massive neck and said to her:
"You may scratch his forehead now."

She hesitated and I saw that her eyes were on the long
curving horns. But she came and touched Labang's forehead
with her long fingers, and Labang never even stopped chewing
his cud except that his big eyes half closed. And by and by, she
was scratching his forehead very daintily.

My brother Leon put down the two trunks on the grassy
side of the road. He paid Ca Celin twice the usual fare from

the station to the edge of Nagrebcan. Then he was standing beside us, and she turned to him eagerly. I watched Ca Celin, where he stood in front of his horse, and he ran his fingers through its forelock and could not keep his eyes away from her.

"Maria—" my brother Leon said.

He did not say Maring. He did not say Mayang. I knew then that he had always called her Maria, and that to us all she would be Maria; and in my mind I said—"Maria"—and it was a beautiful name.

"Yes, Noel."

Now where did she get that name? I pondered the matter quietly to myself, thinking Father might not like it. But it was only the name of my brother Leon said backwards and it sounded much better that way.

"There, is Nagrebcan, Maria," my brother Leon said, gesturing widely toward the west.

She moved close to him and slipped her arm through his. And after a while she said quietly:

"You love Nagrebcan, don't you, Noel?"

Ca Celin drove away hi-yi-ing to his horse loudly. At the bend of the *camino real* where the big duhat tree grew, he rattled the handle of his braided rattan whip against the spokes of the wheel.

We stood alone on the roadside.

The sun was in our eyes for it was dipping into the bright sea. The sky was wide and deep and very blue above us; but along the saw-tooth rim of the Katayaghan hills to the south-west flamed huge masses of clouds. Before us the fields swam in a gold haze through which floated big purple and red and yellow bubbles when I looked at the sinking sun. Labang's white coat which I had washed and brushed that morning with coconut husk, glistened like beaten cotton under the lamp-light and his horns appeared tipped with fire. He faced the sun and from his mouth came a call so loud and vibrant that

the earth seemed to tremble underfoot. And far away in the
middle of the fields a cow lowed softly in answer.

"Hitch him to the cart, Baldo," my brother Leon said,
laughing, and she laughed with him a bit uncertainly, and I
saw that he had put his arms around his shoulders.

"Why does he make that sound?" she asked. "I have
never heard the like of it."

"There is not another like it," my brother Leon said. "I
have yet to hear another bull call like Labang. In all the world
there is no other bull like him."

She was smiling at him, and I stopped in the act of tying
the *sinta* across Labang's neck to the opposite end of the yoke,
because her teeth were very white, her eyes were so full of
laughter, and there was a small dimple high up on her right
cheek.

"If you continue to talk about him like that, either I shall
fall in love with him or become greatly jealous."

My brother Leon laughed and she laughed and they
looked at each other and it seemed to me there was a world
of laughter between them and in them.

I climbed into the cart over the wheel and Labang would
have bolted for he was always like that, but I kept a firm hold
on his rope. He was restless and would not stand still, so that
my brother Leon had to say "Labang" several times. When he
was quiet again, my brother Leon lifted the trunks into the
cart, placing the smaller on top.

She looked down once at her high-heeled shoes, then she
gave her left hand to my brother Leon, placed a foot on the
hub of the wheel, and in one breath she had swung up into
the cart. Oh, the fragrance of her. But Labang was fairly dancing with impatience and it was all I could do to keep him from
running away.

"Give me the rope, Baldo," my brother Leon said. "Maria,
sit down on the hay and hold on to anything." Then he put

a foot on the left shaft and that instant Labang leaped forward. My brother Leon laughed as he drew himself up to the top of the side of the cart and made the slack of the rope hiss above the back of Labang. The wind whistled against my cheeks and the rattling of the wheels on the pebbly road echoed in my ears.

She sat up straight on the bottom of the cart, legs bent so that only the toes and heels of her shoes were visible. Her eyes were on my brother Leon's back; I saw the wind on her hair.

When Labang slowed down, my brother Leon handed to me the rope. I knelt on the straw inside the cart and pulled on the rope until Labang was merely shuffling along, then I made him turn around.

"What is it you have forgotten now, Baldo?" my brother Leon said.

I did not say anything but tickled with my fingers the rump of Labang; and away we went—back to where I had un-hitched and waited for them. The sun had sunk and down from the wooded sides of the Katayaghan hills shadows were stealing into the fields. High up overhead the sky burned with many slow fires.

When I sent Labang down the deep cut that would bring us to the dry bed of the Waig which could be used as a path to our place during the dry season, my brother Leon laid a hand on my shoulder and said sternly:

"Who told you to drive through the fields tonight?"

His hand was heavy on my shoulder, but I did not look at him nor utter a word until we were on the rocky bottom of the Waig.

"Baldo, you fool, answer me before I lay the rope of Labang on you. Why do you follow the Waig instead of the *camino real*?"

His fingers bit into my shoulder.

"Father, he told me to follow the Waig tonight, *Manong.*"

Swiftly, his hand fell away from my shoulder and he reached for the rope of Labang. Then my brother Leon laughed, and he sat back, and laughing still, he said: "And I suppose Father also told you to hitch Labang to the cart and meet us with him instead of with Castaño and the *calesa.*"

Without waiting for an answer, he turned to her and said, "Maria, why do you think Father should do that, now?" He laughed and added, "Have you ever seen so many stars before?"

I looked back and they were sitting side by side, leaning against the trunks, hands clasped across knees. Seemingly but a man's height above the tops of the steep banks of the Waig, hung the stars. But in the deep gorge, the shadows had fallen heavily, and even the white of Labang's coat was merely a dim grayish blur. Crickets chirped from their homes in the cracks in the banks. The thick unpleasant smell of dangla bushes and cooling sun-heated earth mingled with the clean, sharp scent of arrais roots exposed to the night air and of the hay inside the cart.

"Look, Noel, yonder is our star!" Deep surprise and gladness were in her voice. Very low in the west, almost touching the ragged edge of the bank, was the star, the biggest and brightest in the sky.

"I have been looking at it," my brother Leon said. "Do you remember how I would tell you that when you want to see stars you must come to Nagrebcan?"

"Yes, Noel," she said. "Look at it," she murmured, half to herself. "It is so many times bigger and brighter than it was at Ermita beach."

"The air here is clean, free of dust and smoke."

"So it is, Noel," she said, drawing a long breath.

"Making fun of me, Maria?"

She laughed then and they laughed together and she took my brother Leon's hand and put it against her face.

I stopped Labang, climbed down, and lighted the lantern that hung from the cart between the wheels.

"Good boy, Baldo," my brother Leon said as I climbed back into the cart, and my heart sang.

Now the shadows took fright and did not crowd so near. Clumps of andadasi and arrais flashed into view and quickly disappeared as we passed by. Ahead, the elongated shadow of Labang bobbed up and down and swayed drunkenly from side to side, for the lantern rocked jerkily with the cart.

"Have we far to go yet, Noel?" she asked.

"Ask Baldo," my brother Leon said, "we have been neglecting him."

"I am asking you, Baldo," she said.

Without looking back, I answered, picking my words slowly:

"Soon we will get out of the Waig and pass into the fields. After the fields is home,—*Manang.*"

"So near already."

I did not say anything more, because I did not know what to make of the tone of her voice as she said her last words. All the laughter seemed to have gone out of her. I waited for my brother Leon to say something, but he was not saying anything. Suddenly he broke out into song and the song was "Sky Sown with Stars"—the same that he and Father sang when we cut hay in the fields of nights before he went away to study. He must have taught her the song because she joined him, and her voice flowed into his like a gentle stream meeting a stronger one. And each time the wheels encountered a big rock, her voice would catch in her throat, but my brother Leon would sing on, until laughing softly, she would join him again.

Then we were climbing out into the fields, and through

the spokes of the wheels the light of the lantern mocked the shadows. Labang quickened his steps. The jolting became more frequent and painful as we crossed the low dikes.

"But it is so very wide here," she said. The light of the stars broke and scattered the darkness so that one could see far on every side, though indistinctly.

"You miss the houses, and the cars, and the people and the noise, don't you?" My brother Leon stopped singing.

"Yes, but in a different way. I am glad they are not here."

With difficulty, I turned Labang to the left, for he wanted to go straight on. He was breathing hard, but I knew he was more thirsty than tired. In a little while, we drove up the grassy side onto the *camino real.*

"—you see," my brother Leon was explaining, "the *camino real* curves around the foot of the Katayaghan hills and passes by our house. We drove through the fields, because—but I'll be asking Father as soon as we get home."

"Noel," she said.

"Yes, Maria."

"I am afraid. He may not like me."

"Does that worry you still, Maria?" my brother Leon said. "From the way you talk, he might be an ogre, for all the world. Except when his leg that was wounded in the Revolution is troubling him, Father is the mildest-tempered, gentlest man I know."

We came to the house of Lacay Julian and I spoke to Labang loudly, but Moning did not come to the window, so I surmised she must be eating with the rest of her family. And I thought of the food being made ready at home and my mouth watered. We met the twins, Urong and Celin, and I said "Hoy," calling them by name. And they shouted back and asked if my brother Leon and his wife were with me. And my brother Leon shouted to them and then told me to make Labang run; their answers were lost in the noise of the wheels.

I stopped Labang on the road before our house and would have gotten down, but my brother Leon took the rope and told me to stay in the cart. He turned Labang into the open gate and we dashed into our yard. I thought we would crash into the bole of the camachile tree, but my brother Leon reined in Labang in time. There was light downstairs in the kitchen, and Mother stood in the doorway, and I could see her smiling shyly. My brother Leon was helping Maria over the wheel.

The first words that fell from his lips after he had kissed Mother's hand were:

"Father, where is he?"

"He is in his room upstairs," Mother said, her face becoming serious. "His leg is bothering him again."

I did not hear anything more because I had to go back to the cart to unhitch Labang. But I had hardly tied him under the barn when I heard Father calling me. I met my brother Leon going to bring up the trunks. As I passed through the kitchen, there were Mother and my sister Aurelia and Maria and it seemed to me they were crying, all of them.

There was no light in Father's room. There was no movement. He sat in the big armchair by the western window, and a star shone directly through it. He was smoking, but he removed the roll of tobacco from his mouth when he saw me. He laid it carefully on the window-sill before speaking.

"Did you meet anybody on the way?" he asked.

"No, Father," I said. "Nobody passes through the Waig at night."

He reached for his roll of tobacco and hitched himself up in the chair.

"She is very beautiful, Father."

"Was she afraid of Labang?" My father had not raised his voice, but the room seemed to resound with it. And again I saw her eyes on the long curving horns and the arm of my brother Leon around her shoulders.

"No, Father, she was not afraid."

"On the way—"

"She looked at the stars, Father. And Manong Leon sang."

"What did he sing?"

" 'Sky Sown with Stars.' She sang with him."

He was silent again. I could hear the low voices of Mother and my sister Aurelia downstairs. There was also the voice of my brother Leon, and I thought that Father's voice must have been like it when he was young. He had laid the roll of tobacco on the window-sill once more. I watched the smoke waver faintly upward from the lighted end and vanish slowly into the night outside.

The door opened and my brother Leon and Maria came in.

"Have you watered Labang?" Father spoke to me.

I told him that Labang was resting yet under the barn.

"It is time you watered him, my son," my father said.

I looked at Maria and she was lovely. She was tall. Beside my brother Leon, she was very tall and very still. Then I went out, and in the darkened hall the fragrance of her was like a morning when papayas are in bloom.

EPILOGUE TO REVOLT

THERE WAS a great uproar in the village on the day that the four pardoned prisoners arrived from the city accompanied by the town president. A big crowd was at the little station to meet them and, as the four men descended from the train, shouts of *Mabuhay*—long live—filled the morning air. The town president, in a barong Tagalog of embroidered jusi, his narra cane hooked on his left arm, stood on the steps of the train. He waved his buntal hat and shouted, *"Mabuhay si Quezon!"* The crowd took up the cry; many voices wished long and fruitful life upon Quezon, who had on his fifty-eighth birthday pardoned thirty-one Sakdalistas, four of whom came from this village.

The engine whistle blew a piercing blast; the train started to move forward; it puffed and snorted furiously, for some moments drowning the noise of the villagers. The passengers in the coaches stuck their heads out of the windows, waved their hands and hats. And once more the villagers raised their voices in a mighty cheer, *"Mabuhay si Quezon!"* They jumped up and down, stamped on the green grass, waved back to the passengers. Then the train made the turn around the low hill at the southern end of the village and vanished as though swallowed by the earth.

The people of the village were left with the four pardoned prisoners whose names were Julian, Binong, Inggo, and Ansel.

"*Vámonos,*" said the town president who had a fondness for Spanish. "Let us go to the *lechonada.*"

"*Bámonos, bámonos,*" the children cried; they ran through the crowd, chased each other, and rolled on the grass.

A feast had been prepared in the yard of the house of the *teniente del barrio,* barely five hundred meters from the station. If the wind had been right, there would have been wafted to the crowd the delicious odor of young pig roasting whole over a heap of burning coals. More than a dozen chickens had also been slaughtered to provide the soup which even now simmered, golden-brown, inside wide-mouthed iron kettles set above slow fires in trenches dug to one side of the long, hastily improvised table covered with banana leaves.

The town president led the way, his buntal hat firmly set on his head, an unlighted cigar between his lips. At every other step, he poked the ground with his cane which he held in his right hand.

"*Adelante,*" he said.

The four pardoned prisoners walked immediately behind the town president. Julian held his youngest by the hand—a boy of seven, dark-skinned like his father, and with his father's stout, slightly bowed legs. The boy hopped along as fast as he could, not looking at his father, his eyes on the back of the town president.

"Where is your mother?" Julian asked hoarsely, for his throat was raw from having shouted so much at the station.

"She stayed behind, Itay," said the boy, pulling his father's arm. "She is with the other women, cooking the food we shall eat." His small, sweaty fingers slipped like eels from Julian's hand, and he went to join the other children who were now in a noisy group running in front of the crowd. Inggo carried his youngest child on his shoulder, the other two boys having left his side to be with the rest of the children.

"Wait until you grow bigger," said Inggo to the restive child who wanted to be running with the others. "They will step on your navel now."

"When I am big, I shall be a *Sakdalista.*"

"Fool of a child," said Binong, who was walking behind Inggo. "Do you wish to be shot down by soldiers?"

"I will kill them all with my bolo."

"Then you will be put in Bilibid where you will rot like salted fish."

"You are only trying to frighten me," said the child. "Quezon will send me home and we will have *lechon* to eat."

Binong started to laugh. "Ho, ho, ho," he bellowed, his thick shoulders shaking. Binong had no child, having been married barely a fortnight when he had joined the Sakdals and fought with bolos and spears and home-made guns the constabulary soldiers sent down to subdue them. "Ho, ho, ho," he roared, placing an arm around the narrow shoulders of the thin, sensitive-faced Ansel. There were ringworm marks on Binong's wrist and between his fingers—coarse, whitish spots.

Ansel quietly removed Binong's arm from his neck. Binong was shouting with laughter, bending forward drunkenly, stumbling from side to side. He was still laughing, the tears fairly streaming down his hairy face, when the crowd reached the house of the *teniente del barrio.*

The house boasted galvanized iron roofing and *sawali* walls, unlike the surrounding huts of nipa and bamboo. Hanging from the eaves at the windows were different kinds of air plants held in coconut husks painted red. There were no curtains.

"So you have come back," said Petra, Binong's young, buxom wife. "See that at the earliest opportunity you go out again waving your bolo," she said, warding off with quick blows his clumsy attempts to take her into his arms.

"No more of that for me," Binong said. "We promised

Quezon—did we not, Ansel?" slapping the other man's back.

Ansel turned away. He went upstairs where a prayer was to be said before the feast began.

Aling Sabel, Julian's wife, stood before an image of the Virgin Mary at the north end of the small *sala*. In her hand was a big candle which she lighted and placed on the table supporting the Virgin Mary. Then making the sign of the Cross, Aling Sabel knelt down and began to pray in a voice that could be heard clearly in all parts of the house. The women, old and young, fell on their knees behind Aling Sabel. Some of the men who had come up from the yard at the behest of their wives, sat on the window ledges. One or two knelt. The four pardoned prisoners near Aling Sabel squatted on their heels. As the prayer progressed, the crowd mumbling the answers to the words intoned by Aling Sabel, the four men got up on their knees, the thin, sensitive-faced Ansel first.

The voice of the town president, hoarse and peremptory, could be heard coming from the yard. He was telling several of the men left down there and one or two of the younger girls how to place the food on the long table. Now and then the howl of a kicked dog or the fierce snarling of several dogs fighting over a bone dominated every other noise.

The prayer was long. Aling Sabel never once changed her position. Only her fingers carefully telling the wooden beads of her rosary to mark the number of *Ave Marias* she had said, could be seen to move. Her voice was steady and clear. Some of the kneeling women had sunk down on their heels, their knees not proof against the hard bamboo slats of the floor.

Aling Sabel's voice dropped, took on a deep earnest tone of supplication as she began the Litany. *Santa María, Mother of God, pray for the countless souls in torment in the fires of Purgatory, especially for the souls of Potenciano García, Manacis Bautista....*

The women beat their breasts and said, *Mother of God, pray for him,* after each name.

A woman sobbed. It was Marta, the widow of Ansel's older brother, Potenciano, who was among those killed during the Sakdal uprising. Several women began to weep, noisily. But above the tumult of their lamentations rose the clear voice of Aling Sabel. She had reached the invocation: *Kyrie eleison,* she intoned, clasping her hands, the wooden beads of her rosary dangling from her tightly interlaced fingers.

There was a rustling of clothes and a creaking of the floor as everyone now knelt upright and repeated the words after Aling Sabel. Then it was the end and each person made the sign of the triple cross, and Aling Sabel turned around, saying in her ordinary voice, "Good morning to everybody," and the youngsters got up to kiss the hands of the old people, who blessed them.

Julian called his youngest child to him and held him up against his chest, saying, "How tall you are now, my son," and the child said, "That is because you are carrying me." Aling Sabel, going up to them, laid a hand on Julian's arm and said: "Leave your Itay, my child. He must be tired after his long journey. Go now into the yard. Fill up on chicken meat and roasted pig." Julian lowered the boy and he raced down the stairs so fast that Aling Sabel called after him, "Take care, do not fall down and break your neck."

When she turned to Julian, there were tears in her eyes, and she pulled a corner of the kerchief around her neck to wipe them away.

"You old woman," said Julian, gruffly. "Why are you crying like a child? We had a fine time in Bilibid. Ask Inggo here," he said, grabbing Inggo, who nodded his head and laughed, and nodded his head again.

"O, you are a fool, you old man," said Aling Sabel. "Why did not the *constabulario* kill you?"

"Ho, ho, ho," Binong laughed, dragging Petra after him. "Hear that, Julian? Come, let's go down to eat. Come, Aling Sabel, you nearly starved me to death with your long prayer."

"What a shameless one you are, Binong," Aling Sabel said. "Prison has not changed you one bit."

"Nothing will ever change Binong," Ansel said in his quiet manner, and Binong looked at him.

"Well, and how about you?" he asked heavily. "Better be careful how you talk after this. We want no more of your —your changes."

Ansel turned away.

They went down to eat.

On each side of the long, narrow table, the people ranged themselves, standing, and ate with their hands. The *lechon*, chopped into small pieces, lay in mounds in the center of the table; big platters of rice were within reach of everyone. Boiled prawns, thick as a man's wrist, and crabs with huge pincers, were bright scarlet on the green banana leaves. There was *tuba* aplenty, fresh from the nipa groves, and everyone, men, women, and children, drank it from the slender bamboo tubes. People left the table when they had finished eating and others took their place. A ceaseless chatter, broken by loud, unrestrained laughter and the sharp clattering of dishes, enveloped the yard.

The four pardoned prisoners stood near the town president who was at the head of the table. Soon there arose a clamor for a speech. "Speech, speech!" the crowd shouted. And the town president wiped his mouth, picked up his cane which he had laid against a leg of the table, leaned on it a moment, smiled, shook his head, laughed, hooked the cane on his left arm, looked around, and spread his hands in front of him as the people continued to demand a speech.

The president had more gray than black in his short, thinning hair. He had been elected twice to his post; he hoped to be elected again. He coughed and the people grew silent.

"*Compatriotas,*" he began, and his voice rose and fell rhythmically as he went on, dwelling on the vowels, stretching the last syllables of the words. He was interrupted by frequent applause. Whenever the name Quezon fell from his lips, the people shouted, "*Mabuhay si Quezon.*" At one time, the clamorous voices of some children playing to one side of the yard caused him to turn a disapproving glance in their direction. Binong went over and ordered the youngsters to be quiet, cuffing the more obstinate ones, but in a little while they were again running after each other and shouting at the top of their voices.

The town president did not speak very long, because his throat was sore. "In conclusion," he said hoarsely, "permit me, my countrymen, to put into words what is in the heart of every person here: We ask God to reward and bless our good President Manuel Luis Quezon through whose kindness and generosity our four friends are now with us enjoying the freedom of the earth and sky . . . . They have learned their lesson and will in future time be law-abiding citizens . . . ." The end of his speech was punctuated by shouts in which his name, the name of Quezon, and those of the four pardoned prisoners were heard.

When the noise subsided somewhat, it was noticed that Ansel had not joined in the cheering. Too, food lay before him untouched. The town president turned to him saying, testily, "Ha, Ansel, you still think of your brother? He was ten thousand times a fool—God forgive me for speaking ill of the dead! But so are you a fool if you do not change your mind. You have more education than the rest of the men here. Now is your chance to show them how to profit by their mistakes. Eh? *Sinvergüenza!*" And the president glared wrathfully at the silent man.

"Speech, speech, Ansel," Binong yelled, laughing loudly, looking around at the crowd who cried with him, "Speech, Ansel, speech! *Mabuhay si Ansel!*"

Ansel swallowed but did not speak. His hands were clasped behind him, making him appear thinner than ever. His *camisa de chino* hung loosely from his narrow shoulders. At last he opened his mouth to speak. He began in a low voice; the people leaned forward the better to hear what Ansel had to say.

"My words are few. I have not much to say. There is nothing it seems that I can say to you now. You do not really care to hear anything that I have to say. All that you want now is a 'speech' to go with the food that you eat."

An uncomfortable silence fell on the crowd around the table. The children in the yard could be heard distinctly, yelling, chasing each other. The town president frowned angrily; he called Ansel's name in a hoarse, admonitory whisper, but Ansel seemed not to have heard him.

"We pray for the souls of the dead," he went on, his voice unemphatic; he stared straight in front of him, beyond the heads of the people. "Then we stuff ourselves with food bought with money that is borrowed. We do these things better than anything else I can think of. This is what I have learned. Just so long as we can pray and gorge on pig's flesh and chicken meat, the dead can rot in their graves—."

Ansel paused, and a boy wearing a black shirt came running across the yard; he yelled shrilly: "I am a Sakdal, I am a Sakdal. Follow me, follow me." Several other children raced after him; they waved pointed sticks before their faces, intent and eager.

Binong started to laugh. The tension caused by Ansel's words was broken. "Ho, ho, ho," Binong roared. He caught one of the urchins, the one in the black shirt; shook him roughly: "Fool," he leered into the bewildered face of the child. "You want to be shot like your father, ha? Here, give me that," he said, snatching away the stick with which the boy had begun to strike the big thick hands that held him. He gave the child several light whacks, broke the stick in two, threw the pieces away and laughed.

Crying, the boy ran to the side of Ansel. The man placed his arm around the shaking shoulders, comforted the boy in his quiet voice, and led him away from the feasting.

BIENVENIDO N. SANTOS [1911 –]

The Sulucan slums, near the railroad tracks in Manila's Tondo section, are the common home of Emilio Jacinto, intellectual leader of the 1896 Katipunan revolt, as well as of modern "greasegun" gangs; of movie star Rogelio de la Rosa and of Vice-President Diosdado Macapagal; of the now punch-drunk former flyweight champion of the Orient and of Bienvenido Santos, writer and teacher.

In a crumbling nipa hut on an open sewer, Santos watched his father cough out his life and daily before walking to school washed the cancer in his mother's neck with Lysol. While earning his college degree (BSE, 1931) at the University of the Philippines, he rose from messenger to publisher's understudy on a woman's magazine.

In 1941, he was sent as a *pensionado* to the University of Illinois; later he studied creative writing at Columbia and, with I. A. Richards, Basic English at Harvard. When the Japanese bombed Baguio and Manila, Santos was asked by the U.S. Office of Education to tour America and to lecture on the strength and stamina of his people. The loneliness of his enforced separation from his wife brought him closer to his fellow "exiles." On campus after campus, "All I did was talk sincerely, all I did was be myself, liking people, warming up easily in company, and I loved my countrymen, the so-called Pinoys who were simple and good and trusting once they found you were not a snob simply because you went to college." For these "hurt men" and not for officials at the Philippine Embassy who "passed themselves off as South Americans" he collected his stories, *You Lovely People* (1955).

By then he had returned to the Philippines and had become a professor and ranking official of the Legazpi Colleges in Albay, near the end of the government railroad tracks spinning out of Manila. As an administrator he felt uncomfortable always: "I am not so happy," he wrote, "because I cannot always be good to everybody . . . I am afraid to hurt other people because I am so easily hurt myself." In addition, a Palanca award in 1951 and the success of *You Lovely People* in the Benipayo Series on Philippine Contemporary Writing and of his collected poetry, *The Wounded Stag* (1956), encouraged him to believe in himself as a writer.

In 1957, he was appointed president of the Legazpi Colleges; but the following year he resigned and accepted a Rockefeller grant (renewed in 1959), in order to complete several novels at the State University of Iowa. This time his wife Beatriz was able to accompany him. In his absence, a manuscript of earlier Sulucan stories was awarded first prize during the golden jubilee contest conducted by the University of the Philippines in 1958. Later, the same work, *Brother, My Brother,* was published in Manila. In all his writings, there is the sound of endurance, denying that it must drop into silence unheard. Not the death of beauty, but the beauty of beauty even in death, is the writer's burden and signature for Santos as person.

After finishing several drafts of *Villa Magdalena* at Iowa, Santos was awarded a Guggenheim, to permit the writing of a second novel, *The Volcano,* whose setting is international. Simultaneously he became the first visiting lecturer in fiction craft from the Philippines, under the State University of Iowa Foundation in Creative Writing.

THE COMMON THEME

Why should we in our peevish opposition
Take it to heart? Fie! 'tis a fault to heaven,
A fault against the dead, a fault to nature,
To reason most absurd, whose common theme
Is death of fathers . . .

—HAMLET, I, 2.

For a wet season, with the rains coming as early as April soon after Easter, that October in 1941 was a dry month indeed. Even the year-long puddles on the way to Martin's house in the interior of Sulucan were dry. Their surfaces had taken on a dark-green yellowish hue not unlike the Hawaiian sweet potatoes which Andang sold near the Cine Star in the days of her maidenhood. Now she stayed at home with their son Dencio who helped her fashion artificial flowers out of thin wire and cheap crepe paper of many colors. For imitation orchids of the rare Mindanao variety, she used parchment of a quite expensive quality. Finished, they had the cool snobbish splendor of the true *cattleya*. The likeness between the artificial and the real was amazing.

Martin had not ceased to marvel at the magic—it couldn't be anything but that—of Andang's hands fashioning flowers out of wire and paper. Daily as he sat in a corner of the market north of the bolted warehouse surrounded by mounds of slow-burning sawdust, Martin wondered whether indeed the flowers he was peddling were real or not. Sometimes looking at the buds he caught himself waiting for them to burst open, they seemed so live with the promise of growth. And he would smile, thinking of Andang with unusual tenderness. On a clear night, as he walked home from the market, the unsold flowers in the baskets in his arms looked real enough in the moonlight; a woodland fragrance pervaded the air; these were yellow cannas, red roses, pale white lilies, orchids and *champacas,* fresh from a garden, fresh with moonlight.

But tonight all the flowers had been sold. The empty flower baskets dangled on the hook of his arm. He had said, early that morning, there would be many people now looking for artificial flowers to decorate the graves of the poor of Manila. Andang had bought plenty of material, rolls of wire and crepe paper of all colors, imitation parchment, glue, and an extra pair of scissors for Dencio. The boy was learning fast. He didn't mind working after school. That boy would never go hungry, Martin thought with pride. Even now mother and son would be working. He must tell her that red roses were in demand. People asked for roses, they fetched the lowest price. Even he could make them if he tried. People liked them, always asked for them. In their lives, perhaps, no other flowers bloomed but roses; and right here in Sulucan, red should go well with the green of dried up puddles and fungi on stagnant streams. Oh, well, artificial flowers are just right for the graves of men. They last longer than the day set aside for the dead, they need no care, they can dry up and look fresh again after the rain, they don't wilt in the sun. But it is a gift making them, a sort of magic which Andang possessed, which she could give Dencio and him, Martin, whose hands were rough with work, who was too strong and too careless with fragile things like paper flowers.

Martin paused at Chua's store. On the right side of the building was a narrow trail bridged with half-buried stones all the way to the waterless creek beyond which was his house, 1047, interior 12, Sulucan.

"Martin!" called out one of the men loitering in front of the Chinese store, "A letter arrived for you this morning. The postman had a hard time looking for your house."

"Huh?" Martin asked. He could not believe what he heard. He could not remember how far back, these many years, since someone had written him a letter.

"Your boy got it and must have given it to Andang," the man said.

"Where did it come from?" Martin asked.

"I don't know," said the man, "how should I know?"

"That's right," Martin said, smiling shyly, "I was just asking myself."

But now as he stepped on the stones in the alley, he knew who had sent the letter. The thought struck him suddenly like an unexpected tap on the shoulder that made you turn around only to find yourself face to face with somebody dearly beloved and missed so long. Who else could have written him and known where he lived except Gorio, his only brother who resided somewhere in the southern islands?

What could Gorio say, he now asked himself as he walked on through the alley. But nice of him to remember. God, he knew it, Gorio had not forgotten!

Gorio was his elder brother. He worked in a printer's shop in those days when his parents were still living. He studied at night in the Philippine School of Commerce. He would come home very late. Martin would be fast asleep. But he would wake up as Gorio lay down beside him in the dark, smelling of sweat that had soured all day. Gorio would not say anything. He would just push him a little for a bit of space on the floor. They lived in this same one-room shack in the interior of Sulucan. The house was low, two of its posts were in a river bed, the other two on dry land. Sometimes Martin would complain. "You don't have to wake me up every time you come in," but Gorio would only say, "Move over," or sometimes, he would whisper, "Is there food in the house? I'm hungry."

Gorio was unhappy in Sulucan. After a while he stopped going to school. That was soon after their mother's death. Their father died also in less than two years. He was an old man, given to silences, and always infirm. Martin himself was old enough to work, old enough to even marry. When he landed a temporary job at the Manila Railroad Company, he married Andang. Gorio left for the south soon afterwards. In his letters, he said that he worked for a man who was the manager of a provincial branch of an American oil company. There was a letter almost every month during the first year. Around October, he sent money for two electric bulbs, one for Mother's grave, and the other, for Father's.

But the succeeding years brought no more word from Gorio. He had stopped writing. Even after Dencio was born and Martin had asked Andang to write him, Gorio did not write. Since then every time Martin heard that someone in Sulucan had been to the South, he would go to him even if he was a stranger and ask, "Have you seen Gorio, my brother?" Then he would recite particulars which, of course, were not of any use, as in most cases the stranger was not interested or took Martin for what he seemed, an ignorant laborer, too stupid to realize that the southern islands were many and teemed with people. Martin didn't even mind being fooled by those who, seeing in him a likely victim to their fun, pretended they knew Gorio, invented imaginary conversations, and when Martin's eyes glowed with hope that perhaps, here, at last, his search for his brother was ended, they would slap him on the shoulder and confess that they were only joking. Martin swallowed his tears hard, but he didn't care. He never truly gave up hope.

There were bad times for Martin. That year Andang got sick and Dencio himself nearly died. Martin worked as substitute garbage collector for a while. He had always had a weak stomach and the job, for him, was quite an ordeal. He kept vomiting the first few days, but he learned to endure it. After some time the garbage didn't stink too much any more. In those days he prayed hard so Gorio would know, so he would write. He went to church and prayed, "Wherever you are, Gorio, please think of us, we need your help, Andang and Dencio are very sick. We need help. God help us."

God was kind, Andang and the boy got well and soon she was selling cakes and sweet potatoes at the foot of their stairs. But Gorio had not written.

Now, at last, this letter. Oh, please, Martin prayed, let it be a letter from Gorio.

When he reached the house, he found Andang and Dencio squatting on the floor with the kerosene lamp on the trunk giving them the light they needed. Crepe paper and wires lay on the floor. The finished flowers stood in a basket near the kerosene lamp.

"Andang," he said, dropping the empty baskets near the door, "is it true, I have a letter?"

"Yes," Andang answered. "Where's the letter, Dencio?"

Dencio had jumped up from the floor and was now kissing his father's hand. He got an envelope from under the support of a mirror hanging on the wall. "Here, Father," he said, giving Martin the letter.

Martin went over to the trunk where the lamp was, stepping on buds and stems. He knelt as he placed the envelope under the light. Andang and Dencio crowded around him.

"You did not open it?" Martin asked his wife, as he read his name on the envelope.

"No," Andang said, shaking her head, "Dencio said it was not proper."

Martin tried to open the letter at the flap but could not. He tried one side and suddenly he felt weak. His fingers felt like lard.

"Dencio," he said softly, "give me the scissors."

Dencio was quick to obey. Martin's tenseness filled the room. He clipped the side of the envelope. Dencio watched the thin sliced end curl towards him like a white strand as it fell on the floor.

Martin's fingers felt for the paper inside. There was a typewritten sheet; and a money order.

"Money!" Dencio gasped. He had seen those things in school.

Andang stretched her hand toward the pink piece of paper, but Martin drew it away from her towards the light, the better to see.

"Twenty," he read.

"Did it really come from Uncle?" asked Dencio.

"Who else would send us money," said Andang; "President Quezon?"

Martin was looking at the signature. Gorio had signed his full name with a flourish over the typed capital letters GREGORIO T. GARCIA.

"Read the letter now," said Andang, touching her husband's elbow, "read it aloud."

Martin sat on the floor, placed the lamp farther away from the open window through which a soft breeze was blowing, causing the lamp to flicker, making it hard to read.

Martin stared at the words for a while in silence.

"Go on," Andang urged him, "read it aloud, I said."

"P.C. Headquarters, Surigao," Martin began, placing the lamp still farther from the window. The wind had risen. It could be heard sweeping over the *kangkong* fields, shaking the acacia trees like sudden rain. Andang cupped her palm around the letter. Her husband read on: "October 5, 1951. My beloved brother, I hope you are all well as well as I who am now writing you after a long time. I am happy to be able to send you this money, I hope this amount will enable you to buy the things you need. Also, since All Saints Day is approaching, please don't forget to get an electric bulb each for the graves of our dear parents. Include flowers. I am now in the P.C., a sergeant. Many things have happened to me, but let us thank God, I'm still alive, we are all alive. There is a man here, he sells pictures, he says you are neighbors in Sulucan. So you see, I know all about you. I know about Dencio. You see, I also have a son. I am a father now . . ."

"Gorio is a father now!" Martin exclaimed, looking up from the letter. Then the light went out.

"Where's the match?" asked Andang.

The house was in complete darkness. Across the *kang-kong* fields farther away, a bit of sky over the city glowed with light.

"I have no match," said Martin.

"I don't know where the match is," said Dencio.

"Go buy a match from the Chinese store," said Andang, groping for Dencio's hand to give him the money.

Dencio ran down the steps saying, "Surigao!" his voice investing the name with the glamor of distant, unfamiliar things.

"Hurry," Andang's voice came from the darkness.

For a time she sat there, trying to see Martin's face. Martin had not spoken. It seemed he was no longer in the room.

"Martin!" Andang called. "What are you doing?"

"I'm thinking of Gorio," came the quick reply. "So, he's a P. C. sergeant. I didn't know. I thought he was a rich man now. Oh, why did he become a soldier? They say at the market place that there will be a war."

"But perhaps he is all right," said Andang. "This is a big amount. It is the biggest order we have had for flowers."

"Maybe he means real flowers, Andang," Martin said.

"Oh, but he knows. He says he knows about us. Has he ever lived in this house, Martin?"

"Andang, have you forgotten? This has been our only house since my parents came to Sulucan from Pampanga."

"I remember. Yes," Andang replied.

"Say, Andang, do you remember that time on All Saints Day when it rained so hard and so long the cemetery was flooded? It happened at night."

"Yes, yes. I was there, but we were not caught in the rain. We stayed in a friend's house near the cemetery."

"Good for you. We . . . we got wet. The three of us, Gorio and Father and I."

"Your father was still living then?"

"Yes. But he didn't live long after that. Mother died that year. Her grave was a mound of earth covered with grass and planted to hedges on the sides. The earth was fresh and the hedges just recently planted. Gorio and I had worked on it every Saturday and Sunday the whole month of October. Even the cross had a new coat of paint and Mother's name, written in black, stood out clearly. That night we stuck candles all around. Father sat at the foot of the grave and watched the candles. Sometimes he stood to straighten them and, as usual, he was silent.

"Gorio and I wandered around. Sometimes we watched the gay group not far from Mother's grave. They were enjoying a feast. They had chicken legs; and the girls were laughing all the time at the things the boys were saying. The grave was well-lighted. I think it was made of marble. The picture of a gentleman stood on the slab. Over it, like a roof, was spread a canvas which sheltered the picture from the sun in the daytime."

"I have seen the graves of the rich," Andang said when Martin paused. "They say they cost very much." Now she could see Martin sitting there on the floor, recalling things.

"You know what Gorio told me that night? He said, look Martin, we cannot even afford an electric bulb. And look at

Father, what can we do for him? Father sat on the grass, staring at Mother's cross. In the candlelight, he looked like a ghost."

Dencio had arrived with a match, but he paused in the doorway when he heard his father's voice. He listened.

"We did not expect rain that night. But it came, suddenly and hard. There was a scampering for dry places and vehicles. The gay group left quickly in two cars, the girls screaming in delight. Gorio and I went over to Father. He had moved under a huge tree. The candles had been snuffed. It was dark where we stood. I didn't know what to do. Gorio held a newspaper over Father's head. Then when it appeared that the rain would not stop, Gorio made me hold the newspaper. He removed his coat and placed it around Father's shoulders. Father did not say a word. But when the water started to come up to where he was sitting, his body trembled, but not even a sigh came from him. I still held the dripping, now useless newspaper over his head. It made him more wet. Your shirt, Martin, Gorio cried to me. But the water had drenched it. The water was cold on my skin. It's wet now, I said. Oh, my God, said Gorio, this will be bad for Father. Then he ran towards the lighted grave.

"Before I knew what he was going to do, he had ripped the canvas off the steel bars that held it. There was a clatter as the picture fell on the marble, the rain pounding against it. Gorio ran to us with the canvas which he put over Father's head and around his body. The place was flooded now. So we lifted the old man in our arms and waded. The canvas was thick and Father was at last safe from the flood and the rain. Our hands were stiff with cold, but we walked on with Father bundled between us. Once Gorio asked, Father, are you all right? The old man did not answer, but when we peered under the canvas, we heard him crying. My sons, my sons, he sobbed."

"Gorio is a good man," said Andang.

"Here's the match, Father," said Dencio.

As he lighted the lamp, Martin said, "It is not good to be a soldier these days. And Gorio is so rash. He is so brave."

"Gorio is good," Andang repeated. "Imagine, sending us twenty pesos. Perhaps he does not have much money himself."

"Yes, yes, Gorio is good," Martin said, but added, "Why should he be a soldier? At this time? Oh, he is reckless. You don't know him. And everybody is saying, there is a war coming."

"Gorio is good," Andang repeated as though in the fullness of her heart, she could not say anything else. But suddenly her face lighted up. She turned to her husband, their shadows huge on the walls meeting grotesquely, and said, "I will make him flowers. Let us send him flowers. The best flowers I can make. I will make the best for him."

Martin stared at her.

"But, Andang," he began at the same time that Dencio was saying, "But he is in Surigao, Mother. They have lovely flowers there."

"Yes, real flowers!" Andang's voice was suddenly shrill. Her face was flushed as she continued, "But these flowers I shall make him will be lovelier yet . . . I once saw a flower when I was a child. This was in Sta. Cruz, long ago, near the riverside. I have often dreamed of that flower, but I've never dared to make one like it. I don't even know its name. But I know every vein of it. I can make a dozen, two dozen, like it. For Gorio. Let us send him flowers . . ."

Martin had at last found the words to say, "What for?"

Even in her excitement, Andang sensed immediately the angry note in the question. Her hands went to her face. God, she thought, what was I saying?

"What for, Mother?" It was Dencio's voice. He had taken up his father's words. "Aren't these flowers for the dead?"

Martin looked at his son, the anger in his voice now in his eyes, and the hand that held the letter trembled a little as he raised the piece of paper to the light.

The wind was stronger now. Andang went to the window and closed it. As she did so, the pole fell across the basket where the finished flowers stood, crushing the leaves. The floor shook a little. Andang picked up the pole as Dencio crawled on his knees to reach for the flowers. Martin steadied the lamp. Nobody spoke.

Meanwhile, over the *kangkong* fields, the wind had risen, shaking window shutter like a friend, perhaps a stranger, asking to come in because the night outside was cold and filled with dull, uncertain voices.

SCENT OF APPLES

WHEN I arrived in Kalamazoo it was October and the war was still on. Gold and silver stars hung on pennants above silent windows of white and brick-red cottages. In a backyard, an old man burned leaves and twigs while a gray-haired woman sat on the porch, her red hands quiet on her lap, watching the smoke rising above the elms, both of them thinking of the same thought perhaps about a tall, grinning boy with blue eyes and flying hair, who went to war, where could he be now this month when leaves were turning into gold and the fragrance of gathered apples was in the wind.

It was a cold night when I left my room at the hotel for a usual speaking engagement. I walked but a little way. A heavy wind coming up from Lake Michigan was icy on the face. It felt like winter straying early in the northern woodlands. Under the lamp posts the leaves shone like bronze. And they rolled on the pavements like the ghost feel of a thousand autumns long dead, long before the boys left for faraway lands without great icy winds and promise of winter early in the air, lands without apple trees, *the singing and the gold!*

It was the same night I met Celestino Fabia, "just a Filipino farmer" as he called himself, who had a farm about thirty miles east of Kalamazoo.

"You came all that way on a night like this just to hear me talk?" I asked.

"I've seen no Filipino for so many years now," he answered quickly. "So when I saw your name in the papers where it says you come from the Islands and that you're going to talk, I come right away."

Earlier that night I had addressed a college crowd, mostly women. It appeared that they wanted me to talk about my country; they wanted me to tell them things about it because my country had become a lost country. Everywhere in the land the enemy stalked. Over it a great silence hung; and their boys were there, unheard from, or they were on their way to some little known island on the Pacific, young boys all, hardly men, thinking of harvest moons and smell of forest fire.

It was not hard talking about our own people. I knew them well and I loved them. And they seemed so far away during those terrible years that I must have spoken of them with a little fervor, a little nostalgia.

In the open forum that followed, the audience wanted to know whether there was much difference between our women and the American women. I tried to answer the question as best as I could, saying, among other things, that I did not know much about American women, except that they looked friendly, but differences or similarities in inner qualities such as naturally belonged to the heart or to the mind, I could only speak about with vagueness.

While I was trying to explain away the fact that it was not easy to make comparisons, a man rose from the rear of the hall, wanting to say something. In the distance, he looked slight and old and very brown. Even before he spoke, I knew that he was, like me, a Filipino.

"I'm a Filipino," he began, loud and clear, in a voice that seemed used to wide open spaces, "I'm just a Filipino farmer out in the country." He waved his hand towards the door. "I left the Philippines more than twenty years ago and have never been back. Never will perhaps. I want to find out, sir, are our Filipino women the same like they were twenty years ago?"

As he sat down, the hall filled with voices, hushed and intrigued. I weighed my answer carefully. I did not want to tell a lie, yet I did not want to say anything that would seem platitudinous, insincere. But more important than these considerations, it seemed to me that moment as I looked towards my countryman, I must give him an answer that would not make him so unhappy. Surely, all these years, he must have held on to certain ideals, certain beliefs, even illusions peculiar to the exile.

"First," I said as the voices gradually died down and every eye seemed upon me. "First, tell me what our women were like twenty years ago."

The man stood to answer. "Yes," he said, "you're too young . . . Twenty years ago our women were nice, they were modest, they wore their hair long, they dressed proper and went for no monkey business. They were natural, they went to church regular, and they were faithful." He had spoken slowly, and now in what seemed like an afterthought, added, "It's the men who ain't."

Now I knew what I was going to say.

"Well," I began, "it will interest you to know that our women have changed—but definitely! The change, however, has been on the outside only. Inside, here," pointing to the heart, "they are the same as they were twenty years ago, God-fearing, faithful, modest, and *nice*."

The man was visibly moved. "I'm very happy, sir," he said, in the manner of one who, having stakes on the land, had found no cause to regret one's sentimental investment.

After this, everything that was said and done in that hall that night seemed like an anti-climax; and later, as we walked outside, he gave me his name and told me of his farm thirty miles east of the city.

We had stopped at the main entrance to the hotel lobby. We had not talked very much on the way. As a matter of fact, we were never alone. Kindly American friends talked to us, asked us questions, said goodnight. So now I asked him whether he cared to step into the lobby with me and talk shop.

"No, thank you," he said, "you are tired. And I don't want to stay out too late."

"Yes, you live very far."

"I got a car," he said, "besides..."

Now he smiled, he truly smiled. All night I had been watching his face and I wondered when he was going to smile.

"Will you do me a favor, please," he continued smiling almost sweetly. "I want you to have dinner with my family out in the country. I'd call for you tomorrow afternoon, then drive you back. Will that be all right?"

"Of course," I said. "I'd love to meet your family." I was leaving Kalamazoo for Muncie, Indiana, in two days. There was plenty of time.

"You will make my wife very happy," he said.

"You flatter me."

"Honest. She'll be very happy. Ruth is a country girl and hasn't met many Filipinos. I mean Filipinos younger than I, cleaner looking. We're just poor farmer folk, you know, and we don't get to town very often. Roger, that's my boy, he goes to school in town. A bus takes him early in the morning and he's back in the afternoon. He's a nice boy."

"I bet he is," I agreed. "I've seen the children of some of the boys and their American wives and the boys are tall, taller than the father, and very good looking."

"Roger, he'd be tall. You'll like him."

Then he said goodbye and I waved to him as he disappeared in the darkness.

The next day he came, at about three in the afternoon. There was a mild, ineffectual sun shining; and it was not too cold. He was wearing an old brown tweed jacket and worsted trousers to match. His shoes were polished, and although the

green of his tie seemed faded, a colored shirt hardly accentuated
it. He looked younger than he did the night before now that
he was clean shaven and seemed ready to go to a party. He was
grinning as we met.

"Oh, Ruth can't believe it. She can't believe it," he kept
repeating as he led me to his car—a nondescript thing in faded
black that had known better days and many hands. "I says to
her, I'm bringing you a first class Filipino, and she says, aw,
go away, quit kidding, there's no such thing as first class
Filipino. But Roger, that's my boy, he believed me immediately. What's he like, daddy, he asks. Oh, you will see, I says,
he's first class. Like you, daddy? No, no, I laugh at him, your
daddy ain't first class. Aw, but you are, daddy, he says. So
you can see what a nice boy he is, so innocent. Then Ruth
starts griping about the house, but the house is a mess, she
says. True it's a mess, it's always a mess, but you don't mind,
do you? We're poor folks, you know."

The trip seemed interminable. We passed through narrow lanes and disappeared into thickets, and came out on
barren land overgrown with weeds in places. All around were
dead leaves and dry earth. In the distance were apple trees.

"Aren't those apple trees?" I asked wanting to be sure.

"Yes, those are apple trees," he replied. "Do you like
apples? I got lots of 'em. I got an apple orchard, I'll show you."

All the beauty of the afternoon seemed in the distance,
on the hills, in the dull soft sky.

"Those trees are beautiful on the hills," I said.

"Autumn's a lovely season. The trees are getting ready
to die, and they show their colors, proud-like."

"No such thing in our own country," I said.

That remark seemed unkind, I realized later. It touched
him off on a long deserted tangent, but one ever there perhaps.
How many times did the lonely mind take unpleasant detours
away from the familiar winding lanes toward home for fear of

this, the remembered hurt, the long lost youth, the grim shadows of the years; how many times indeed, only the exile knows.

It was a rugged road we were traveling and the car made so much noise that I could not hear everything he said, but I understood him. He was telling his story for the first time in many years. He was remembering his own youth. He was thinking of home. In these odd moments there seemed no cause for fear, no cause at all, no pain. That would come later. In the night perhaps. Or lonely on the farm under the apple trees.

In this old Visayan town, the streets are narrow and dirty and strewn with coral shells. You have been there? You could not have missed our house, it was the biggest in town, one of the oldest, ours was a big family. The house stood right on the edge of the street. A door opened heavily and you enter a dark hall leading to the stairs. There is the smell of chickens roosting on the low-topped walls, there is the familiar sound they make and you grope your way up a massive staircase, the bannisters smooth upon the trembling hand. Such nights, they are no better than the days, windows are closed against the sun; they close heavily.

Mother sits in her corner looking very white and sick. This was her world, her domain. In all these years I cannot remember the sound of her voice. Father was different. He moved about. He shouted. He ranted. He lived in the past and talked of honor as though it were the only thing.

I was born in that house. I grew up there into a pampered brat. I was mean. One day I broke their hearts. I saw mother cry wordlessly as father heaped his curses upon me and drove me out of the house, the gate closing heavily after me. And my brothers and sisters took up my father's hate for me and multiplied it numberless times in their own broken hearts. I was no good.

But sometimes, you know, I miss that house, the roosting chickens on the low-topped walls. I miss my brothers and sisters. Mother sitting in her chair, looking like a pale ghost in a corner of the room. I would remember the great live posts, massive tree trunks from the forests. Leafy plants grew on the sides, buds pointing downwards, wilted and died before they could become flowers. As they fell on the floor, father bent to pick them and throw them out into the coral streets. His hands were strong. I have kissed those hands . . . many times, many times.

Finally we rounded a deep curve and suddenly came upon a shanty, all but ready to crumble in a heap on the ground, its plastered walls were rotting away, the floor was hardly a foot from the ground. I thought of the cottages of the poor colored folk in the south, the hovels of the poor everywhere in the land. This one stood all by itself as though by common consent all the folk that used to live here had decided to stay away, despising it, ashamed of it. Even the lovely season could not color it with beauty.

A dog barked loudly as we approached. A fat blonde woman stood at the door with a little boy by her side. Roger seemed newly scrubbed. He hardly took his eyes off me. Ruth had a clean apron around her shapeless waist. Now as she shook my hands in sincere delight I noticed shamefacedly (that I should notice) how rough her hands, how coarse and red with labor, how ugly! She was no longer young and her smile was pathetic.

As we stepped inside and the door closed behind us, immediately I was aware of the familiar scent of apples. The room was bare except for a few ancient pieces of second-hand furniture. In the middle of the room stood a stove to keep the family warm in winter. The walls were bare. Over the dining table hung a lamp yet unlighted.

Ruth got busy with the drinks. She kept coming in and out of a rear room that must have been the kitchen and soon the table was heavy with food, fried chicken legs and rice, and green peas and corn on the ear. Even as we ate, Ruth kept standing, and going to the kitchen for more food. Roger ate like a little gentleman.

"Isn't he nice looking?" his father asked.

"You are a handsome boy, Roger," I said.

The boy smiled at me. "You look like Daddy," he said.

Afterwards I noticed an old picture leaning on the top of a dresser and stood to pick it up. It was yellow and soiled with many fingerings. The faded figure of a woman in Philippine dress could yet be distinguished although the face had become a blur.

"Your..." I began.

"I don't know who she is," Fabia hastened to say. "I picked that picture many years ago in a room on La Salle Street in Chicago. I have often wondered who she is."

"The face wasn't a blur in the beginning?"

"Oh, no. It was a young face and good."

Ruth came with a plate full of apples.

"Ah," I cried, picking out a ripe one, "I've been thinking where all the scent of apples came from. The room is full of it."

"I'll show you," said Fabia.

He showed me a backroom, not very big. It was half-full of apples.

"Every day," he explained, "I take some of them to town to sell to the groceries. Prices have been low. I've been losing on the trips."

"These apples will spoil," I said.

"We'll feed them to the pigs."

Then he showed me around the farm. It was twilight

now and the apple trees stood bare against a glowing western sky. In apple blossom time it must be lovely here, I thought. But what about wintertime?

One day, according to Fabia, a few years ago, before Roger was born, he had an attack of acute appendicitis. It was deep winter. The snow lay heavy everywhere. Ruth was pregnant and none too well herself. At first she did not know what to do. She bundled him in warm clothing and put him on a cot near the stove. She shoveled the snow on their front door and practically carried the suffering man on her shoulders, dragging him through the newly made path towards the road where they waited for the U.S. mail car to pass. Meanwhile snowflakes poured all over them and she kept rubbing the man's arms and legs as she herself nearly froze to death.

"Go back to the house, Ruth!" her husband cried; "you'll freeze to death."

But she clung to him wordlessly. Even as she scrubbed her arms and legs, her tears rolled down her cheeks. "I won't leave you, I won't leave you," she repeated.

Finally the U.S. mail car arrived. The mailman, who knew them well, helped them board the car, and, without stopping on his usual route, took the sick man and his wife direct to the nearest hospital.

Ruth stayed in the hospital with Fabia. She slept in a corridor outside the patients' ward and in the day time helped in scrubbing the floor and washing the dishes and cleaning the men's things. They didn't have enough money and Ruth was willing to work like a slave.

"Ruth's a nice girl," said Fabia; "like our own Filipino women."

Before nightfall, he took me back to the hotel. Ruth and Roger stood at the door holding hands and smiling at me. From inside the room of the shanty, a low light flickered. I had a last glimpse of the apple trees in the orchard under the darkened sky as Fabia backed up the car. And soon we were on our way back to town. The dog had started barking. We could hear it for some time, until finally, we could not hear it any more, and all was darkness around us, except where the head lamps revealed a stretch of road leading somewhere.

Fabia did not talk this time. I didn't seem to have anything to say myself. But when finally we came to the hotel and I got down, Fabia said, "Well, I guess I won't be seeing you again."

It was dimly lighted in front of the hotel and I could hardly see Fabia's face. He had not come down from the car, but he had moved to my side, and I saw his hand, extended. I gripped it.

"Tell Ruth and Roger," I said, "I love them."

He dropped my hand quickly. "They'll be waiting for me now," he said.

"Look," I said, not knowing why I said it, "one of these days, very soon, I hope, I'll be going home. I could go to your town."

"No," he said softly, sounding very much defeated but brave. "Thanks a lot. But, you see, nobody would remember me now."

Then he started the car, and as it moved away, he waved his hand.

"Goodbye," I said, waving back into the darkness. And suddenly the night was cold like winter straying early in these northern woodlands.

I hurried inside. There was a train the next morning that left for Muncie, Indiana, at a quarter after eight.

N. V. M. GONZALEZ [1915–]

The uneasy interval between changing shore and flowering surf seems an unlikely counterpart to jade touchstones clutched in meditation. Yet it is N. V. M. Gonzalez' preference for this intersection of things in flux and things fixed which makes him—despite a lifelong fondness for fishing—not sportsman so much as writer. On a different scale, Hemingway learned the rhythm of necessity and the patience of a craftsman from pan fish in Michigan. For Gonzalez, in each reflex of sun, each turn of wind an angle of past is exposed—of those days that his father, a supervising teacher, went from Romblon to pioneer Mindoro island, off the mouth of Manila Bay, as *The Winds of April* (prize novel in the 1940 Commonwealth Literary Contest) recalls. With some small exception, the most memorable of Gonzalez' fiction has been concerned not with English-speaking peoples among his urban readership, but with the *kaingin,* tentatively culivated rice fields at the cleared edge of jungle or mountain.

While he was still a high school student in Mindoro, Gonzalez' work was accepted by the *Graphic* (a Manila magazine on whose editorial staff he was later to serve for six years, prior to the war). He was not yet of age, when *Poetry* published a group of his verses. Consequently, although he went to Manila to study law in conventional aspiration to white-collar status, it was inevitable that he should end as a writer-teacher. After the war he edited the *Evening News Saturday Magazine* and later the *Manila Chronicle* supplement, *This Week.* In 1947, twelve stories which he had completed for the *Philippine Magazine* were published in book form as *Seven Hills Away,* by the Swallow Press in Denver. Two years later, under Rockefeller auspices, he was enrolled in Wallace Stegner's courses at Stanford; and briefly attended the University of Denver, Kenyon College, the University of Kansas Writers' Conference, and Breadloaf.

On his return to Manila, Gonzalez taught writing at Sto. Tomas, the Philippine Women's University and, finally, the University of the Philippines. Almost singlehandedly at the state university he made the new *Diliman Review* equal to creative-critical journals the world over (it is classified by the Library of Congress).

Gonzalez has traveled throughout Southeast Asia and the northern fringes of the Far East on Rockefeller grants, lecturing, observing, writing. As a result, his works are read widely in translation, from Indonesia to Japan (and occasionally in Mexico). Although the characters in his second book of short stories, *Children of the Ash-Covered Loam* (1954) believe in *anting-anting* charms and ghostly *anitos*, they are interesting not because they believe themselves instruments of some dark misfortune, but because in the midst of suffering they assert their worth, and care bravely for one another. Since then he has published two novels, *A Season of Grace,* tracing the ritual of the pioneer's daily sacrifice of living in spite of life (1956), and *The Bamboo Dancers,* an international novel aware that death too, whether by radiation or otherwise, is part of man's natural cycle.

In 1954, he received the first Republic Award in literature, from President Magsaysay, for "advancement of Filipino culture in the field of English literature"; and in 1960, the first Cultural Heritage Award, for *The Bamboo Dancers.* He has served as the first president of the Philippine Writers Association.

Although Gonzalez' stories have appeared in a number of American magazines—*Poetry,* the *Sewanee Review,* the *Pacific Spectator,* the *Hopkins Review*—and in Martha Foley's Honor Roll (1952), he has long encouraged the Filipino writers' search for and stimulation of local readers. He has been influential in the organization of such projects as the Benipayo Series on Philippine Contemporary Writing in the mid-1950's; the translation of major literary works into native languages; and formation of Kuwan (Thingamajig) Publishers, to put into print overlooked volumes such as Alejandrino Hufana's collection of poems, *Sickle Season.*

WHERE'S MY BABY NOW?

ALTHOUGH for the past nine years Mrs. Bilbao has had nothing to conceal from her husband, she feels she must keep this one a secret. To speak about the matter will be embarrassing, to say the least. How will she begin? And, having begun, and persevered, what of this thing which she will have succeeded in confiding to him?

Bilbao is a busy man; a free-lance accountant can be a very busy man. And he's the quiet type: you can hardly tell what's behind all the diligence which he observes going through the musty books of some small merchant trying to avoid his taxes. Such hours he keeps at times at some downtown office stuffy with the smell of ink and typewriter oil; and towards the twentieth or twenty-first of the month, how he sweats it out in some dingy mezzanine in the company of a pale little nervous bookkeeper exuding from some secret spot under his shirt the aroma of imported cigarettes. Then, for an entire week, Bilbao is grubby and sullen, a dull fire smouldering in his eyes.

She can't understand it. But she must admit he's a wizard at budgeting his time, so much so he can find two or three hours each day for watching the children in the courtyard the while ostensibly going over some baker's balance sheet or some ice-cream parlor's journal-ledger. Mrs. Bilbao thinks this is rather unusual. No man ought to take such interest in the games children play.

She will have to think, forgetting the children's convenience entirely, about moving out to a new neighborhood. For there's nothing here for her, nothing to speak of. Unless, of course, you can feel nice about the streets in this part of the city being named after flowers.

Theirs is apartment 177-F, Jasmine Street, the sixth from the gate. A thoughtful man, the landlord has built an adobe wall around the block, as if anticipating that some day his tenants may elect to keep away from all society. And there's the courtyard, too, for the children. Although hardly fifteen feet wide, it's covered with smooth concrete with trapezoids and triangles of varying sizes simulating flagstones, thanks to some fanciful mason. The one feature Mrs. Bilbao approves of is the length of water-pipe like an inverted U, at the end of the courtyard, from which a grilled door swings stiffly upon its hinges; and it's the fresh purple paint, so fetching in the morning sun, of which she's really proud.

She couldn't say that the others feel the same way. The Poncianos, for instance. Well, perhaps, they can feel good about other things. They occupy 177-A, the apartment nearest the street, and thus enjoy the advantage of having two extra windows. But this is offset by their having to serve as gate-keepers ex officio. If they are annoyed over this, they do not indeed show it. On coming home, in the late evenings, Bilbao has to call their servant to request that the bolt be unfastened. Being the person he is, her husband, Mrs. Bilbao thinks, approves of the Poncianos' preferring to provide this service to risking the chance of a burglar's visit. Pedro, the servant, having slipped in the bolt, clamps on the lock that he has been carrying in his pocket all day, and then shuffles away lifting his brow with an air of fulfillment.

The true pleasures of this life are so few and far between you have to snatch them perforce? Her husband is very pleased with this arrangement over the gate, it is true. "The children will be safe," he says. They have three of them, two of kindergarten age. And the courtyard, he has often remarked, is just the sort of over-sized play pen that the young ones need. The landlord, bless his soul, has left a strip of earth shaped like a fat cigar in the center; here some colorful and fragrant rosebush can be grown. But Mr. Bilbao likes it bare; he likes his pleasures all of one kind. The children, says he, can run about freely. And Mr. Ponciano agrees with him. The Ponciano girls, aged four and six, have led their mother to say: "We needn't worry about them, so long as our Pedro's around to watch the gate." Doubtless, she has in mind the rickety jeeps that cruise up and down Jasmine Street, raising a cloud of dust that has the same thickness, the same consistency always, regardless of the time of day; and although helpless against the dust, the children are spared effectively from those reckless drivers.

Mrs. Bilbao understands all this. What really puzzles her is her husband's interest in the children's games. "Do you know," he says, the legs of his cane chair scraping the cement. He finds working in the mornings in the shade of the wall quite pleasant these days. "Do you know? A rumor has spread. There's famine abroad. And the children have made a game of it."

Mrs. Bilbao has brought out her basket of wash. It's no game, in so far as she's concerned; this is Saturday, and she is too busy to listen to talk of this kind.

But Bilbao perserveres. "I recall how it was in my day," he says, having fixed his chair where the sunlight slants so, making huge diamonds of the broken lemonade bottles embedded on top the adobe bricks. It will not hurt his eyes to sit there and go over several books of Buenos Dias Co., successors to De Luxe Bakery. "Yes, yes," he says, spreading one thick journal before him, his feet propped upon a wooden box. "We used to fly kites. But only during certain months of the year, mind you. After seven, did you play with dolls?" he asked her suddenly. "Children make good prophets, you know."

The impertinence, the impudence of it! He knows she has work to do, a clothesline to fasten properly. There's the nail on the wall to which she can tie the line, but to do this properly she must stand on that chair, better yet on that box. But does he offer to help? Instead, he asks again: "After seven, did you still play with dolls?"

"I don't remember," she says, concealing her petulance.

"And when was it you played Man and Wife? And Housekeeping, let's say?"

"I don't recall. And I don't care to," she says, reaching for the nail on the clammy wall—because if there's a will there's a way.

Then, uncoiling the clothesline after her, she crosses to the other side of the court. Here the drainpipe is on the same level as that nail; and he need not help, no. There ought to be no need for him ever. There's one hopeless fellow for you; he keeps asking "When? When?" Instead of saying "What's next?" he pesters you with "Do you remember? Do you recall? Why, in my day—" He speaks as though he were sixty, a re-tired cigar-smoking bureau chief, on a fat pension.

She hangs the wash, trappings that have survived the years, upon the line. His white shirts (he loves white) her chemises and slips, the children's clothes, then the sheets that had been soiled the night before. "Here, can't you help a bit?" she calls, for the first sheet is heavy and causes the line to sag.

Mr. Bilbao pushes the wooden box from under his feet. There's some chivalry left in him after all. She props the line tentatively with a trembling arm. "Quick! Give me a hand!"

He's so sweet about it. He has run to the house and brought back the long broomstick that the maid Concha fashioned against the day for sweeping the cobwebs that have gathered up the kitchen ceiling and the back porch's eaves.

"There, does it work? It does!"

"Thanks."

But at what price! You've to listen more to talk, and it's not about the clothesline either.

"The courtyard is bare now. The effects of the rumor are evident. Not only have the children forgotten hopscotch, they have put their other toys away. The tricycles are gone; the four-wheeled wagon belonging to the clubfoot in 177-D is gone."

"What does it all mean?" she asks, bringing out the second sheet soap-suddy white in the basket. "Give me a hand!"

"What does it mean? Why, I used to be pleasantly disturbed in my work. You remember the children used to play ball. 'Safe! Safe!' they'd shout, in the midst of their game, really softball simplified with two bases instead of four, at which Pedro presides both as umpire and retriever, for the ball often rolls off to the street. But now my mornings have become quiet. You do not know, you're often out of the house."

That's the first of his many hints. For the moment she must hide her feelings.

"And also, the children used to play a game called Storekeeper. The favorite place for it used to be the front of 177-C. The children gather there in the shade of the wall, our own as well as the Ponciano and Gomez children. Somebody plays storekeeper, after the model set by the Chinaman who owns the general store at the street corner. I used to pause in my work to watch them. They have their own version of buying and selling, of haggling, of going into debt, of holding up the storekeeper for a gain of garlic or a bulb of onion. Pedro says it's the way with some characters in the neighborhood; they make it their business to mortify the Chinaman. I'm surprised you've never observed this. Never?"

He insists on knowing. Impatient, she relents. "No, I've

noticed nothing at all," she says, stretching the white sheet upon the line, right between the wall and her frillies.

"You're away much too often," he says with a smile so innocent as to seem without malice. "But just watch them of a morning as soon as they're back from kindergarten."

That's how it is: he gets the children involved. It is somewhat difficult to nourish her petulance into disgust, and, under the circumstances, perhaps into hate.

"Now, give me a hand! And don't be so clumsy, please. There, careful now!"

And it's all her fault. So says that look in his eyes. She ought to have known better. She ought not to have moved the prop so, making the line more taut.

"Concha! Concha!"

The girl must rinse the sheets again. There she is at the door, and she peeks at the sunshine and runs, runs, runs to Mr. Bilbao's rescue—with not a look of protest in that servant-face.

Bilbao's is an expressionless, almost an indifferent face. Mrs. Bilbao confronts it calmly. "You've to fix the line yourself."

"It was bound to snap," he says, picking up the loose ends of the string. Then, as he begins to knot them: "Why, in the old days you could get genuine clothesline—not this sort of thing. . . . I was speaking about this new game of the children's. Was watching them the other afternoon, you know. Where were you then? At some meeting or other? Which was this one now?"

"The Mother's Civic League," she replies.

"I was there, watching. Was telling Mrs. Ponciano, across the courtyard, that her eldest boy will perhaps grow up to be a leader. For there he was, urging the children to till the strip of earth over there at the center; and then they planted corn—no, simply sticks at first. Later, Pedro came with real corn—goodness knows where he got them. The children, gathering about him, thinking he had something other than familiar boiled peanuts in that tiny paper bag for them, began digging into his pockets. You should have been here. Pedro might have stood there all morning, himself a seven-year-old all over, with the pure wonder of the giver burning in his eyes. . . . There, you've as good a knot as can be made with this string."

Mrs. Bilbao watches him stretch the clothesline to a new tautness. For him, this must seem truly an admirable accomplishment. Suddenly she feels tender towards this man who is her husband, this man for whom she has borne three children. But a mother's instincts are beyond cavil. You cannot reason down a woman's fears. And Mrs. Bilbao fears that three children establish her claim to motherhood quite eloquently. Whether it is an angel or the spirit of God itself in her blood that cries, "Enough! Enough!" she does not know. But it is a stern and urgent voice, with its one stern and urgent message. A mother listens with her heart.

As if she hasn't been listening to his talk: must she admit it? A sentiment, nevertheless, escapes her: "Sometimes I can't help feeling sorry for the children," she says. "Why, as a child—" No, she corrects herself: "As a girl . . . in a farm." . . .

It is her favorite memory. She's afraid, lest she launches upon a more substantial evocation of a childhood long since gone, irrecoverable like pin money squandered upon some trifle in a bazaar.

"Now give me a hand," she says, for Concha has returned with the re-rinsed sheets.

"I've it from Mrs. Ponciano that once in a while the children refuse to eat. Part of their game. They'll carry it as far as that, you know. And I've been waiting for this: they'll bring in pails of water out here, and cry out loud: 'Flood!

Flood!'—meaning there's flood all over the land, crops will perish, there'll be hunger everywhere."

Mrs. Bilbao can't help laughing, the fun bubbling from deep within her. So this is why he sits there! Well, if it pleases him, let him be.

She remembers that the children will be home from kindergarten. It's no matter. She must hurry off, this time to that symposium on Progressive Education. These lectures and civic club activities are her only bid for widening her horizon. And there are several in the offing, now that the town's full of visiting American professors.

She picks up her clothes basket, which is too large for tucking under her arm like a book, and starts for the apartment. But Mr. Bilbao, now back in his chair, feet propped upon the empty box, detains her.

"I've heard the Ponciano children have amassed a supply of biscuits," he starts all over again, turning, eyes fixed so upon the empty basket by her side. "The father has been in the habit of bringing home two-pound tins of biscuits, which he's fond of himself; and no sooner is he at the gate than his little girls rush for the present and without so much as a 'Thank you, papa,' run off to the house with this fresh addition to their stock. I've Mrs. Ponciano's word; the girls have built in her closet a pyramid of red-yellow and cellophane-sealed tins of biscuits marked 'Eat Well Brand. Made in U. S. A.' 'That high already,' she says, blushing."

"And you're waiting, hoping to see those little girls harass their father again?"

"Yes," Mr. Bilbao says calmly, "if you want to put it that way."

How exasperating! And with Bennie and Bobby home now, the pink dimity pinafore of the girl no more soiled than the boy's sailor suit. "What? Are you home already?" But it is as though she has said: "This is my cue. Now I must go."

"Oh, no, darling! You'll spoil my dress," Mrs. Bilbao retreats, warily, to spare the really stunning thing she has on, for Bennie's embrace can be disastrous. The dress is of fine linen; the Chinese collar makes her ever so attractive. "Now be a good girl," she says.

Yet, in a moment, she presses her cheeks upon Bobby's (because he is her favorite, although he looks every inch like his father) and then upon Bennie's. "Go wipe yourself with a towel," she tells the girl, for Bennie has brought home with her the familiar aroma of Jasmine Street sunshine.

Mr. Bilbao drags his cane chair back to the house. "You have this other luncheon meeting?" he asks, and then turning to the children: "Oh, Bennie, Bobby—now tell Daddy what you've learned in school today."

It's a ceremony which, Mrs. Bilbao knows, is more a matter of form than of substance. The upshot of it will be that the two-year-old, who's been serenely asleep all this while, will soon be sniveling in his wet bed.

"Hssshh!" she exhorts them, peeking from the bedroom door at the tiny bed in the corner. "Johnny's still asleep. And it's the Women's Social Action Committee, Daddy. I've forgotten to tell you." She says "Daddy" with a special flavor, for the children's sake. They will know, they're bound to know. She adds, even more casually yet: "And after the meeting, that other symposium I've mentioned. (Has she, indeed, told him?) Some congressmen will be present."

Now, how stuffy the house seems! Has she suddenly filled it with imaginary people—congressmen, lecturers, members of the WSAC? She crosses the *sala* and the dining room, escaping to the kitchen at last. Now the last-minute instructions for Concha. There's an extra bottle of milk for Johnny-boy in the refrigerator—he'll need that soon. The maid must heat some sausages for the children's lunch; those finger-shaped ones will do, leftovers from breakfast though they are. "Times are hard, Concha. Never waste the slightest scrap. And mind the faucet. We still have the water bill to pay."

She is aware that she has become Good Housekeeping and Vigilance personified. Efficiency and a high sense of responsibility exude from her like Heavenly Colonial, say, or some such imported perfume which, though but sparingly used, keeps its scent for an agreeably long time, enhancing the realization—the fulfillment even—of womanhood.

It is this thought that propels her out of the kitchen, which after all is really Concha's world. Bennie and Bobby, their necks flushed from rubbing with the towel, are waiting for their father at the doorway. Mr. Bilbao has brought out Johnny-boy: the two-year-old has been wide awake, it seems, these past five minutes at least. But what a well-disposed little fellow. He ought to whine as most children do on getting up from bed. But there he is, perched so proudly upon his Daddy's arm, his soft cheek against Daddy's cavernous nostrils.

For she feels jealous of Daddy. And it's Mr. Bilbao the accountant, not Daddy at all, who, now with a smile, holds the door open for her.

There's a distinction there. In applause for the thought, the bright sunshine in the courtyard sweeps upon her white linen dress, lays siege upon her in a transport of rapture. She makes three—four—careless steps. Then suddenly she remembers. She must have a more studied and purposive air.

She tries it—head held high, arms swinging artfully, cutting across some imaginary ribbon before her. There, directly in front of her leatherette belt! And the small black purse tightly clasped in her one hand. Down, down the length of the courtyard, and she knows with each pressure of her heels that the flagstones are what they really are.

Mr. Bilbao's wheedling voice, which seems to belong to some aspect of his nature that she has never quite discovered, reaches her: He's chanting: "Say 'bye-bye' to Mummie. Say 'bye-bye'."

But Johnny-boy only squints at the sunshine. And from Bobby and Bennie, who are much older and can therefore be trusted to understand: " 'Bye-bye Mummie,"—Daddy there at their side, their shy voices clear across the courtyard.

She cannot open her palm (it's the hand with the purse) as she waves to the children. Actually, she is describing an arc with her fist.

Scenes like this are a concession she must give. She must be impartial with her love, such as it is. She doubts whether she loves Daddy as Daddy at all: it is middle-age creeping in? All the same it's her wish to be always one step ahead: after such words at the lectures as "troglodytical" and "archetype" how self-conscious and yet how alert and aware one can become: it can't now be said that although a mere housewife she isn't progressive—this fact she feels has become the essence of her life—and to be forever interested in the significant and new, to be always in search of facts to investigate and evaluate that other beautiful world and not sit there watching children all day long at some old game but rather to cut the heart open and probe into its secrets.

LUPO AND THE RIVER

THE BIG *lauan* log was still some distance upstream. Pisco stood at the riverbank watching it. Already Lupo had gone to the fish trap at the river's mouth. Pisco saw him reach the trap in time to pull out of the water three *hangaray* sticks which supported the bamboo-work. Lupo got a fourth stick out of the mud and shoved the approaching log with it. The log slipped through the opening, carrying the dirt along.

"Let me help!" Pisco called from the bank, ready to push his own *banca* into the stream.

"Go home!" Lupo shouted back. "Get busy elsewhere!"

Soon Lupo had enough of those *hangaray* sticks out of the way, and the debris from the *kaingins* in the interior—banana trunks, pieces of *hinagdong* and bamboo—rushed freely through. Pisco smiled and walked home.

His father's hut was a stone's throw from the river. It was a small one; it was no different from the other fifteen or twenty huts which comprised the barrio of Malig. Here was the same nipa-shingled wall, the same rooftree with cabonegro stuck into place at the ridge by spear-shaped bamboo sticks. The roof extended over to one side for that portion of the hut called the *sulambi* or sleeping place, the floor of which dropped about one foot below that of the main room. Nipa shingles also walled the lean-to, which one entered from the kitchen by way of a three-runged ladder. From the *sulambi* to the lean-to was another entrance, but this was without stairs of any sort. To enter the *sulambi* from this side, one heaved over—as though the doorsill were a fence to sit on.

Wet from standing a long time in the rain, Pisco entered the kitchen. He swung himself over into the *sulambi*, moistening the doorsill with the damp seat of his denim shorts. It was dark inside; the little room had only one window and it was still closed. The door that led to one side of the house threw in a rectangle of half-light which fell to the floor and then straggled a few inches up the wall. Pisco's foster sister Paula, who was twenty, had just wakened and was still rubbing her eyes as she got up from her mat. He watched her for a moment. She had rolled up her sleeping mat, and was standing it against the wall, right behind the corner post. As she turned around, her bare shoulders appeared heavy-set in the half-light. With her foot she pushed her pillows out of the way, then she took a dress from off a clothesline that hung across the length of the room, and hurriedly put it on over her loose cheesecloth chemise. The light from the door limned well her large legs. As she walked to the door, Pisco caught a glimpse of the full and firm curves of her breasts.

She must have heard him enter, but before her eyes could meet his—and he knew she could stare at him in such a fierce and frightening way—he had himself looked in the direction of the stove fire. It would seem as if he had simply rushed up the house to avoid the rain which slithered in from the yard.

He began to whistle. But it sounded absurd and he stopped. Still, he couldn't help wondering now how much more womanlike his foster sister would look in better light. Although he was only nine, he wished he could see her with Lupo's eyes. Lupo was almost twenty-five; if he had not married, so people said, it was because the girls were afraid of him. Unlike his sister Tía Talia, in whose house he stayed, Lupo did not live a quiet, uneventful life. Tía Talia was the kind of person who would nurse her hurt and grievances in silence. Lupo was ill-tempered; he drank great quantities of *tuba*, which made matters worse. It was a surprise that they had got him to help build and look after the fish trap. Pisco had heard his father say that they were lucky to have him around. It occurred to him now that he knew what kept Lupo coming to the hut again and again. It was not usual for one to set out for the river in the flood and in the rain. One did those things for certain reasons, and Pisco wondered whether his father also knew. The more he thought of the matter the more he grew certain that his father had had thoughts of this kind.

The flood swelled that morning and Crispino Olarte acknowledged that Lupo's presence of mind had spared the fish trap from damage. As for him, Pisco said to himself, he missed the crowd that gathered in the hut every morning whenever the catch was brought in.

No less than half the barrio would gather there; people collected near the stove, sat on the bamboo steps, even clambered up the doorsill entrance to the *sulambi,* and waited for Unday to be done with the partition of the day's catch. On days when the catch was extremely good, people from Bakawan up the river came down in their *bancas* or took the trail through the swamps; then there in the kitchen they crowded and spilled out into the yard.

Often a length of bamboo, its rind moist with *tuba* spume, found its way into the kitchen. Numerous *buri* and sugar palms grew in Bakawan, and as a practical method of clearing the land the *kaingin*-makers collected the palm sap; in this way they killed the trees. Meanwhile, they collected the palm sap in big earthen jars which they hoisted to the improvised platforms atop the trees, and then they filled their containers and brought *tuba* home to the barrio.

Pisco's father hardly missed his share. If no one came he was likely to send Pisco to Bakawan. People knew how it was to go without fish, and they did not mind filling Pisco's container to the brim. At home, his stepmother had always a word or two to say about his father's drinking. *Tuba* made Crispino many friends, and it was difficult to get one's friends to pay for the fish that they took home with them. Pisco could be sure, however, to see his father hand over a big string of fish to whoever had been so thoughtful as to provide him with his portion of *tuba* for the day. Sometimes Unday drank a little herself "Just to make me a little more talkative," she would admit. It was then she did not care any more where the fish went. By now Crispino Olarte had drunk enough to warm, as he put it modestly, the very pit of his stomach. Reminiscences of the Insurrection and of the Constabulary would be then in order; his father's stories never seemed to stale, and Pisco drank also and listened.

If his stepmother Unday had succeeded in keeping his foster sister away from someone who might make her a good husband, then perhaps it would not now be for long. His Manding Paula had caught Lupo's fancy. How often he must have seen her wearing her mother's *patadiong;* he must have seen her knotting her long black hair exactly as the older woman did. How this must have made her look five or even six years older than her twenty years. But perhaps Lupo did not mind. From under a coconut tree he would watch her go down to the barrio well, which was back of the house of the midwife Tía Orang. This explained, Pisco told himself, why he often found Lupo at the old midwife's place. With wash under her arm and a long bamboo water-container or a jar on her shoulder, Paula was the very picture of diligence. Truly, she needed a husband to protect and cherish her. Pisco thought Lupo could be one such husband.

In a shed outside the fence that protected the well from stray pigs and carabaos, Paula did her washing. There, too, she bathed—leaving the place perhaps two hours later, with

her hair lustrous from a shampoo of the juice from pounded
gogo bark. Sometimes she used lime; its pulp had a scent
which, perhaps for Lupo, traveled far. The *patadiong*, now
wet and fastened tight around her armpits, hugged her body
unembarrassedly. There would be the wash to take home,
along with the water-container. Lupo would come round directly, yet as if from nowhere, and then offer to help her. If
after the first two trips to the well Lupo did not fill all the
jars, he then made a third or perhaps even a fourth trip with
the water-container.

It continued to rain the whole afternoon and there was
scarcely anything one could do to keep busy. Fortunately, his
Manding Paula brought out a winnowing basket heaped with
palay to be pounded and the husks saved for the pig that Unday was fattening. The pen was behind the kitchen lean-to
and its occupant squealed intermittently. She did not have to
tell Pisco to bring to the kitchen the heavy *narra* rice mortar
and two pestles. Usually they set up the rice mortar there in
the yard, and the instant Lupo heard the thump of their pestles
he would stop in the middle of a *cara y cruz* or whatever game
he might be playing with the other young men of the barrio;
even if it happened to be a card game over at Tía Orang's place,
he would go straight to the Olarte house all the same. The
moment he had arrived he would pick a heavy pestle from
among those under the bamboo steps and would proceed to
help at the mortar. It was impossible to see Lupo too often at
this chore and mistake his intentions.

But now Pisco and his Manding Paula had been pounding the *palay* for over half an hour in the kitchen lean-to and
not a sign at all that Lupo might come. Perhaps it's because
of the rain, Pisco said to himself, looking out now and then
at the door. A pool had formed at the doorway and one would
have to leap over to cross.

Perhaps his Manding Paula suspected what was in his mind, for she said rudely: "Well, if you expect any help, better think again."

"Oh, but wouldn't you want him to come?" Pisco teased her.

"Who? That fellow?" Pisco was glad she did not look offended. "He can't even talk!" She laughed.

This was quite true. Pisco had observed that whenever Lupo happened to be anywhere near Manding Paula the fellow behaved as if dumb. For that matter, Manding Paula could not look at Lupo directly. Together they would be busy pounding rice and she would keep her eyes to the ground; or Lupo would appear at the kitchen door with a basket of fish on his shoulder and Paula, who would be at the stove building a fire, could be depended upon to turn her back.

That evening, a little after supper—indeed the tin plates they had used were still scattered about the bamboo floor— Tía Orang the midwife paid the Olartes a visit. The rain had changed to a drizzle and the old woman appeared excited over something. She had brought along with her, besides a kerchief with which she protected herself from the drizzle, a basket which contained a black pot; so very sooty it was, one couldn't think it was chicken *adobo;* but it was. Presently Lupo arrived with his father and mother—Lupo and his father Tio Longinos in neat white *camisa de chinos,* and Tía Pulin in a dark starched-stiff cotton skirt and a hempen *camisa.* The two old people had no doubt come all the way from Bakawan in the flood, and Pisco wondered why he had not seen them paddling down the river. They had brought along some *tuba,* and each of them had carried a frond of *buri* for umbrella.

"This can only mean one thing," Pisco heard his father tell his stepmother. Then his father whispered something into Tía Unday's ear; and she ran up to the house, to tidy the room a little before asking their visitors in.

Amidst the clatter of the tin plates, for Tía Unday seemed so clumsy, Tía Orang remarked: "It seems that youth is tongue-tied."

"Very well then," Pisco's father said, keeping the guests in the kitchen a little while longer. Finally Tía Unday gave him the signal, and he bade them come up the hut.

Pisco was about to join them, but his father said: "Go out there to the riverbank—it seems to me this rain has stopped. See that nobody goes off with our *banca!*"

Like a *hangaray* stick at the fish corral, he was being pulled away. Lupo, then, was the big *lauan* log rushing down? He was looking at him now, smiling.

"We'll be needing the *banca* to visit the fish trap sometime tonight," Pisco's father said.

Somewhat nettled, Pisco lingered in the kitchen. He could have done anything to be able to see the matchmaking at first hand.

When the weather had cleared and the river was green again, they added more *hangaray* sticks and bamboo at the trap, letting its arms spread wider than before. Lupo could not help very much, Pisco's father said, because he was going to be busy building a hut of his own. Although that night no date for the wedding had been set, it was known all over the barrio that Tía Unday had asked that the would-be groom provide a hut for his bride and that for a start they ought to have on hand between the two of them twenty-five *cavanes* of *palay*.

It seemed that Lupo had acquired a different standing now. He was even more often at home than elsewhere, and when Pisco cooked rice for their noon meal one day his father reminded him: "Add now an extra *chupa*. Lupo eats with us."

Pisco set the pot on the stove and fixed the wood in order that the heat would come evenly under the pot. Then he walked over to Lupo, who was busy at the whetstone, which was behind the two big water jars. He was sharpening his bolo.

"What do you think, Manong," he began. "The *palay* will be plentiful this year?"

"The rains must have harmed the crop a little, if that's what you mean," Lupo replied.

He stopped working the blade of the bolo up and down the length of the whetstone and gave Pisco a queer look. "But if you are thinking of the twenty-five *cavanes*," he added, "then have no worries about that."

After a long pause, Pisco asked: "What are you sharpening the bolo for?"

Lupo let the blade of his bolo cut against his thumb nail and blinked his big deep-set eyes. He seemed quite satisfied with his bolo blade. But what Pisco wondered at was that look in his eyes. Pisco felt uncomfortable noticing how Lupo held the bolo with his thumb and forefinger, gently rubbing the blade. Suddenly he lunged forward, crying "Shsst!" His thumb and forefinger caught Pisco's throat. The boy fell back, trembling.

"Now be off to your work. See that your rice pot boils well," Lupo said, laughing.

The bolo, of course, was for going to the swamps, in the mud and among the mosquitoes; it was for cutting posts and beams and rafters out of *dungon, tangal,* and *hangaray*—and the names of the woods pleased Pisco's ears.

That afternoon, seeing Lupo following Paula down to the well, Pisco recalled a remark Tía Unday had made: "His eating here with us—what will people say?" Paula, who was then in the *sulambi,* getting together the dirty rags to wash, had not perhaps heard her mother. Pisco thought his father had looked annoyed then, as if the matter ought not have come up at all. "He works for us," Pisco's father had argued. "A meal or two every day, what does that matter?"

ANISTO

Pisco took a water container with him, just in case Lupo should wonder what he might be up to. He had not reached the tamarind tree in Tía Orang's yard when he saw him sitting quietly at the midwife's kitchen doorstep. Perhaps Lupo meant to see for himself from that distance that no one came within ten yards of the washing-shed. Himself he did not care to get any closer, as if afraid he would see his betrothed in her wet *patadiong* and thus have too soon a surfeit for her.

When Lupo saw Pisco coming, there was nothing the boy could do but walk on ahead with the water container on his shoulder.

"But I thought I filled all the water jars this morning?" said Lupo, looking quite perplexed.

Pisco lied. "It's water for the drinking jar that we need," he said. The words came to him quite quickly enough.

"What do you mean? Are you saying I did not fill those jars this morning?"

"It's not that, Manong," Pisco said. His knees felt weak.

"Step over here, then!" Lupo ordered.

Dragging the bamboo container after him, Pisco retreated instead.

"Don't you slip away now, I'm telling you!" the other commanded. "Over here!" His big toe made an "x" on the ground, on a spot not more than one foot from where he stood.

To gain time, Pisco gently laid his bamboo water container on the ground. He pressed a foot down to keep the container from rolling over and watched the left-over water trickle out of the opening.

"Be quick about it," Lupo said.

Pisco found himself standing on the marked spot. It was as if his feet had moved forward of their own accord. Cold sweat stood now on the nape of his neck, on his temples. His hands seemed to hang limp from his shoulder joints. It was hardly the prize for being too curious.

"Say, 'You filled the water jars early this morning!' Say it ten times!"

Lupo grabbed him by the neck and the big callous hands closed in. "You filled the water jars early—" Pisco mumbled.

"Say it out loud; and then ten times!" Lupo insisted, tightening his grip. "Out loud so the whole world will hear!"

As Pisco's eyes began to moisten, a mere gasp emerged from his throat. Down toward the corner of his lips a tear fell and it tasted brackish. "You filled the water jars—"

"Say, 'Every one of them, including the one for drinking water!' "

" 'Every one of them, including—' " Pisco repeated. Keeping count with his fingers, he said the sentences again and again: " '—the one for drinking water . . .—for drinking water . . .' "

Pisco hardly ever saw Lupo idle afterward. In the evenings Lupo stayed sober, too, so that he might work longer and harder the following morning. He began his mornings as always with the filling of the water jars; or, if the woodpile back of the kitchen had become a foot high, he cut and split *tangal;* then he set out for the swamps again.

On a Friday morning he announced he would use the *dalapang.* This was the big outriggerless *banca* that lay bottom-side up behind the kitchen lean-to. It was only for hauling rice that they used this *banca,* Pisco remembered. Now it seemed that Lupo had his wood ready—perhaps all that he needed for his hut.

They helped him launch the *dalapang.* After breakfast he was off, perched like a little boy at the stern, the tip of his paddle hardly reaching the water.

It had meant hard work, not only cutting the wood but piling them piece by piece near some bank, perhaps that of one of the three Ambaols. Being without outriggers, the *dalapang* could go up any of the small creeks that filled the Malig with brackish wash from the swamps. The creeks not being navigable in the ordinary outrigged *banca,* Lupo had insisted on the *dalapang,* unwieldy though it was.

Toward noon Tío Longinos Basco arrived from up the river. He had a bolo at his waist—he had come to work.

"Lupo not yet back?" he asked. "He told me to come, to help him."

But Lupo was still in the swamps, somewhere. Tío Longinos was anxious. He had come by way of Ambaol Creek, he explained, for it was there he knew the pile of mangrove wood to be. Lupo himself had told him. From Ambaol Creek, it would be a matter of an hour and then the wood would be in the barrio.

Tía Unday said could Pisco set the tin plates on the bamboo floor for their noon meal? It was a good way to make Tío Longinos feel he was not only welcome but that he was at home, truly.

"This son of mine," Tío Longinos said, sighing, "sometimes it is as if he's like Pisco over there. So restless, and not quite knowing, I must say, what he is about! If it were but October and harvest time now, there would be no end to his saying, 'Father, let us bring down the twenty-five *cavanes* to the barrio—today, this very minute!' "

Pisco dropped the plates he had brought in from the kitchen. He heard someone out there in the river, yelling.

He ran to the water's edge. Nothing there in the September sun this hour toward midday but the green water. And because of the high tide, the water looked greener than ever. Where the tide had reached far up the mangrove-covered bank, on the other side of the river, the trees did not hang their roots over the water's edge any more. The nipa palms held their fronds limp as if they had struggled to keep above water and failed.

Pisco found his father and Longinos standing beside

him. "But that's our *dalapang*—over there—*Tatay!*" he told them, pointing to the long black thing where a thick strip of nipa palms partly concealed the river bend. Half like a crocodile and half like a long black log it looked; and what was strange was that it should be floating but not quite getting any nearer downstream.

They could see the floating coconut that Lupo's head had become as he swam in the water. The *dalapang* had capsized, all that wood had fallen into the river. All that material for the hut—posts, rafters, perhaps even the wrist-sized *hangaray* sticks for the kitchen wall—the river had now claimed. A kingfisher flew across the river, shrieking, and disappeared at the palm-covered bend.

But he succeeded in getting the boat right side up. As he trod water, he swung and rocked the boat, and water somehow leaped from prow and stern. Now he was boarding the boat, now shoveling out, and perhaps with much scraping of his paddle blade, the rest of the water in the boat. Then he began diving for the wood he had lost. The floating coconut that his head had been disappeared, and then came the first piece of *hangaray*—it was lifted as by some invisible force. Pisco wished he was out there; he imagined himself in the boat, receiving every stick retrieved.

Lupo had secured the boat to a mangrove tree, no doubt with a length or two of strong vine. Now it kept turning and turning, as if eager to get caught in the stream, like some dark-spirited and restless creature.

About the first week of October, a peddler came to the barrio of Malig. It was Pisco and his father who took him in their *banca* from the other side of the river.

"Pedro Aguacil, at your orders," the peddler said, looking very friendly; even his eyes were smiling.

Unlike most peddlers who visited Malig, he did not

carry a *palmabrava* cane. Neither did he display under his belt the frighteningly long fan-knife one expected of traveling tradespeople.

Pisco carried the pandan-leaf *tampipi* that the peddler had brought along; and, arrived in the hut, where they took him at once, Aguacil showed them his merchandise. Tía Unday left the stove where she was cooking supper, and called to Manding Paula, who dropped the empty pail for hog feed as she stepped into the kitchen and joined her mother.

"Come," Tía Unday said, "perhaps he has something nice for a dress!"

"After all, with her wedding day only to be set—" Tatay said.

"*Si Tatay naman,*" said Manding Paula, shy about it all. "Now, Father. What exactly does that mean?"

"So she's the bride?" the peddler said, smiling, his eyes on Paula.

They gathered eagerly around him. He smelled of sweat —so far away he must have come from. A small, wry-faced man, he had cheeks that looked remarkably sharp. His lips were thin, but when he smiled they became quite expressive. A strange look animated his eyes and the small black in them might have been catlike were he less a pleasant-enough person, the kind who could tell one many things about goings-on in the world, about towns he had been to and people he had met.

Aguacil unknotted the string which bound the *tampipi.* He had come all the way from Pinagsabangan—if only he knew, he said, that there was in these parts a handsome girl planning to get married. . . .

"That's truly nothing to be certain about," Manding Paula protested.

"Then, perhaps, you have some trousers and shirts for

my menfolk," Tía Unday asked. "Something to use so that every now and then they won't look like the river people that they are?"

Aguacil said he was sorry. "Truly my fault—" and he looked as if his regret was great.

He had the *tampipi* now and what did he have indeed but a few combs and bracelets and earrings! "These!" He sought their sympathy. "But how could I have known? Tell me?"

His own clothes were in the bottom of the *tampipi,* and he dug into them. After the clothes emerged a carefully wrapped package, and what were all these but some holy pictures?

Pisco was disappointed. The pictures were those of the *Nuestra Señora de Buen Viaje,* the *Sagrada Familia,* the *San Antonio,* the *San Josep—*Tía Unday could identify each of them, and Aguacil said they cost six *gantas* of *palay* each. What, then, were six measures of rice compared to the lot of good one would have by having some holy pictures to hang about the house? Pisco listened to Aguacil's pleasantries but without interest.

When, after supper, Tía Unday told her stepson, "Show him where Tía Orang's house is. Perhaps the old woman will want to have a good look at the pictures," Pisco frowned, and said:

"Perhaps the old midwife isn't home tonight."

But Tía Unday was not to be disobeyed. Without eagerness, then, Pisco accompanied the peddler, letting him carry his own *tampipi.* Tía Unday shouted to Pisco, who had already crossed the yard: "What impoliteness!" And to the peddler: "Let the boy carry the *tampipi,* Mang Pedro."

But the peddler said it was all right, and took but three of those bow-legged steps of his to clear the yard and get down to the street.

"One must carry one's own burden, is it not?" he called back.

After a week in the barrio, during which time he managed to dispose of all his holy pictures, Aguacil left for Pinagsabangan, going by way of Dias, whence he had come. He would be back in Malig, he promised, perhaps even before the harvest season was over.

Lupo was at his father's clearing in Bakawan at the time of Aguacil's arrival and had remained there ever since. Their *kaingin* rice was said to look very well; the place must be guarded at night against wild hogs and stray carabaos that roamed around and destroyed the crop. It was everyone's problem, getting the crop in. And when one succeeded, one did not forget the Olartes. The people from Bakawan who came down for fresh fish brought now new rice, their very clothes sometimes exuding the fragrance of it.

There were those, of course, who were either too busy to come or, as Tía Unday put it, "who had forgotten, because their time of need had passed." And to the clearings of those people Pisco and his father went. "So that you'll know how things are," Tatay seemed to say as he steered the *banca* up the river in silence. Sometimes Pisco's thoughts went elsewhere. He wondered whether in some way Lupo had arranged for the purchase of Manding Paula's wedding dress. Since Aguacil was coming back, Pisco reasoned, the matter of a suitable dress was perhaps more important than ever.

With empty rice sacks on their shoulders, they visited the *kaingins* then, and people told Pisco's father: "Ipin, you have the wisdom. You do not work the land; you do nothing but tend your fish corral. But it is as if you're a *kaingin* right here, beside this one of ours."

"I have no way with the soil, that's why," Tatay admitted. "My father was a sailor, exactly as his father had been before him. I learned the making of fish corrals from an uncle, that's the reason. Every bolo to its own sheath, what do you think?"

"True. Then what about Pisco here?"

At this point, the boy would look the other way, shy about being spoken about.

Once his father said: "That perhaps it is for him to see which suits him best—the river or the land."

Pisco thought about the matter for a long time. It occupied his mind as they trudged along from one clearing to another. The thought followed him on the trail toward the landing in Bakawan. It was pleasant to do the thinking while paddling, the *banca* smooth in the water, and somehow the little noises which outriggers and paddles made in the water seemed something of an answer. Someday he would understand it all completely, he said to himself. At the moment, the answer was somewhat uncertain in the soft drone of the mosquitoes.

When the rice harvest was being threshed, Aguacil returned. One burning midday, he came up the river in a *parao*. The beach was deserted; boatmen poled up the river yelling and shouting, as if in that way they could dispel the heat. There was Aguacil indeed on the *parao's* deck. Pisco recognized him instantly. But so severe was the heat Tía Unday would not let the boy leave the hut until the *parao* had come directly in front of the kitchen lean-to. Only then did Pisco run to the water's edge, as though Aguacil had promised him a present.

The peddler did bring two hampers, large ones both of them. In the first one were ready-made dresses and undershirts and cheesecloth and denim; in the other were packages of matches and soap. Also there were two tins of petroleum, contained in a fragrant pine-board crate, that the men from the *parao* brought up the house. As before, Aguacil stayed with the Olartes.

"Help him if he needs you," Crispino told his son; for

Aguacil said he might set up some kind of a stall. A shed, perhaps? The extension of the kitchen roof, propped up so that two benches could be set up under it! There the men might sit around; from a counter, Aguacil would wait upon them.

Two days passed, then three. Pisco waited for Aguacil to say: "Go to the swamp, boy. Get me some wood. And for an undershirt that I'll give you, build me that shed." But Aguacil said nothing of the sort.

Instead, he brought the petroleum tins up the house and posted them beside the two hampers, like guards. Whenever the neighbors came to see what goods Aguacil had, he would push the tins to the wall to open the hampers and then display his merchandise on a mat which Tía Unday had given him to use.

The family was not incommoded at all. There was Manding Paula to help Tía Unday. They had underestimated Manding Paula; she liked tidying up the hut and did not mind having visitors about. Lupo had seen a good housekeeper in her. He was a far-seeing person, this Lupo.

People from up the river came to see the ready-made dresses, to feel the rough cheesecloth between their fingers, to sniff the gummy smell of denim; and because it was not always that Aguacil was around to talk to them, Manding Paula it was who sometimes attended to them. She opened the hampers herself and discussed prices and terms.

"Do you have the peddler's permission?" Tía Unday might ask.

"Have no fear, Mother," Manding Paula would reply.

Mornings, while splitting firewood in back of the kitchen, Pisco could hear them talk:

"But that would be twenty *gantas*. What do you say?"

"Five for this undershirt, is that it? Three for the soap and matches? Isn't that a little too much?"

"But it is a bargain!"

"Three *gantas* for the bar of soap? You call that a bargain?"

"And the matches go without charge! What more can you say?"

On bringing in the wood he had cut, Pisco saw Tía Unday and his father in the kitchen. The two had been listening, too. His father was shaking his head, Pisco noticed.

"Maybe we ought to open a store. We have a shopkeeper right here with us," Tatay said.

"No, not that," Tía Unday said. "But we ought to encourage Lupo—let him set up a store. Let him engage in some small business, as soon as the two of them are settled down. 'Open a *tienda.*' Tell Lupo that."

"He'll have the shopkeeper for this shop, true enough," Tatay agreed.

It was said that Lupo's father had threshed sixty *cavanes* of *palay*—a good number, considering that there had been but two *cavanes* of seed-rice planted. Pisco wondered how much rice would be left in Tío Longinos' house after the twenty-five *cavanes* promised for Lupo and Manding Paula had been brought to the barrio.

Now because the work in the *kaingin* was all over, too, Tío Longinos himself came to the barrio to help his son build the hut. Father and son worked steadily, quietly—"Like grave-diggers!" Pisco heard his father say. But Pisco liked it there in the mornings; he liked sitting round, watching Tío Longinos and Lupo looking so busy. If Tatay, as people in the *kaingins* had said, had the wisdom concerning the river and fish corrals, Pisco felt certain that Tío Longinos had something of the kind concerning houses and the earth. A *peseta* had been buried with each of the principal posts; the main doorway was to be such it would face the river and the east; there would be an odd number of steps, never even, for the bamboo stairs. Pisco lingered round, picking up this and that bit of lore, soaking all of them in, as though he were the wick of a *lamparilla*.

"You know how it is done, boy?" Lupo once said.

They were working with the center beam. Lupo had tied it at one end to the center post, and the result was a neat, if elaborate-looking matter of weaving and looping of rattan. Pisco gaped in wonder.

"Go up there, and I'll show you," Lupo said.

Pisco climbed the post, held with his upturned foot one end of the heavy beam Lupo had lowered, bent over and caught the wood with his loop of rattan and pulled. Lupo taught him how to work the rattan this way and that, never sacrificing pattern for strength, never losing your purpose and yet taking every care to make out of something ordinary a beautiful thing. Below, in the broken shade that the house-parts made on the ground, Tío Longinos worked with mallet and chisel, watching the two. Pisco could not help feeling that it was from him all this wisdom of the rattan had come, and then he thought he saw the father smile quietly all to himself.

From where he was perched, Pisco could see far out along the barrio street in the quivering half-shade of the coconut trees. The peddler Pedro Aguacil was walking home—it seemed he had gone to Tía Orang's. As Aguacil drew nearer, he looked more bow-legged than ever.

"How about going home now and helping your Manding Paula cook the noon meal?" Lupo suggested.

Pisco reluctantly slid down his perch and regarded from below the beautiful rattan work he had done on the beam and post. His reluctance to leave simmered away, as he discovered now for himself from this distance the intricate pattern in rattan he had made. His elation came like a *santol* seed that stuck in his throat. Feeling that way, he thought, he could go anywhere and could do anything Lupo told him.

"Yes, Manong Lupo—yes!" he heard himself, saying, as he ran home.

When his Manding Paula brought out that afternoon the rice to be pounded, Lupo left his work looking a bit out of sorts.

"There's a pestle for you," Manding Paula pointed to the pestles stacked under the *sulambi* door.

Lupo picked one and began pounding, lifting and dropping the pestle desultorily. Pisco joined, followed by his Manding Paula, who, as she dropped her pestle, kept bending and scraping in with her free hand the rice grains that scattered round the mortar's mouth. It was a broken one-two-three rhythm that they made pounding, and one far from pleasant to hear.

"It's your fault!" Lupo pointed to Pisco. The boy could not answer back.

The rice kept spilling.

"If that's how the two of you work," said Paula, "I'll have to ask you to stop."

Pisco decided to be a little more careful. Then, after the mortar had been emptied, Manding Paula gathered the husks in a torn *buri* mat that had been sewn into a basket. Pisco brought out from behind the kitchen door the old tin pail they used for mixing hog feed in. Manding Paula poured the rice husks into it now, and Pisco picked up a stick with which to stir the mixture. Manding Paula smiled up at him.

"There, take it to the pig," she said.

He was out walking to the pigpen back of the kitchen, the pail heavy in his hand, when he heard them quarreling. By the time he was done, they were shouting at each other back and forth in low but angry voices; and he could hear them above the grunts of the pig, its mouth deep in its trough. Thinking it would embarrass him to return to the kitchen, Pisco left the pail in the pen and went to the riverbank. A little later, he saw Lupo with a water container on his shoulder and walking out into the street.

Pisco returned to the kitchen after Lupo had returned from Tía Orang's well. As if nothing had happened, Manding Paula helped Lupo fill the water jar. She held one end of the bamboo water container against the mouth of the jar so that the water would not spill.

"About my helping Aguacil, what about that?" Manding Paula demanded.

"That you must stop, I say," Lupo answered.

Manding Paula tried to hold the bamboo container more firmly against the jar's mouth. Already Lupo had tilted the container and the rush of the water down the joints of the bamboo left a hollow sound in the air.

"I'll do as I please." Manding Paula's voice was shrill.

"What I say is, you stop!"

"Why, are you my husband already? My master?" Manding Paula let go with one hand and suddenly the bamboo water container slipped down the round of the jar's mouth and struck the dirt floor.

"Just watch out!" Lupo said, raising the bamboo container and standing it against the corner wall. "I've warned you!"

Lupo was already at the river bank when Pisco got there in the slow-lifting dawn twilight. At the fish trap, tiny crabs slithered up the platform and down the sides of the *bunuan*. The splash of fish threw sparkling blobs of light on the water.

It was Lupo who got down and Pisco lowered the hand-net to him. "Throw all those crabs away! What we want are the fish!" he cried, as he splashed about inside the trap.

Pisco got the paddle and brushed the crabs down the length of the platform. They scattered like pebbles into the water.

"Be ready up there with this catch!" Lupo called.

With him inside, the *bunuan* looked full. He dipped and rose as if to feel with his hands each and every mudfish and mullet that thrashed and spun round. Bubbles rose and broke on the surface, and finally the handnet came, two hands holding it up, and Lupo shouting: "It's heavy, it's full!"

In order to take advantage of the low tide, they stayed in the river even after Tatay, who had followed them, had brought home the catch. There were several *hangaray* poles that stood loose in the mud bottom and had to be replaced if the bamboowork could be expected to withstand the rush of the tide at high noon. Then again Tatay came to see that the work was done well.

"What now?"

Pisco saw his father chuckling. It was one of the few occasions when he heard that chuckle. Tatay had found Tío Longinos in the hut, and was asking him: "You offering to barter fish for rice?"

"And how else? That seems to be the way things are," said Lupo's father.

"You, like all the others? What has come?"

It occurred to Pisco that perhaps something had gone wrong; he could feel it in the somewhat childish way Tío Longinos spoke.

"It is as if you are some other person. Here your son works and works, and he has a good share—which of course he sends up the river to your house. Does he?"

"That's the truth," Tío Longinos admitted. "But today, this morning, it was as if I were stranger here!"

Tatay laughed, perhaps to make what he might say seem unimportant. "But, *balaye!* How does this happen? How does life make a stranger of you in my house?"

"Ipin," Tío Longinos said, clearing his throat. "You are a sensible person. Now listen. I've been at Lupo's hut working, fitting this bamboo window and that. It's the hut where some day our two young people will make their home. It's there I work, as I've just said. Then I come in here to your house, judging from the voices of the womenfolk that fish has arrived. For a man needs fish, even a working man. But I am a busy person, and when I work, I like to finish my work. That portion of it, at least, which I had promised to myself I'd finish. So here I come to your kitchen and I am quite late. . . . "

"I do not understand you at all, *balaye*. But continue. Your *balaye* listens intently," Taytay said.

"All right then. Listen, *balaye*. What happens is, your stepdaughter mistakes me for a customer of Aguacil's."

"Impossible! Paula doing that?" Tatay protested. "I cannot believe it. Shall I call her this very minute?"

"No need for that, *balaye*. But this I must tell you," Longinos went on. "She asks, shouting from the *sulambi*: 'What do you want? Soap, matches?' My fault, of course, because I come after those who have gotten fish have all of them gone. Still, I am too dumbfounded to speak. Imagine a prospective father-in-law being treated that way. I do not utter one word in reply. I keep my words, *balaye*. From upstairs, in the *sulambi*, this Paula of yours—"

"But she is no daughter of mine, really!" Tatay said, putting his forefinger to his lips, half-whispering.

"All right, then. But still she says, shouting: 'You wait there, there in the kitchen. I'll be with you in a minute. Perhaps you've heard that it is well past harvest-time now, and you can't get goods unless the *palay* is right there along with you. Have you got the *palay* then? *Mano a mano*, as they say?' "

"Why, where was Segunda?" Tatay demanded. Segunda? Paula—where's your mother? And you there, staring like that!"

Pisco saw that his foster sister had heard all, had indeed

stepped out of the *sulambi* to be sure that she caught every word of Tío Longinos' complaint. She posted herself at the *sulambi* door.

Tío Longinos did not change his tone. Nor did he speak of other things. "There she is!" he pointed. "She'll admit it, if she's honest!"

It was as if Manding Paula was too surprised to speak. She merely stood there, she could not even move. Pisco felt like telling her to go away. Suddenly he disliked her. She did not look to him anywhere the darkly provoking full-breasted grown woman he had seen in the dimness of the *sulambi* many weeks back. The fierceness he had feared then returned. It seemed to have taken this old form, her silently standing there, as if daring Lupo's father to speak further.

"She was standing like that," Tío Longinos continued, in an even tone, "and that means, she knew who it was. . . . God's my witness. What she said I've told you, *balaye*. Now what am I, an old man—the father of one who might be your son-in-law—what am I to do?"

Then he burst out laughing, as if to say: "There, now! Since I've unburdened myself, forget what I've said!" On the overturned rice mortar he sat down and pulled out his small buri basket under his rattan belt; from this basket he drew out his chewing things—*buyo* leaf, lime and betel nut. He handed the chewing things to Tatay, who accepted them.

"Well, think nothing of it," Tatay said, giving him three mudfish, so live still they were too slippery and difficult to hold. Tío Longinos picked up a piece of *buri* with which to string up the fish through the gills. The loop was heavy enough.

"Pisco," Tatay said, "give your Tío Longinos a better piece of string!"

And as he was looking for some pieces of *buri* in the

yard, Pisco saw other people from Bakawan arriving in their *banca*.

His father greeted them warmly: "You've come late! Very late!" Tatay met them in the kitchen, "But let's see what can be done for you."

On account of some customers of Aguacil's, the whole house that evening was astir till quite late. People crowded in the kitchen. At his father's behest, Pisco built a smudge in the yard. After the men had gone and, along with them, Aguacil—who seemed to be pressing some sale—dogs started barking in the street and down the river bank. Then, above the noise of the dogs, there rose the clear and languid notes of a guitar.

Perhaps Tía Unday was the person most startled of them all. She sat up on her mat, which she had hastily spread after Aguacil's customers had gone. The serenaders were approaching from across the back yard. Pisco looked out the window; the smudge had died.

Now the guitar-player was right by their window, and his father asked: "Will you let him in?"

What could that mean? Pisco asked himself the question, remembering the betrothal. Perhaps, he thought, letting the serenaders come might mean the breaking of the betrothal. Where could Lupo be at that moment? Perhaps, back there at Tía Talia's? Yes, at his sister's house and sound asleep! What if the guitar should wake him up?

"Paula," said Tía Unday in a whisper. "You'd better light the *lamparilla*."

Manding Paula got out the small kerosene lamp, and scratched a match.

"Nanay," she said, "perhaps we should open the window."

Tía Unday looked across the room, in Tatay's direction. There was neither consent nor approval forthcoming from

his father, Pisco noticed. The *lamparilla* light flickered miserably. His father's face hardly helped. It was a tired man's
face. When he stirred from where he sat in the corner, it was
to roll his own sleeping mat—a mere concession.

"Well—" Tía Unday hesitated.

Manding Paula said: "I'll open the window then, Nanay.
Please help me," she added, picking up one of the two bamboo
props that would set the window shutter up. It hung oddly
until, for her portion of the window, Tía Unday had adjusted
the prop. That was her part in the opening of the window and
a sudden breeze from the river all but extinguished the newly
lighted *lamparilla*.

A chorus of respectful "Good evening's" followed the
song, and from that moment on, Manding Paula had to sit at
the window, holding the *lamparilla* in her hand.

"They are *constabularios*, Nanay," she told her mother.

After they had sung their fourth song, Tía Unday said:
"Ask them then to come up the house."

Pisco sighed; it was done at last. He heard his father
grumbling: "You might just as well."

Profuse "Thank you's" and then the clatter of rifles, as
the four men clambered tiredly up the stairs.

They seated themselves more tiredly upon the bamboo
floor. Manding Paula laid the *lamparilla* in the middle of the
floor, then seated herself opposite the men. She stared at the
lamp, which stood unsteadily, for the bamboo floor slats moved
as the men stirred in their seats. Pisco noticed they looked at
him too, as though fixing in their minds where they had seen
him last. He was sure he had not seen them before.

"We have to spend the night somehow," one soldier
began.

"Such is a soldier's life," said another.

"My husband, there," said Tía Unday, "he was once
with the *constabularios* himself. Only that was long ago.

The conversation was like a *banca* that had struck, it seemed, a sandbar in the stream; the soldiers tried to push it forward. They had come from Palaon and they had stopped at Tía Orang's, they said. The midwife had wanted to trouble herself about preparing supper, for they must be hungry. But, truly, they had had supper in Palaon. Were they not pushing on to Dias, just ahead? Yes, but this night seemed so restful: there was a moon. They could not pass up this chance, truth to tell, of meeting pretty barrio girls. Ay, soldiers are such lonely people! That they ought perhaps to look up someone to serenade, some young girl, a pretty one, if such person could be found! And they had found her? On this point they argued, apparently for sheer argument's sake. It was as though their conversation had run into a whirlpool. Then one solider poled it out of the danger-spot; all four of them were young unmarried men, he revealed. One owned the guitar, had carried it on many a journey like this through the length and breadth of Sipolog Province. He had tied the guitar on to his back and covered his pack with *buri* leaves when it was too hot on the beach or when it rained. And truly all four of them were good listeners. Could Paula favor them now, with a song?

The guitar player started strumming his instrument again, and they coaxed and begged.

"Let us hear all four of you first of all," she said smiling vaguely.

"And then it will be your turn?"

She blushed, half turning her head, as if to avoid their seeing her face in the flickering light of the *lamparilla*.

One by one they sang. Then the soldier with the guitar crossed over to Manding Paula's side of the room, clumsily folded his two legs beneath him, balanced the guitar across his lap, and commenced a *pasacalye*. It was one he had not used before. Manding Paula watched his fingers dancing on the fingerboard. Perhaps what specially struck her fancy, Pisco thought, was the seashell ring on the soldier's finger; perhaps she thought of sailboats and distant places. Oh, how tired those soldiers must be, what with their long journey from the south. Yet of course they had come with guitar music and the idea that they were begging of her something of great value, a song from her lips, from her very heart . . . it could touch anyone deeply.

The guitar player repeated the *pasacalye,* and then from Tía Unday came the shattering harshness: "If you intend to sing, then sing!"

Pisco himself jerked back from his corner near the door-step. He saw Manding Paula clear her throat before words came to her lips, before the tune could take shape.

> *Oh, how the beggars make merry*
> *In our town called San Roque,*

she sang, and her voice quivering:

> *Oh, how the blind one*
> *Watches the dancing of the lame!*
> *Oh, how the deaf one*
> *Listens to the song of the dumb!*

The soldiers did not return to Tía Orang's hut, where they said they would spend the night, until it was well past midnight. Momently, Pisco expected Lupo to come; it would be no trouble coming from over there, across the back yard, from his sister Tía Talia's house. But he did not come. Pisco peeked through the kitchen door, and found but darkness across the yard, the triangular lump, which was the roof of Tía Talia's house, looking thin against the bulkier gray of the moonlight under the coconut trees.

Dogs started barking again as the soldiers, their guns

slung loose on their shoulders, walked down the street. Pisco followed them across the yard and down the street. Was that somebody there behind a coconut tree? Pisco thought the soldier with the guitar peered into the half-dark himself and then, on finding no one, walked on down the street.

The next morning, Lupo appeared at the Olarte kitchen door. Pisco and his father were preparing to go to the trap and they had been indeed rather impatient; Lupo had never been quite so late before. But, well, here he was. Only, what was this he was wearing if not a scowl? And Tía Unday asked: "What do you mean by that Good Friday look?"

Lupo did not say one word.

"Here, you take something warm, both of you," Manding Paula said to Lupo and Pisco, offering ginger tea.

Then Tatay went down to the riverbank. Still scowling, Lupo held the bowl of ginger tea in his hand. Pisco could see Lupo's hand trembling. It could be the ginger tea was so hot Lupo couldn't take a sip. But also it could be something else; his eyes began to look wet; he blew into the bowl noisily and sniffled, as if he couldn't avoid sniffling.

"I am going away," he told Manding Paula, putting down his bowl.

"Where?" Manding Paula answered quickly. "To Pinagsabangan? To San Roque, perhaps? Or to the river? In fact, you're already late!"

"Anywhere. What will it matter to you?"

"It's not true," Manding Paula said.

"Just wait," Lupo said.

"Then, perhaps, it is because you want me to cry and say, Oh, please, don't go!"

"Just wait," Lupo said again, his eyebrows narrowing.

Except for Pisco, there was no one in the kitchen. Tatay was still at the river bank; Pisco could hear him bailing out the water in the bottom of the *banca* with a coconut shell. The slushing of the water and the scraping of the coconut shell combined to make a strange sound; it was as if something was being ripped open.

His overhearing the quarrel had made Pisco uneasy. He felt like leaving for the river bank now; at the same time he couldn't help it if they had started to quarrel while he was here in the kitchen, looking for a paddle to take along with him to the *banca*. Now he pretended to be busy with some ropes piled in back of the stovebox. As he stirred, the bamboo siding yielded motes that fluttered in the air. A sneeze caught him, but he stifled it by rubbing his nose. He wished Tía Unday were in the kitchen, too. But then, he told himself, it did not really matter; she could be watching, for all he knew, peering from behind some chink in the *sulambi* wall.

"Just wait! What do you mean?" Manding Paula demanded. But Pisco missed what Lupo said then. The voice was different, Lupo was not himself.

Pisco pulled out a paddle from under the ropes and got up from behind the woodpile. It was as if that movement had a relation with what he now saw Lupo to be doing, as if he and Lupo were both tied on one rope and someone had jerked the rope. Except that the pull on the rope had pushed Lupo forward. And then there he was holding Paula, drawing her to him, tightly.

He might have thrown back his head at least; but no, he didn't. Pisco forgot thinking about imaginary ropes and wondered why Lupo held Manding Paula so close, no doubt he could smell now the scent of lime and *gogo* bark in her hair. He might have thrown back his head at least, but instead he held her even tighter, and then his tongue was laving her neck and chin. Finally, their lips met; and Pisco shuddered. He imagined Lupo and Paula's teeth knocking together, for it was as if Lupo felt a beastly, uncontrolled urge to bite her. She resisted and managed to turn her head away. Now Lupo had ripped her blouse open, and they tussled for a minute.

Manding Paula, defenseless now, looked limp and weak, her back to the wall. But she did not cry out for help, she only bit her lips and closed her eyes. Lupo suddenly stepped back, the fear to touch other parts of her body perhaps growing in him. Manding Paula managed to turn about and face the wall. Hands covering her face, she began to sob. Lupo caressed her. Her hair, although completely disheveled now, looked soft in his hands. Lupo held her on the shoulder tenderly, and then she lifted her gaze to him. Perhaps something in that look changed him, for instantly he kissed her again. She yielded, holding on to him tightly, her hands digging into his shoulder blades. It was as if she would not let him go, but Lupo drew himself away. When he was free, he said, loud enough for anyone to hear!

"There! Who will ever marry you now?"

Pisco rushed out of the kitchen, dragging the paddle behind him. He ran to the river bank in one bound, crossing the strip of sand from the doorstep to his father's *banca* at the water's edge.

Whether or not his stepmother had seen what had happened, Pisco couldn't say, but he thought—and Lupo's words kept ringing in his ears—of how Manding Paula's life would be from now on, now at last as Lupo's wife. Surely, Lupo must marry her. But he had dashed out of the kitchen and, following the path through the *chichiriki* and *sentimiento,* he had crossed to the empty lot where the hut he had been making for Paula stood. He would not stop there, Pisco feared. Lupo would run until he had reached the swamp and disappeared behind the *piyapi* trees.

Tatay came hurrying into the kitchen. "Why, what's happened?" he demanded, seeing Manding Paula crying. She was standing behind the Y-shaped stand which held the small earthen jar containing drinking water, and she was shaking convulsively. It was as if above the sobs Pisco could hear her saying, "Now, I'm not pure any more!" He thought her trouble was like that of the water-gatherer of the folk tale who had broken her jar.

"Now, Paula!" Tatay cried angrily. "Can't you ever stop!" He called to Tía Unday: "Segunda, make her stop! Don't you be making a scandal of it, for the whole barrio to talk about!"

Pisco knew then that his father had understood. "You go down over there," Tatay told him, pointing to the edge of the swamp. "See which trail he's taken."

"Let him alone in the swamp, where he belongs—that beast!" said Tía Unday, coming down from the *sulambi*, her hair flying about.

Pisco hesitated. He could not see any good in his following Lupo now into the swamp. He stood in the yard, gaping at the sunshine, feeling this might be the first time he would disobey his father.

It was about this time that fish from the corral was ready, and either the neighbors had come for that or they had heard the cries; but anyway they were gathering now in the kitchen.

"What is this I hear mention of my brother's name?" Tía Talia demanded. She had come running from across the *chichirika* patch, carrying her four-month-old baby astride her hip. Flor and her sister Little Ana had come, too, the latter clinging to the edge of their mother's *camisa*.

"A beast is a beast, whatever food you feed it with," Tía Unday said.

"Be reasonable, Manang Unday," Tía Talia begged. "Tell us first what this is that my brother's done."

A confusion of voices, of answers and questions, and everyone eager to speak—all but Tatay. To Pisco he had whispered, "Better go fetch the catch yourself," and had sat at the doorstep and remained silent there.

And then started the talk about sending someone to Palaon, to fetch the Justice of the Peace, Juez Tupas. Two men from Kakawan had come to see Aguacil the peddler, and Tatay broke his silence finally and asked could these two try and get Lupo. Perhaps, he would stay in the swamps, Aguacil said, repeating what he had claimed a few minutes before: "If only I had been home, nothing would have happened." As if, Pisco thought, Lupo might have paid any attention to the peddler. But, anyway, Aguacil sat near the whetstone and worked on a coconut shell, one of these "over which the moon had passed" and had neither meat nor water, that he had picked up in the grove two days back. There he worked Tatay's bolo up and round the shell, to remove every shred of coir and make it clean and shiny. To Tía Talia who stood by watching, perhaps wondering why Aguacil could be so much with them and yet so apart, he explained he intended to cut through the hard shell some kind of a slit afterwards; it would serve so well as a container for his pesetas and centavos. Tía Talia stared, and Aguacil did not seem to mind; he worked on the coconut shell with the awful interest of a little child.

Pisco had picked up his paddle reluctantly. Flor made way for him as he left the crowd in the kitchen. Little Ana sidled to the wall and gave him a sidelong glance—rather a startling look, because the girl had a white spot in one eye. It was said to be growing, that already it was the size of a grain of rice, that it might grow so large she would become blind. Yet Little Ana did look at him so, Pisco decided, if only perhaps to say that this would be the first time he would get the catch in the corral himself.

He hurried to the *bunuan*, each stroke of his paddle bringing to his ears, it seemed, the sound of Lupo's feet in the muddy trail, past the growths of nipa and corkwood. He would be nearing Bakawan now, Pisco calculated. Half an hour more, and Lupo would be at Tío Longinos' clearing; or perhaps he would be up on some *buri* palm and drinking. It wouldn't take any time to get him properly drunk and perhaps barely able to get down the bamboo ladder; and most likely he would be shouting to the *buri* trees: "I've ruined her already! Who will ever marry her now?"

Pisco asked himself did he really want to see that Lupo and his Manding Paula become man and wife. But instead his mind kept asking did he pity his Manding Paula; now? He was seven when his father married Tía Unday, Manding Paula's mother. She had often beat him up with whole lengths of coconut midrib, if not with the entire swishing broom itself. It had been that way all through that year his father was with the Constabulary and had left Pisco with Unday in Sinukuan. Later, when Tatay got his discharge, the year after his marriage, the family moved from Sinukuan to Malig, traveling across the province by way of the mountain trails. The journey had taken seven days, and Manding Paula, already fifteen then, rode the skinny cow that his father had bought for the journey. Then, pasturing the cow in Malig had been a problem afterward, for there was very little grass on the side of the river where the barrio was. The cow had to be taken across the river to the grass in another coconut grove; and every time Pisco forgot to swim the cow over, or whenever he allowed the cow to remain on the other bank for the night, he was sure to receive from either Tía Unday or Manding Paula a tweak in the ear. A good thing Tatay sold the cow to buy some bamboos from Palaon and hire some labor; somehow this ended, Pisco realized, the "burning" of his ears. At the same time, of course, he had become five—then seven, and then eight. When they got Lupo to help with the fish trap, somehow both Manding Paula and Tía Unday became much kinder people. Pisco's thoughts as he paddled to the *bunuan* reproduced vague pictures of his own mother, whom he had heard Tatay call Berta and who had died—Tatay said—when he, Pisco, was only two. A long line of aunts and uncles—in such places as Nawan, Alag and Buhanginan, where Tatay said he himself had spent his youth—moved before Pisco's mind as he paddled and tied the boat fast to a *hangaray* pole and grabbed his basket and his handnet, and then he climbed up the platform. He was in the water in no more than a minute, and was quietly manipulating the handnet exactly as he had seen Lupo do it before.

Oh, but Lupo was back! In running to the swamp, directly after what happened, it was for him as if only in answer to a call of nature.

On returning from the fish corral, Pisco saw him in the half-finished hut. He was busy setting up a portion of the wall. Actually, he could not do much for he did not have a bolo with him. They saw him moving about, setting up this *hangaray* pole and that, putting this one to that side and this other pole to the other side. Sorting them? If he could go back to Tía Talia's house and pick up his bolo, or if someone could bring him a bolo—

But Tía Talia reprimanded Pisco for the thought. "Don't you see a bolo in his hands may be dangerous?"

Still with the coconut shell in his hand, Aguacil nodded. "Yes, true enough," he muttered, although no one had sought his opinion.

When Tatay's back was turned to the others, Pisco went up to him and whispered. "Lupo's hungry. I'll bring him some food."

Tatay did not answer at once but walked out to the yard, from where they could see Lupo and his hut better. But Lupo was gone.

"Isn't he that one now?" Pisco pointed to a *banca* that

was quietly disappearing behind the palm-covered bend of the river.

"He'll return," Tatay said calmly.

The two men who had been sent to Bakawan returned about noon. Tío Longinos had not seen his son's shadow, and from this fact it would seem that Lupo had gone up some *buri* tree and drunk *tuba* and perhaps taken a nap up there for good measure.

All afternoon, Pisco lingered about the beach restlessly. About sundown he saw a *parao* sailing east from somewhere down Lumawig Point, five miles south of the mouth of the Malig River. Perhaps it had come from Palaon; its sail of *buri* leaves was dark-gray in the sunset glow. Pisco wondered whether Lupo had meant what he said about going to Pinang-sabangan, or somewhere faraway. A spell of loneliness seized him, and he hurried back to the hut to help his Manding Paula pound rice and feed a pig in the pen behind the kitchen.

Impatient for its food, the pig squealed and Pisco thought of Juez Tupas. Perhaps he could come in a day or so; and if there was going to be a wedding, surely Tía Unday's pig would have to go. It was no doubt against such a day as that that Tía Unday had raised and fattened the pig, and he remembered now that his stepmother had been so strict about feeding the animal regularly and properly.

Now, who of them at home had had a good night's sleep, Pisco could not say; but he recalled Tatay reminding him about fetching the catch early the following morning and asking where the handnet was. They could not find it anywhere round the house, and Pisco decided that he must have left it in the *bunuan*.

It was not yet light when he set out; he paddled hurriedly. The soft wheezy sound of the crabs crawling about the bamboo-work greeted him as he tied the *banca* to a *hangaray* pole, but before he could climb up the *bunuan* there was the hand-net, heavy and full, over the side.

"It's you, Manong Lupo?" he asked, breathlessly.

"Go back, quick!" the other said from behind the bamboo-work. "Don't bother me."

Pisco emptied the contents of the handnet into his *banca*, and before he knew it Lupo had let the boat loose. "Shall I bring some food?" he called weakly.

"No, only the bolo," Lupo replied.

"I'll try," Pisco heard himself saying faintly.

But Tía Unday, following a tack all her own, had kept Tatay's bolo, his small fan-knife and axe—everything sharp about the house, all because Manding Paula kept to herself in the *sulambi* all this time, afraid that people would see the mark —if there was any—Lupo's lips had left on her cheeks; and it was possible, Pisco thought, that since Manding Paula's shame was great—was greater, in fact, than Lupo's—because it was she, the bride-to-be, who, in effect, was being spurned; because even if she did not love him, she had been pledged to him and now she had been shamed and abandoned; and the hut and the fish corral and the river being things Lupo now preferred; and because of all this, perhaps Tía Unday feared that Manding Paula might do something to herself.

No word came from Palaon about Juez Tupas. It was as if in his wisdom the Justice of the Peace had decided that Malig ought to settle its troubles first before even looking toward Palaon. The day passed tensely; once more Pisco saw a *banca* slip past the palm-covered river bend; and although in the brightness of the sun it was not possible to say exactly that that was Lupo's head, that that shoulder was Lupo's shoulder, that that way of lifting the paddle was Lupo's way, he felt sure about him. The *buri* palm would nourish him, and the river would keep him. He had shamed his betrothed because she had broken her troth, and maybe in the end the river would counsel him, would tell him what to do.

The second day was over, and the sound of rice-pounding was over. Even the occasional barking of dogs was gone. Malig was slipping quietly into evening now. The streets darkened early; in the coconut grove the *chichirika* and *sentimiento* bushes looked shapeless.

It was a cool windless night. For November, it was fraught with silence—like a night in Maytime, with everyone in the barrio gone to the clearings up the river for the planting season. Pisco remembered the evening of the soldiers with the guitar and it seemed he could hear guitar music again. If there was a place whence it might come, this was the swamp: the trees were illumined by fireflies.

Down the bend of the river came a *banca*, the two persons in it shouting, quarreling perhaps even as they paddled, and one listened to the voices and they were voices that echoed and re-echoed in the mangrove trees. A few more strokes of the paddle, however, and the two became Tía Pulin and Tío Longinos, the woman at the prow and now shouting at the mangrove trees that no wind stirred or rustled:

"Now, what else could they want? The house is being built, soon it will be completed. Our Lupo is no turtle!" And then Longinos, taking a different view:

"But that is the way people are. First one thing, then another! There's the house, yes. Then the twenty-five *cavanes*. Remember the twenty-five *cavanes*? Now, they want no wedding set, and then suddenly this sending for the Juez—"

And from Tía Pulin: "What does that make of us?"

Tío Longinos: "People to be pulled this way and that!"

Tía Pulin: "As if, then, without thinking heads of our own."

"But quiet now. Keep your thoughts!" It was Tío Longinos, trying to speak softer, but altogether without control of his voice. "Maybe, the Juez is down there, right now!"

They were coming to a turn and the prow hit sand. It was Tía Pulin who got up first, staggering knee-deep in the water.

"Careful, Longinos," she told him. "After this, never darken their doorstep again!"

The other said, pulling up the *banca*, "Tonight, what must be must be. But, afterward—"

"This can mean that tomorrow you bring down the rice. Twenty-five *cavanes*, no less—" Tía Pulin's voice strident.

"But what must be must be," Tío Longinos repeated.

Fireflies glowed over their heads as they walked from the river, following the edge of the swamp—taking care, Pisco realized, not to pass anywhere near twenty yards of the Olarte hut. And then to Tía Talia's hut they went. Pisco saw them round the yard where Lupo's unfinished house stood, and from there across the *sentimiento* the old couple hunched their way to their daughter's hut. If they had spoken loud their thoughts, with the mangrove and river listening, now they had the silence of the clam. Then they were like shadows entering Tía Talia's kitchen.

Pisco kept to himself what he had heard and what he knew; it was his secret. Although he wanted very much to tell his father about the couples' arrival, he sensed that there were possibly other things he would get around to say, and all this time in his mind the figure of Lupo again roaming about the swamps obsessed him. He imagined he saw him sitting under a *piyapi* tree by the river bank and beckoning to him and asking:

"Well, now, can you look after the fish corral all by yourself."

"Why, then, you are going away?"

"Truly, I am."

"It is true, then, about your wish to go to Pinagsabangan, to San Roque?"

"Well, yes. Since you are there and big enough to be of help."

"Ay, think of the difficulty in the flood—should there be one."

"That'll be next rainy season, and you'll be a much bigger fellow then!"

The words kept coming, sometimes in whispers, sometimes loud enough for anyone to hear. He imagined himself seeing Lupo go, in the dark, following the trail whence Pedro Aguacil the peddler had come. This was the trail that began at the other side of the river and took you to Dias, whence you could go to Pinagsabangan by *parao*—or to wherever you wished. And Pisco followed Lupo to the wide world where you lived with such wisdom in your head as Tatay had—and perhaps it was what Lupo had wanted to learn—about the river and fish corrals, or such as Tío Longinos had about houses and the earth.

He had two dreams that night. In the first one, a stranger came down from over Tía Talia's place across the back yard and was holding something in his hand for Pisco to see. It was a bundle and Pisco unwrapped it. A pair of long trousers and a shirt. "Here, something for you!" the stranger had said; and Pisco's leg had jerked in his sleep, and he awoke at precisely the moment his hands felt the weight of the cloth. He slept on, though, and the second dream came. It was full of vague figures and harsh voices and fireflies throwing their lamps into the *sentimiento* and *chichirika*. Pisco got up and opened a window wide and looked out. Nothing but the night out there in the river.

To his left among the *piyapi* trees the fireflies were burning their lamps as mindlessly as before in the cool and windless air. Would Lupo spend the night in his unfinished hut? Later, staggering under the weight of a half-filled bamboo container for *tuba* that he might have brought down from Bakawan, how he could very well come and ask Manding Paula's forgiveness. If he came, thus, at this hour, no one would see him. No one would hear the stir of the *chichirika* leaves that brushed his legs dryly—if he but walked home at that hour. He might walk, thus, down the street and the path under the coconut palms and under the arches that their fronds, silent in the listless darkness, formed; and then on toward the beach he might go, to linger there until dawn, for afterward he might see to the fish trap which had become so much the navel and the heart, as the river was the body, of all these days and nights.

Directly after a streak of white bared the black wall of the sky, as though a door had been opened there to let a visitor in, Pisco left the hut for the river. The air was sodden with the smell of mangrove leaves and tanbark in the brackish water of last night's tide. There was also a burnt smell somewhere, as though all of last night's fireflies had died; and Pisco, lingering at the river bank for a moment, breathing in these smells, looked around for the *banca*. At the water's edge, the *banca* waited. He spaded the water out with his paddle blade, and he pushed the *banca* into the stream and paddled to the fish corral.

On the platform there lay an empty bamboo container, hardly two joints long. Pisco remembered that it was from here where Lupo had last lowered the handnet to him. The dawn light came fuller now, rippling the water as though it were the breeze.

In this half-light, Pisco saw the body. Broad and bare, Lupo's back had risen from the heart of the trap, clear above the water. The water now rocked him gently.

Pisco pressed his lips and willed himself not to cry.

A WARM HAND

HOLDING ON to the rigging, Elay leaned over. The
dinghy was being readied. The wind tore her hair into wiry
strands that fell across her face, heightening her awareness of
the dipping and rising of the deck. But for the bite of the *noroeste,* she would have begun to feel faint and empty in her belly.
Now she clutched at the rigging with more courage.

At last the dinghy shoved away, with its first load of
passengers—seven boys from Bongabon, Mindoro, on their way
to Manila to study. The deck seemed less hostile than before,
for the boys had made a boisterous group then; now that they
were gone, her mistress Ana could leave the crowded deckhouse for once.

"Oh, Elay! My powder puff!"

It was Ana, indeed. Elay was familiar with that excitement which her mistress wore about her person like a silk
kerchief—now on her head to keep her hair in place, now like
a scarf round her neck. How eager Ana had been to go ashore
when the old skipper of the *batel* said that the *Ligaya* was too
small a boat to brave the coming storm. She must return to the
deckhouse, Elay thought, if she must fetch her mistress'
handbag.

With both hands upon the edge of the deckhouse roof,
then holding on to the wooden water barrel to the left of the
main mast, she staggered back to the deckhouse entrance. As
she bent her head low lest with the lurching of the boat her
brow should hit the door, she saw her mistress on all fours

clambering out of the deckhouse. She let her have the right of way, entering only after Ana was safe upon the open deck.

Elay found the handbag—she was certain that the powder puff would be there—though not without difficulty, inside the canvas satchel that she meant to take ashore. She came dragging the heavy satchel, and in a flurry Ana dug into it for the bag. The deck continued to sway, yet presently Ana was powdering her face; and this done, she applied lipstick to that full round mouth of hers.

The wind began to press Elay's blouse against her breasts while she waited on her mistress patiently. She laced Ana's shoes and also bestirred herself to see that Ana's earrings were not askew. For Ana must appear every inch the dressmaker that she was. Let everyone know that she was traveling to Manila—not just to the provincial capital; and, of course, there was the old spinster aunt, too, for company—to set up a shop in the big city. It occurred to Elay that, judging from the care her mistress was taking to look well, it might well be that they were not on board a one-masted Tingloy *batel* with a cargo of lumber, copra, pigs, and chickens, but were still at home in the dress shop that they were leaving behind in the lumber town of Sumagui.

"How miserable I'd be without you, Elay," Ana giggled, as though somewhere she was meeting a secret lover who for certain would hold her in his arms in one wild passionate caress.

And thinking so of her mistress made Elay more proud of her. She did not mind the dark world into which they were going. Five miles to the south was Pinamalayan town; its lights blinked faintly at her. Then along the rim of the Bay, dense groves of coconuts and underbrush stood, occasional fires marking where the few sharecroppers of the district lived. The *batel* had anchored at the northernmost end of the cove and apparently five hundred yards from the boat was a palm-leaf-covered hut the old skipper of the *Ligaya* had spoken about.

"Do you see it? That's Obregano's hut." And Obregano, the old skipper explained, was a fisherman. The men who sailed up and down the eastern coast of Mindoro knew him well. There was not a seaman who lived in these parts but had gone to Obregano for food or shelter and to this anchorage behind the northern tip of Pinamalayan Bay for the protection it offered sailing vessels against the unpredictable *noroeste*.

The old skipper had explained all this to Ana, and Elay had listened, little knowing that in a short while it would all be there before her. Now in the dark she saw the fisherman's hut readily. A broad shoulder of a hill rose beyond, and farther yet the black sky looked like a silent wall.

Other women joined them on the deck to see the view for themselves. A discussion started; some members of the party did not think it would be proper for them to spend the night in Obregano's hut. Besides the students, there were four middle-aged merchants on this voyage; since Bongabon they had plagued the women with their coarse talk and their yet coarser laughter. Although the deckhouse was the unchallenged domain of the women, the four middle-aged merchants had often slipped in, and once had exchanged lewd jokes among themselves to the embarrassment of their audience. Small wonder, Elay thought, that the prospect of spending the night in a small fisherman's hut and with these men for company did not appear attractive to the other women passengers. Her mistress Ana had made up her mind, however. She had a sense of independence that Elay admired.

Already the old aunt had joined them on deck; and Elay said to herself, "Of course, it's for this old auntie's sake, too. She has been terribly seasick."

In the dark she saw the dinghy and silently watched it being sculled back to the *batel*. It drew nearer and nearer, a dark mass moving eagerly, the bow pointing in her direction.

Elay heard Ana's little shrill cries of excitement. Soon two members of the crew were vying for the honor of helping her mistress safely into the dinghy.

Oh, that Ana should allow herself to be thus honored, with the seamen taking such pleasure from it all, and the old aunt, watching pouting her lips in disapproval! "What shall I do?" Elay asked herself, anticipating that soon she herself would be the object of this chivalrous byplay. And what could the old aunt be saying now to herself? "Ah, women these days are no longer decorous. In no time they will make a virtue of being unchaste."

Elay pouted, too. And then it was her turn. She must get into that dinghy, and it so pitched and rocked. If only she could manage to have no one help her at all. But she'd fall into the water. Santa Maria. I'm safe. . . .

They were off. The waves broke against the sides of the dinghy, threatening to capsize it, and continually the black depths glared at her. Her hands trembling, Elay clung tenaciously to the gunwale. Spray bathed her cheeks. A boy began to bail, for after clearing each wave the dinghy took in more water. So earnest was the boy at his chore that Elay thought the boat had sprung a leak and would sink any moment.

The sailors, one at the prow and the other busy with the oar at the stern, engaged themselves in senseless banter. Were they trying to make light of the danger? She said her prayers as the boat swung from side to side, to a rhythm set by the sailor with the oar.

Fortunately, panic did not seize her. It was the old aunt who cried *"Susmariosep!"* For with each crash of waves, the dinghy lurched precipitously. "God spare us all!" the old aunt prayed frantically.

And Ana was laughing. "Auntie! Why, Auntie, it's nothing! It's nothing at all!" For, really, they were safe. The dinghy had struck sand.

Elay's dread of the water suddenly vanished and she said to herself: "Ah, the old aunt is only making things more difficult for herself." Why, she wouldn't let the sailor with the oar lift her clear of the dinghy and carry her to the beach!

"Age before beauty," the sailor was saying to his companion. The other fellow, not to be outdone, had jumped waist-deep into the water, saying: "No, beauty above all!" Then there was Ana stepping straight, as it were, into the sailor's arms.

"Where are you?" the old aunt was calling from the shore. "Are you safe? Are you all right?"

Elay wanted to say that in so far as she was concerned she was safe, she was all right. But she couldn't speak for her mistress, of course! But the same seaman who had lifted the old aunt and carried her to the shore in his arms had returned. Now he stood before Elay and caught her two legs and let them rest on his forearm and then held her body up, with the other arm. Now she was clear of the dinghy, and she had to hold on to his neck. Then the sailor made three quick steps toward dry sand and then let her slide easily off his arms, and she said: "I am all right. Thank you."

Instead of saying something to her the sailor hurried away, joining the group of students that had gathered up the rise of sand. Ana's cheerful laughter rang in their midst. Then a youth's voice, clear in the wind: "Let's hurry to the fisherman's hut!"

A drizzle began to fall. Elay took a few tentative steps toward the palm-leaf hut, but her knees were unsteady. The world seemed to turn and turn, and the glowing light at the fisherman's door swung as from a boat's mast. Elay hurried as best as she could after Ana and her old aunt, both of whom had already reached the hut. It was only on hearing her name that that weak, unsteady feeling in her knees disappeared.

"Elay—" It was her mistress, of course. Ana was standing outside the door, waiting. "My lipstick, Elay!"

An old man stood at the door at the hut. "I am Obregano, at your service," he said in welcome. "This is my home."

He spoke in a sing-song that rather matched his wizened face. Pointing at a little woman pottering about the stovebox at one end of the one-room hut, he said: "And she? Well, the guardian of my home—in other words, my wife!"

The woman got up and welcomed them, beaming a big smile. "Feel at home. Make yourselves comfortable—everyone."

She helped Elay with the canvas bag, choosing a special corner for it. "It will rain harder yet tonight, but here your bag will be safe," the woman said.

The storm had come. The thatched wall shook, producing a weird skittering sound at each gust of wind. The sough of the palms in back of the hut—which was hardly the size of the deckhouse of the *batel*, and had the bare sand for floor—sounded like the moan of a lost child. A palm leaf that served to cover an entrance to the left of the stovebox began to dance a mad, rhythmless dance. The fire in the stove leaped intermittently, rising beyond the lid of the kettle that Obregano the old fisherman had placed there.

And yet the hut was homelike. It was warm and clean. There was a cheerful look all over the place. Elay caught the old fisherman's smile as his wife cleared the floor of blankets, nets and coil after coil of hempen rope so that their guests could have more room. She sensed an affinity with her present surroundings, with the smell of the fish nets, with the dancing fire in the stovebox. It was as though she had lived in this hut before. She remembered what Obregano's wife had said to her. The old woman's words were by far the kindest she had heard in a long time.

The students from Bongabon had appropriated a corner for themselves and began to discuss supper. It appeared that a prankster had relieved one of the chicken coops of a fat pullet and a boy asked the fisherman for permission to prepare a stew.

"I've some ginger tea in the kettle," Obregano said. "Something worth drinking in a weather like this." He asked his wife for an old enameled tin cup for their guests to drink from.

As the cup was being passed around, Obregano's wife expressed profuse apologies for her not preparing supper. "We have no food," she said with uncommon frankness. "We have sons, you know; two of them, both working in town. But they come home only on week ends. It is only then that we have rice."

Elay understood that in lieu of wages the two Obregano boys received rice. Last week end the boys had failed to return home, however. This fact brought a sad note to Elay's new world of warm fire and familiar smells. She got out some food which they had brought along from the boat—*adobo* and bread that the old aunt had put in a tin container and tucked into the canvas satchel—and offered her mistress these, going through the motions so absent-mindedly that Ana chided her.

"Do offer the old man and his wife some of that, too."

Obregano shook his head. He explained that he would not think of partaking of the food—so hungry his guests must be. They needed all the food themselves, to say nothing about that which his house should offer but which in his naked poverty he could not provide. But at least they would be safe here for the night, Obregano assured them. "The wind is rising, and the rain too . . . Listen. . . ." He pointed at the roof, which seemed to sag.

The drone of the rain set Elay's spirits aright. She began to imagine how sad and worried over sons the old fisherman's wife must be, and how lonely—but oh how lovely!—It would be to live in this God-forsaken spot. She watched the students devour their supper, and she smiled thanks, sharing their thoughtfulness, when they offered most generously some ·chicken to Ana and, in sheer politeness, to the old spinster aunt also.

Yet more people from the *batel* arrived, and the four merchants burst into the hut discussing some problem in Bongabon municipal politics. It was as though the foul weather suited their purposes, and Elay listened with genuine interest, with compassion, even, for the small-town politicians who were being reviled and cursed.

It was Obregano who suggested that they all retire. There was hardly room for everyone, and in bringing out a rough-woven palm-leaf mat for Ana and her companions to use, Obregano picked his way in order not to step on a sprawling leg or an outstretched arm. The offer of the mat touched Elay's heart, so much so that pondering the goodness of the old fisherman and his wife took her mind away from the riddles which the students at this time were exchanging among themselves. They were funny riddles and there was much laughter. Once she caught them throwing glances in Ana's direction.

Even the sailors who were with them on the dinghy had returned to the hut to stay and were laughing heartily at their own stories. Elay watched Obregano produce a bottle of kerosene for the lantern, and then hang the lantern with a string from the center beam of the hut. She felt a new dreamlike joy. Watching the old fisherman's wife extinguish the fire in the stove made Elay's heart throb.

Would the wind and the rain worsen? The walls of the hut shook—like a man in the throes of malaria chills. The sea kept up a wild roar, and the waves, it seemed, continually clawed at the land with strong, greedy fingers.

She wondered whether Obregano and his wife would ever sleep. The couple would be thinking: "Are our guests comfortable enough as they are?" As for herself, Elay resolved, she would stay awake. From the corner where the students slept she could hear the whine of a chronic asthma sufferer. One of the merchants snorted periodically, like a horse being plagued by a fly. A young boy, apparently dreaming, called out in a strange, frightened voice: "No, no! I can't do that! I wouldn't do that!"

She saw Obregano get up and pick his way again among the sleeping bodies to where the lantern hung. The flame was sputtering. Elay watched him adjust the wick of the lantern and give the oil container a gentle shake. Then the figure of the old fisherman began to blur and she could hardly keep her eyes open. A soothing tiredness possessed her. As she yielded easily to sleep, with Ana to her left and the old spinster aunt at the far edge of the mat to her right, the floor seemed to sink and the walls of the hut to vanish, as though the world were one vast dark valley.

When later she awoke she was trembling with fright. She had only a faint notion that she had screamed. What blur there had been in her consciousness before falling asleep was as nothing compared with that which followed her waking, although she was aware of much to-do and the lantern light was gone.

"Who was it?" It was reassuring to hear Obregano's voice.

"The lantern, please!" That was Ana, her voice shrill and wiry.

Elay heard as if in reply the crash of the sea rising in a crescendo. The blur lifted a little: "Had I fallen asleep after all? Then it must be past midnight by now." Time and place became realities again; and she saw Obregano, with a lighted matchstick in his hand. He was standing in the middle of the hut.

"What happened?"

Elay thought that it was she whom Obregano was speaking to. She was on the point of answering, although she had no idea of what to say, when Ana, sitting up on the mat beside her, blurted out: "Someone was here. Please hold up the light."

"Someone was here," Elay repeated to herself and hid her face behind Ana's shoulder. She must not let the four merchants, nor the students either, stare at her so. Caught by the lantern light, the men hardly seven steps away had turned their gazes upon her in various attitudes of amazement.

Everyone seemed eager to say something all at once. One of the students spoke in a quavering voice, declaring that he had not moved where he lay. Another said he had been so sound asleep—"Didn't you hear me snoring?" he asked a companion, slapping him on the back—he had not even heard the shout. One of the merchants hemmed and suggested that perhaps cool minds should look into the case, carefully and without preconceived ideas. To begin with, one must know exactly what happened. He looked in Ana's direction and said: "Now please tell us."

Elay clutched her mistress' arm. Before Ana could speak, Obregano's wife said: "This thing ought not to have happened. If only our two sons were home, they'd avenge the honor of our house." She spoke with a rare eloquence for an angry woman. "No one would then dare think of so base an act. Now, our good guests," she added, addressing her husband, bitterly, "why, they know you to be an aged, simplehearted fisherman—nothing more. The good name of your home, of our family, is no concern of theirs."

"Evil was coming, I knew it!" said the old spinster aunt; and piping out like a bird: "Let us return to the boat! Don't be so bitter, old one," she told Obregano's wife. "We are going back to the boat."

"It was like this," Ana said, not minding her aunt. Elay

lowered her head more, lest she should see those man-faces before her, loosely trapped now by the lantern's glow. Indeed, she closed her eyes, as though she were a little child afraid of the dark.

"It was like this," her mistress began again, "I was sleeping, and then my maid, Elay—" she put an arm around Elay's shoulder—"she uttered that wild scream. I am surprised you did not hear it."

In a matter-of-fact tone, one of the merchants countered: "Suppose it was a nightmare?"

But Ana did not listen to him. "Then my maid," she continued, "this girl here—she's hardly twenty, mind you, and an innocent and illiterate girl, if you must all know. . . . She turned round, trembling, and clung to me. . . ."

"Couldn't she possibly have shouted in her sleep," the merchant insisted.

Obregano had held his peace all this time, but now he spoke: "Let us hear what the girl says."

And so kind were those words! How fatherly of him to have spoken so, in such a gentle and understanding way! Elay's heart went to him. She felt she could almost run to him and, crying over his shoulders, tell him what no one, not even Ana herself, would ever know.

She turned her head a little to one side and saw that now they were all looking at her. She hugged her mistress tighter, in a childlike embrace, hiding her face as best she could.

"Tell them," Ana said, drawing herself away. "No, go on —speak!"

But Elay would not leave her side. She clung to her, and began to cry softly.

"Nonsense!" the old aunt chided her.

"Well, she must have had a nightmare, that's all," the merchant said, chuckling. "I'm sure of it!"

At this remark Elay cried even more. "I felt a warm hand

caressing my—my—my cheeks," she said, sobbing. "A warm hand, I swear," she said again, remembering how it had reached out for her in the dark, searchingly, burning with a need to find some precious treasure which, she was certain of it now, she alone possessed. For how could it be that they should force her to tell them? "Someone,"—the word was like a lamp in her heart—"someone wanted me," she said to herself.

She felt Ana's hand stroking her back ungently and then heard her saying, "I brought this on," then nervously fumbling about the mat. "This is all my fault . . . . My compact, please . . . ."

But Elay was inconsolable. She was sorry she could be of no help to her mistress now. She hung her head, unable to stop her tears from cleansing those cheeks that a warm hand had loved.

RONY V. DIAZ [1932—]

Rony Diaz was born in Cabanatuan, Nueva Ecija, in the central rice plains. However, most of his childhood was spent in coconut country southeast of Manila—San Pablo, Laguna. There his father, refusing to farm, managed a *jueteng* den (equivalent to the "numbers racket" in America) for his uncle, until a fire swept the city and burned their house to the ground.

When his father decided next to operate the Manila end of another uncle's lumber business on Mindoro, just beyond Manila bay, the Diaz family moved to Tondo next to the mouth of the Pasig River. Rony remembers how "boats from Mindoro would pole their way in at high tide to unload lumber right in our yard. People here were so poor that we had to hire two bullies to stop children from stealing lumber." Until the outbreak of war, home meant "the smell of poverty, a detrital and fecal odor that shrouded shacks made of crating wood and tin, the reek of a decaying beach at low tide, the estival aroma of drying fish, the sour stench of unwashed children." After Clark Field was bombed, the family moved permanently to Mindoro island.

Rony acknowledges that "Mindoro is central in my life because it was there that I first became aware of the fact of annihilation." His stories make clear that the reference is not just to the bombing and strafing, the sporadic guerrilla fighting, the beheadings, but to other kinds of savagery as well, of terrible inhuman waste. "Once I saw a village slaughter a river of spawning mullets; for days, the people feasted on roe and fish, but they had more roe and fish than they could possibly salt, or dry, or smoke, or feed to the dogs and so they dumped the dead fish back in the river and the crocodiles came. Vast stands of ancient trees were fed to sawmills and the Mangyans would come and cut the main root of the stumps so that the trees could not resurrect themselves and after a year or so they would return to the decayed stumps to dig out grubs which they swallowed whole. I don't know why machines looked more monstrous, more powerful, more naked in Mindoro than anywhere else. A sawmill in the middle of a jungle looks like an armor-plated spider spinning a web of deadly sound."

In 1949, he returned to the main island of Luzon to attend the University of the Philippines, bombed into rubble in the port area and rebuilt in suburban Quezon City which was intended as the new capital site. Rony drifted from zoology, into foreign service, into literature; and he began to write. "I learned literary cunning from Joyce, Flaubert and Chekhov, literary passion from Lawrence, and from Giono I acquired a certain facility in thinking with my nerves." From Lewis Mumford he learned "the nature and implication of progress"; Thorstein Veblen he read "for the humor." After graduation in 1953, he was a political propagandist for President Quirino until the latter's defeat by Ramon Magsaysay. Temporarily Rony helped assemble economic bibliographies at the university's Social Science Research Center; then he was hired as assistant instructor by the English department.

He had already won several Palanca awards in short fiction and had served as co-editor of *Signatures,* the first Philippine poetry magazine (founded in 1955), when he received a Smith-Mundt grant for the study of linguistics and comparative literature at the University of Indiana, in 1959. The following year he was awarded a Rockefeller grant, at the same institution, to complete his first novel, tentatively called *All Others Are of Brass and Iron.*

168

DEATH IN A SAWMILL

YOU CAN CLEAVE a rock with it. It is the iron truth. That was not an accident. That was a murder. Yes, a murder. That impotent bastard, Rustico, murdered Rey.

You have seen the chain that holds the dogs that keep the logs on the carriage in place. Well, that chain is controlled by a lever which is out of the way and unless that lever has been released, the chain cannot whip out like a crocodile's tail and hurl a man to the whirling, circular saw.

I was down at our sawmill last summer to hunt. As soon as school was out, I took a bus for Lemery where I boarded a sailboat for Abra de Ilog. Inong met me at the pier with one of the trucks of the sawmill and took me down.

The brazen heat of summer writhed on the yard of the sawmill which was packed hard with red sawdust.

My father met me at the door of the canteen. He took my bags and led me in. I shouldered my sheathed carbine and followed. The canteen was a large frame house made of unplaned planks. My father's room was behind the big, barred store where the laborers of the sawmill bought their supplies. The rough walls of the small room looked like stiffened pelts.

My father deposited my bags on a cot and then turned to me. "I've asked the assistant sawyer, Rey Olbes, to guide you."

The machines of the sawmill were dead. Only the slow, ruthless grinding of the cables of the winches could be heard.

"No work today?" I asked my father.

"A new batch of logs arrived from the interior and the men are arranging them for sawing."

Then a steamwhistle blew.

"They are ready to saw," my father explained.

The steam machine started and built solid walls of sound that crashed against the framehouse. Then I heard the saw bite into one of the logs. Its locust-like trill spangled the air.

"You'll get used to the noise," my father said. "I've some things to attend to. I'll see you at lunchtime." He turned about and walked out of the room, shutting the door after him.

I lay on the cot with my clothes on and listened to the pounding of the steam engine and the taut trill of the circular saw. After a while I dozed off.

After lunch, I walked out of the canteen and crossed the yard to the engine house. It was nothing more than a roof over an aghast collection of soot-blackened, mud-plastered balky engines. Every inch of ground was covered with sour-smelling sawdust. The steam engine had stopped but two naked men were still stoking the furnace of the boilers with kerfs and cracked slabs. Their bodies shone with sweat. I skirted the boilers and went past the cranes, tractors and trucks to the south end of the sawmill. A deep lateral pit, filled with kerfs, flitches and rejects, isolated like a moat the sawmill from the jungle. Near the pit, I saw Rey. He was sitting on a log deck. When he saw me, he got up and walked straight to me.

"Are you Rustico?" I asked.

"No, I'm Rey Olbes," he answered.

"I'm Eddie," I said, "my father sent me."

He was a tall, sunblackened young man. He had an unusually long neck and his head was pushed forward like a horse's. His skin was as grainy as moist whetstone. He stopped and picked up a canter and stuck it on the ground and leaned on it. Then he switched his head like a stallion to shake back into place a damp lock of hair that had fallen over his left eye. His manner was easy and deliberate.

"Your father told me you wanted to go hunting," he said slowly, his chin resting in the groove of his hands folded on the butt end of the canter. "Tomorrow is Sunday. Would you like to hunt tomorrow?"

"Yes, we can hunt tomorrow."

Inside the engine shed the heat curled like live steam. It swathed my body like a shirt. "It's hot here," I said. "Do you always stay here after work?"

"No, not always."

Then I saw a woman emerge from behind one of the cranes. She was wearing a gray silk dress. She walked toward us rapidly.

"Rey!" she bugled.

Rey dropped the canter and turned swiftly about. The woman's dress clung damply to her body. She was fair; her lips were feverish and she had a shock of black electric hair.

She faced Rey. "Have you seen Rustico?"

"No," Rey answered. There was a small fang of frenzy in his voice.

"Tonight?" the woman asked.

Rey glanced at me and then looked at the woman. He reverted to his slow, deliberate manner as he said: "Dida, this is Eddie. The son of the boss."

Dida stared at me with frenetic eyes. She did not say anything.

"He's a hunter too," Rey continued.

Then I saw a man striding toward us. He walked hunched, his arms working like the claws of a crab. Tiny wings of sawdust formed around his heels. He was a small squat man, musclebound and graceless. He came to us and

looked around angrily. He faced the woman and barked: "Go
home, Dida."

"I was looking for you, Rustico," Dida remonstrated.

"Go home!" he commanded hoarsely.

Dida turned around, sulking, and walked away. She
disappeared behind the boilers and the furnace that rose in
the shed like enormous black tumors. Rustico set himself
squarely like a boxer before Rey and demanded almost in a
whisper: "Why don't you keep away from her?"

Rey looked at him coldly and answered mockingly: "You
have found a fertile *kaingin*. Why don't you start planting?"

"Why you insolent son of the mother of whores!" Rustico screamed. He reached down to the ground for the canter
and poised it before Rey like a harpoon. I bounded forward
and grappled with Rustico. I was able to wrest the canter from
him. He pushed me. I sank to the sawdust; Rustico leapt forward to heel me on the jaw. Rey held him.

"Keep calm," Rey shouted. "That is the son of Mang
Pepe."

Rey released him and Rustico dropped his arms to his
side. He looked suddenly very tired. He continued to stare
at me with eyes that reflected yellow flecks of light. I got up
slowly. What a bastard, I thought. Rustico wheeled about and
strode to the whistlebox. He opened it and tugged at the cord.
The steamwhistle screamed like a stuck pig.

"All right, men," he yelled. "It's time. Load the skids
and let us start working."

Rey picked up his canter and walked toward the log
carriage. Rustico was supervising the loading of the log deck.
He was as precise and stiff as a derrick as he switched levers
and pulled clamps. He sparked like a starter and the monstrous conglomeration of boilers, furnaces, steam machines,
cranes and winches came alive. I walked away.

When I reached the door of the canteen, I heard the teeth of the circular saw swarm into a log like a flight of locusts.

The next day, Rey, carrying a light rifle, came to the canteen. He pushed open the door with his foot and entered the barred room. He stood near my father's table. His eyes shifted warily. Then he looked at me and said: "Get ready."

"I did not bring birdshot," I said.

"I thought you wanted to go after deer?" he asked.

I was surprised because I knew that here deer were hunted only at night, with headlamps and buckshot. The shaft of the lamps always impaled a deer on the black wall of night and the hunter could pick it off easily.

"Now? This morning?" I asked.

"Why not? We are not going after spirits."

"All right. You are the guide." I dragged the gunbag from under the cot and unsheathed my carbine. I rammed the magazine full with shells, pushed it in, and got up. "Let's go."

We entered the forest from the west end of the sawmill and followed a wide tractor path to a log station about four kilometers from the sawmill. The forest was alive with the palaver of monkeys, the call of the birds and the whack of the wind. Then we struck left uphill and climbed steadily for about an hour. The trail clambered up the brush. At the top of the rise, the trail turned at an angle and we moved across the shoulder of an *ipil-ipil* ridge.

Rey walked rapidly and evenly, his head pushed forward, until we reached the drop of the trail. I looked down into a valley walled on all sides by cliffs that showed red and blue-gray gnashes. Streaks of brown and green were palmed across the valley. Islands of dark-green scrubs rose above the level rush of yellow-green grass. On the left side of the valley, a small river fed clay-red water to a grove of trees. At the north end, the valley flattened and sky dropped low, filling the valley with white light and making it look like the open mouth of the jungle, sucking at one of the hot, white, impalpable breasts of the sun. We descended into the valley.

Rey's manner changed. He became tense. He walked slowly, half-crouched, his eyes searching the ground. He examined every mound, bush and rock. Once he stopped; he bent and picked up a small rock. The rock had been recently displaced. He raised his hand to feel the wind and then he backtracked for several yards and crept diagonally to a small clump of brush. I followed behind him.

"Urine," he said. The ground near his feet was wet. "Work in a cartridge," he told me, "and follow as noiselessly as possible." I pulled back the bolt of my rifle.

We crept on half-bent knees toward a grove of trees. Rey, carrying his rifle in the crook of his arm, was swaying gently like a weather vane. I looked around. I saw nothing save the trees that rode to the sky like smoke and the tall grass that swirled with the breeze. Rey was intent.

Then he stopped and stiffened.

"Remove the safety," he whispered. I heard the safety of Rey's rifle click off. I pushed mine off.

"There is your deer," he said in a low voice. We were still crouched. "Near the base of that tree with a dead branch. Only its head is visible but its shoulder is somewhere near that dry patch of leaves. Shoot through that. Do not move until I tell you to do so."

I did not see the deer until it moved. It turned its head toward us. Its antlers were as brown as the dead branch of the tree. The deer regarded us for a long time. Then it dropped its head and quickly raised it again. We did not move. The deer, reassured, stepped diffidently out of the shadows.

"Now!" Rey said, falling to his knees. The deer stopped and looked at us, its antlers scuffling against the leaves. I raised my rifle and fired. The deer went high in the air. Then, dropping its head, it crashed through the trees and vanished.

"Your aim was too high," he told me quietly. He was still on his knees. "Too high," he said softly. "But you got him."

He stood up slowly, pushed down the safety of his rifle and walked toward the grove of low trees.

We found the deer. It was stretched out on the ground. Its neck was arched upward as though it had tried to raise its body with its head after the bullet had ripped a hump of flesh off its back. Blood had spread like a fan around its head. Rey sat down on the ground and dug out of his pocket a small knife. He cut an incision at the base of the deer's neck. He stood and picked the deer up by its hind legs. Blood spurted out of the cut vein.

"You got your deer," he said. "Let's turn back."

Rey hauled the deer up and carried it around his neck like a yoke.

I felt my nerves tingle with triumph. The earth was soaking up the blood slowly. I had a crazy urge to mash my body with the blood. I felt that it would seep into my body and temper my spirit now forging hot with victory. I looked at Rey. He was smiling at me. In a strained voice I said: "I'll try to to do this alone."

"You'll learn," he said. "The forest will surely outlive you."

We walked out of the valley.

After about an hour's walk, we came to a *kaingin.* Rey was sweating. We crossed the charred ground. At the edge of the *kaingin,* Rey stopped. He turned around. The deer had stiffened on his shoulders.

"This used to be deer country," he said. We surveyed the black stumps and half-burned branches that lay strewn on the ground. The bare soil looked rusty.

"You know these parts very well, don't you," I asked.

"I grew up here. I was a logger for your father before I became a sawyer."

His rifle slipped from his arm. I picked it and carried it for him.

"It is the sawmill," Rey continued. "It is the sawmill that opened the forest. The sawmill has thinned the jungle miles around." I stared at him. He continued meditatively, veins showing on his long powerful neck, "But I do not think they can tame the forest. Unless they can discover the seed of the wilderness and destroy it, this place is not yet done for."

"Don't you like your job in the sawmill?" I asked.

He shot a glance at me and grimaced. "I do not complain. You do not have to tell this to your father but Rustico is making my stay very trying. You saw what happened yesterday."

"Yes," I said. "What made him so mad?"

Rey did not answer. We crossed a gully and worked our way to the end of a dry river bed before he answered. The shale crumbled under our feet. The trees that grew along the bank of the river were caught by a net of vines. Rey, yoked by the deer, was now panting. Under a *kalumpit* tree, he threw his burden down and sank to the ground.

"You know why?" he asked. "Because his wife is pregnant."

"Dida? So?"

"He's impotent."

The revelation struck me like a slap.

"And he suspects you," I asked tentatively, unsure now of my footing.

"He knows. Dida told him."

"Why doesn't he leave her then," I said, trying to direct the talk away from Rey.

"He wouldn't! He'd chain Dida to keep her!" Rey flared.

I shut my mouth. It was noon when we reached the sawmill.

Late that afternoon we left to shoot fruit bats. Rey knew a place where we could shoot them as they flew off their roost. He had several tubes of birdshot and a shotgun.

It was almost eight o'clock when we returned. We followed the road to the sawmill. The shacks of the laborers were built along the road. Near the motor pool, a low grass hut stood. We passed very close to this hut and we heard suppressed, angry voices. "That is Rustico's hut," Rey said.

I heard Rustico's voice. He sounded strangled. "I want you to drop that baby!" The words were spewed out like sand. "Let me go!" Dida screamed. I heard a table or a chair go. It crashed to the floor. "I'll kill you," Rustico threatened. "Do it then! Do it!" The yellow wings of light that had sprouted from a kerosene lamp trembled violently.

Rey quickened his steps. He was carrying a bunch of dead bats. One of the bats had dropped, its wings spread. It looked like a black gule on Rey's side.

The next morning, I heard from the men who were huddled near the door of the canteen that Dida had run away. She had hitched a ride to town on one of the trucks.

I was eating breakfast in the store with my father when Rustico entered. He approached my father carefully as though his feet hurt. Then he stood before us and looked meekly at my father. He was gray.

"Mang Pepe," he began very slowly, "I want to go to the town. I will be back this afternoon or early tomorrow morning."

"Surely," my father said. "Inong is driving a load of lumber to the pier. You can go with him."

"Thank you," he said and left at once.

After breakfast, my father called in Lino, the foreman. "Tell Rey to take charge of the sawing today. Rustico is going to town. We've to finish this batch. A new load is arriving this afternoon."

"Rey left early this morning," Lino said. "He said he will be back tomorrow morning."

"Devil's lightning!" my father fumed. "Why didn't he tell me! Why is everybody so anxious to go to town?"

"You were still asleep when he left, Mang Pepe," Lino said.

"These beggars are going to hold up our shipment this week!" my father flared. "Eddie," my father whirled to face me, "look for Rustico and tell him that he cannot leave until Rey returns. We've to finish all the devil's logs before all these lightning-struck beggars pack up and leave!"

I walked out of the canteen to look for Rustico. I searched all the trucks first and then the engine house. I found him sitting on the log carriage. He was shredding an unlighted cigarette.

"My father said he is sorry but you cannot leave until Rey comes back from the town. We have a lot of work to do here. A new load of logs is expected this afternoon." I spoke rapidly.

He got up on the carriage and leaned on the chain that held the log clamps. He acted very tired.

"It is all right," he said. "I've plenty of time." He spat out a ragged stalk of spittle. "Plenty of time." I turned about to go but he called me back.

He looked at me for a long time and then asked: "You are Rey's friend. What has he been saying about me?"

"Nothing much," I lied. "Why?"

"Nothing much!" he screamed, jumping off the carriage. His dun face had become very red. "He told you about my wife, didn't he? He delights in telling that story to every-body." He seized a lever near the brake of the carriage and yanked it down. The chain lashed out and fell rattling to the floor.

Rustico tensed. He stared at the chain as though it were

a dead snake. "Now look at that chain," he said very slowly.

He mounted the carriage again, kicked the clamps into place and pulled at the chain. The chain tightened. He cranked the lever up and locked it.

He was trembling as he unlocked the lever and pulled it down with both hands. The chain lashed out again like a crocodile tail.

"Just look at that chain," he mused.

TWO BROTHERS

At DAWN, the two brothers left the town. Carrying spear-guns and open-mesh rattan baskets, they walked barefooted along the edge of the sliding sea toward the dock. The sea, still weighted by the wind, slid in long unbroken swells toward the shore where it broke and dragged away the footprints and the delicate whorls left by the crabs on the black sand of the beach. The boys walked rapidly, the older brother one or two steps ahead, tugging, it seemed, in his momentum his smaller and lighter companion whose quick, awkward strides resembled those of a fleeing, wingless bird.

The whirling whips of the sun advanced and mangled darkness crouched behind the mountains, staining them into solidity with coagulated shadows.

The two brothers had reached the elbow of the beach, jawed rocks spray-cowled at this time of tide, from where the bay curved away from the town to follow a tall, harsh cliff of clay at whose rocky base the dissolving world of the sea abruptly ended. They walked on a rocky stretch of beach.

With the thrust of the sun, the wind that had settled, gray and heavy, on the surface of the sea, soared and released its herd of white-maned waves, and yellow light stroked the black beach.

The rocks ended in front of a small turtle-shaped cave and once more they were on sighing, salt-dashed sand.

Without stopping, the older brother handed to his companion his speargun and basket. He unbuttoned his shirt, stripped it off and wore it slung in a knot about his hips. The wind was heavy and cold. The smaller boy looked at his brother as he gave him back his gun and basket. His body was dark and tightly muscled. He was looking at the sea. The tide was coming in and the waves slid on in rhythmic rolls. The boy could tell that his brother was satisfied.

"Give me your *antipara*, Simo," his brother said.

Simo reached into a pocket of his short pants and pulled out a pair of goggles. He gave them to his brother. His brother stopped and began to examine the goggles closely. He ran the nail of his forefinger along the caulking that held the oval-cut glass to the wooden frame.

"The caulking has dried," he said softly. "I think it will hold. But I'll try them out for you first before you use them."

They had gone spearfishing at the mouth of the river last week and the caulking of Simo's goggles had come loose in a strand. The glass fell off and saltwater dashed into his eyes. Simo swam to the bank of the river, his eyes smarting. His brother pulled him up and gave him his pair. "Enjoy yourself," he had said. "I'll keep watch over you." Simo caught two *samarals*, which made his brother chuckle gleefully. Going home, the fish stringed through with black *nito*, his brother promised to make a new pair for him. That evening his brother started to whittle the goggles from a seasoned block of *santol* wood.

When they reached the breakwater, his brother stopped. Simo stepped close to him and waited. His brother dropped his spear and basket on the sand, unbuttoned his pants, unknotted the shirt and stepped into the sea in a pair of faded woolen trunks. He stopped at waist deep, snapped on the goggles over his eyes and plunged into the sea.

He broke for air near the middle of the breakwater. He clung loosely to the rocks for several moments and then vaulted up, shaking off drops of water that spangled his dark body.

He straightened abruptly and in that moment he seemed to stand on the horizon, his head touching the sky. Like a lighthouse, the image reared in Simo's mind. He pulled off the goggles and walked toward Simo. From the way he walked and dangled the goggles, Simo knew that everything was all right. The goggles had satisfied his brother.

"It'll do," his brother confirmed, handing back the goggles to Simo. He hitched up his pants, picked up his shirt, speargun and basket and they strode on toward the wharf.

Riding his brother's shadow, Simo felt a blood-measured thrust of pride and elation pulse through his body. He felt safe, wrapped in his brother's shadow as in an imminent cocoon.

This was the first time he would fish the piers. He was happy and he wanted to talk. He groped about in his mind for something to say to his brother. Then he remembered the *kaltang*.

He knew everything about that fish. He and his friends had talked interminably about it, its habits, shape, and augury. It was one of the town's recent legends of peril and mystery. Suddenly, burdened by a necessity still unclear to him, he wanted to hear his brother talk about it, probably to hear his voice deliver the exorcium that would dispel the mystery and danger of this unknown fish.

"Do you think we'll see the *kaltang*?" Simo asked, timorously.

His brother looked at him and smiled. "I don't know. Probably we won't. Nobody has seen it since it appeared once in these waters and that was years ago."

"It is dangerous, isn't it?" Simo pursued.

"It hasn't harmed anyone yet, as far as I can remember. You see, it appeared when this wharf was being built." Simo knew that; and still, striding with his brother, he searched his lips and eyes for the cabalistic image, the twitch or the gesture that would make the unfamiliar predictable. "One of the engineers," his brother continued, voice uninflected, "was standing on the piles when a low-swinging derrick knocked him off into the sea. His head was crushed. Several laborers dived in to get him and almost all of them saw this fish, which they call a *kaltang*, dark, wide-mouthed and horned, swimming about the dead man, weaving in and out of the bloodstained water. That was all and the *kaltang* remains to this day a pretty mysterious fish. Nobody has seen it again." All that Simo knew, and still he waited; but it did not come, and his brother's voice floated before them like smoke which the wind shook and snatched away.

They had reached the dock now. From where they stood, the causeway, built of cairned stones held together by poured concrete and corraled by glinting, low copper rails, looked like a white, crutched appendage that had been grafted to the harsh torso of the cliff. The squat concrete piers that supported the wharf were clobbered with dark extrusions of oyster spats. Two motor launches were berthed along the pierhead. An old steamboat was moored along the left side of the wharf. Sailboats were anchored several yards away from the pier, their masts rising and falling with the wheeling horizon like buoy poles.

They climbed up to the causeway and walked toward the pierhead. Several mangy-looking, sleep-logged stevedores were loafing in front of a canteen, away from the wind. They were smoking and drinking coffee out of dark metal cups. They all looked at the two brothers save one who was watching his cigarette unwind its skein of blue smoke.

"*Hoy*, Litoy," one of them shouted in greeting when they saw his brother.

"Going fishing? It's too early. The tide is just starting to flow in."

"Yes," his brother said disinterestedly. Then the smoke

watcher suddenly rose and approached them. He put his arm
on his brother's shoulder. He walked with them.

"Litoy, I've a favor to ask from you." He flicked away
his cigarette.

"Let's hear it," his brother said, annoyed, Simo could
tell, by the arm on his shoulder. Simo knew at once that whatever that stevedore would ask for, his brother would deny.
He was annoyed and he would say no, Simo told himself; he
felt embarrassed for the man.

"I heard," the stevedore said slowly, "that your uncle
got the contract for that bridge at Alag."

"Yes?" his brother said almost angrily.

"You are going to oversee it, aren't you?"

"Of course. What about it?"

"I just thought you might have a job for me," the stevedore said.

"We've filled up all the positions," Litoy said. "You
should have talked to me earlier. But I'll send for you when
we need more men."

"Thank you, Litoy. But no job now?"

"None at the moment. I said I'll send for you when we
need more men," his brother growled. By now Simo was uncomfortable.

"Thank you. Thank you." He disengaged his arm and he
began to talk effusively. He started to tell them about likely
spots where there would be fish and he even offered to help
them look for fish.

"I know this place. You do not have to tell me where to
fish."

His brother quickened his pace and the stevedore dropped off. Simo looked back and he saw him walk back slowly
to the canteen, his shoulders hunched and his hands in the
pocket of his denim jacket.

A truck loaded with lumber roared past them and turned

alongside one of the motor launches. Three stevedores mounted the open truck and began to push off the lumber.

The two brothers stopped near the old steamboat. A pile of split mangrove trunks was neatly stacked near the gangplank. Gray smoke blew through a blunt smokestack. It was an old boat, spanned from bow to stern with an old, unsealed, rachitic-looking lumber roof. The steersman's seat was above the engine room. They saw that the wheel was lashed to two cleats on the wall. Below the wheel was an open hatch which led to the engine room. From the engine room an old man emerged, picked up pieces of *rajita* that were strewn on the deck and returned below.

Litoy stepped up close and looked in.

"They are firing up this junk," he said to Simo. "I wonder why?"

"Hey you!" Litoy called down. The old man reappeared, peered at them and walked up the gangplank.

"Ah, Mang Orto. Have you bought this junk?" Litoy asked.

"No, Ninoy fixed the engine last night because the Attorney wanted a boat to carry a load of rice to Mamburao. Have you seen Ninoy?" The old man stopped, then he continued: "He saw me this morning and asked me to fire the furnace for him. I know next to nothing about steam engines and the furnace is going full blast. I wish he would come back."

"Ninoy? Hah, he's probably asleep somewhere," Litoy said.

"I wish he would come back. I'm hungry and this pig of a boat looks ready to come apart."

"Just keep the furnace going. He'll be back in time."

Litoy walked off to the opposite side of the dock, Simo trailing after him.

They stripped off their clothes and prepared for the dive.

Litoy tested the rubber of his speargun and then spat onto his goggles. He rubbed the spittle on the glass. He pulled the goggles around his head.

"Stay close to me," he told Simo. "In case you get the cramps I can pull you out." He picked up a coil of rope, lashed it to one of the mooring-heads, tied the baskets to the end of the rope and gently lowered it. A glistening net of oil floated on the water. They slid down the rope, the spear-guns tucked under their armpits, into the water.

They broke through the net of oil, which instantly enveloped them and raised a rank, hot smell. His brother swam carefully around the concrete piles. Treading water, he turned to Simo and said, "It is light enough underwater, we can see." Then he plunged in a spume of spray. Simo inhaled deeply, jacked double and followed after him. The cold water crashed against his belly, and the air inside his chest webbed into thin strands that tautened with every stroke he took. Simo stayed down as long as he could, then turned, broke water, and dived in again.

His brother had looked up and when he saw Simo dive again, he turned head on and swam for the floor of the sea.

Simo heard the sea sigh into his ears and thereafter sealed all sound. He could feel the beating of his blood against his temples.

At ten feet, he felt a wedging sense in his ears, but the soft splayed-looking body of his brother ahead tugged him on and he sounded headlong, until the pressure became a cold, molten metal in his head which he discovered was relieved by hard swallowing. Each swallow he took tightened the webbed strands of air in his chest.

This was the first time he had gone this deep and although he wanted to break surface again he also wanted to impress his brother.

At first, everything at the bottom looked green and even

the bright, murrey corals were only dark horns that defied rigidly the mobility of the sea. It was light enough, as his brother had said, but gliding over the white sand and dark corals, Simo noticed that his brother cast no shadow. The pressure had made him a little giddy and this fact occurred to him without surprise, as though somehow he had expected it. The shadowless domain of the undersea slipped on for several yards and was lost in a hazy, amorphous horizon. Then the corals flamed, and yellow and green seaweeds strove upward in the mote-flecked water, and banded cowries and bright spiny shells stained the white sand. Objects were stretched into exaggerated sizes and shapes. His brother's body looked flat and enormous though not a blot on the bright scape but assimilated, blended into the scene by the encompassing sea.

Simo swam carefully trying to look for fish. He saw his brother stop, only his legs undulating. He swam up to him in time to see him let loose a spear. It shot forward in a feather of bubbles. Ahead, Simo saw a small red fish thrash and lie still, then it thrashed again and swam for the corals where it was lost. His brother raised his arms and he rose, Simo following closely. Under the wharf, where shadow shouldered the piers, his dark brother beamed at him. He gasped for breath and then said excitedly: "I got one. Did you see it?"

"Yes. It hid among the corals."

They dived again for the impaled fish. It was Simo who found it. He slowly pulled at the spear and the dead fish and then signalled his brother.

"It's a *maya-maya*," his brother said.

Simo pushed the fish into one of the rattan baskets that they had tied to the end of the rope. His brother was preparing his speargun for the next dive.

They treaded water for some time. His brother swam behind Simo and told him to dive ahead.

Simo plunged in, dragged the weight of air and water after him, his lungs and heart fluttering with his strokes and his ears ticking off the pressure. He skated smoothly in the water, swaying his head from side to side looking for fish. *Ambassids* swam with him.

Then he saw a black *lapu-lapu* flit briefly behind a branch of coral and stayed still. Simo raised his speargun and swam forward. He approached the *lapu-lapu* as closely as he could and he saw its wide mouth half open, its fins quivering, its large shallow eyes staring at him. He aimed his speargun. The sea tugged at it. He steadied it, aimed at its red-studded pectoral fin, and pressed the trigger. The steel shaft drove forward trailing a flume of bubbles. Another fish gallied off at the soundless strike of bubbles.

His brother slapped him on the buttocks. They swam up and smiled broadly. He peered closely at Simo through his water-fogged goggles and said happily: "That was a big one. This will be a day."

Simo dived alone to get the fish. Swimming up he brushed against one of the piers and he felt oyster shells rasp against his skin. There was no pain but he knew he had cut himself. He gave the fish to his brother. "I cut myself," he told him.

"Come up and let's have a look at it," his brother said, pushing the dead *lapu-lapu* into Simo's basket.

They pulled themselves up by the rope. On the concrete floor of the wharf, the sun had imbedded spikes of heat. Litoy knelt down beside Simo to look at the wound. Simo sat on one of the anvil-shaped mooring-heads. The oyster shells had scraped off the skin. He began to bleed.

"That is nothing," his brother said. "It won't hurt underwater. Seawater is as thick as blood. Let's dive."

That was an old superstition but Simo was startled by

the meaning that flew out of Litoy's unwilling, caged intonation and he sensed its shadow hover hawklike over the idea of his wound.

They slid down the rope and fished continuously for an hour.

Simo was starting to feel the chill of the water when an explosion racked the sea.

The tide had come in completely and the water had pushed nearly four feet up to the ceiling of the wharf. Beneath, the sea was shot through with currents of cold water.

Simo was stalking a striped *maya-maya* when the explosion froze into an instantaneous block about his head. He felt a solid wall of water hit him and his body became numb. Before that moment when he completely lost muscular control, he felt a violent kick strike him on the face. He rolled in the water and he crashed against one of the oyster-pitted piers. The shells flenched cleanly into his skin; he felt his cheek split open and blood glided before his eyes which the crepuscular light of the undersea turned into a momentary purplish blob. He rolled over and he saw the fleeing feet of his brother, attacking with frightened flutters the moiling water.

The block that encased his head melted into his brain and he gasped, salt burning his mouth and nose and he lay crushed by the remorseless wall of the stricken sea. Then his body stiffened.

When his reflexes returned, he sucked in his belly and the taut webs of air in his body slackened; the sea buoyed him up. A sharp pain pierced his ears; a series of minute implosions rang in his head. He felt as though his skull had burst, but fear had cleared his brain and with great deliberation, a feeling that his mind had been wrenched from his body, he turned over and began to swim, his blood slowly thinning in his lungs, for the surface.

It was then that he saw his brother. He was swimming toward him, headlong, looking soft and splayed in the shadowless world of the undersea, afloat above him. His fear-strengthened mind perceived his brother, saw his bubble-scaled body and expressionless glass-walled eyes peering cruelly at him, his mouth pulled wide, and his hair pressed by the sea into a black, sharp horn. Blood was again cast before his eyes and his brother disappeared. He felt Litoy's body brush against his and his hands close around his waist. With his remaining strength, he jerked loose and swam swiftly, pushed by the water, to the surface of the sea.

Gripping one of the oyster-pitted piers, he ripped off his goggles and through shocked, salt-burned eyes saw the old steamboat kneel and sink into the unctuous shadeless sea.

Pushed by the sun against the shagreen floor of the wharf, Simo lay stretched, his hands pressed on his guttered cheek.

Litoy knelt beside Simo and tried to press his shirt on the wound. Simo feebly resisted his help.

Their eyes met and softly Simo accused Litoy: "I saw you. I saw you swimming towards me."

"I came for you," Litoy said. "I came back for you."

"Back! How could you say that? Why did you have to come back?" Simo shouted. Tears of pain came to his eyes.

The tangled voices of the people, who had knotted them in, ceased whirring and hung suspended, unhitched, above them waiting to absorb the next strike.

Then Simo heard one of them say: "The jeep is ready, Litoy. Let's take him to the hospital."

But Litoy seemed not to hear because he lifted his face to them and pleaded: "He's delirious. Can't you see he's delirious!"

"Calm yourself, bridge-builder," the familiar voice of a stevedore mocked. "You *really* brought him back."

"Shut up!" Litoy cried hollowly.

"But you should have seen Mang Orto," the stevedore continued. "What was left of his body was scalded beyond recognition."

Simo closed his eyes at this revelation. His whole body was kindled by a pain more intense than the one that spunked on his cheek, as he felt himself merge with the hurled figure of Mang Orto, his skin peeled off. His body quivered with suppressed sobs. The pain of emergence was unbearable.

Simo heard the jeep start and roar away. "They're taking his body away," the stevedore said.

EDITH L. TIEMPO [1919—]

Until Edith Tiempo returned to Bayombong, Nueva Vizcaya, as a third-year high school student, her memories of her birthplace had been largely borrowed ones. She had followed her father, a provincial auditor, from town to town at government whim, before she had even celebrated her first birthday. Only after his death in 1932, did the family return to the "green contours of hills, high, narrow winding mountain roads, ravines, cold morning fog on the last lap of the trip from Manila . . . rushing green winds. . . . "

For one year, after graduation from high school, she lived deep in Moro-land, on the southern frontier in Surigao whose mining camps figure in *A Blade of Fern,* serialized years later in the *Weekly Women's Magazine.* Later she worked in Manila's downtown business offices, but became interested in the writing circle of which her husband, Edilberto, formed a part. With him she moved, in 1940, to Silliman University in the Visayan Islands at the heart of the archipelago. Within a year they were part of an underground army. During World War II they lost two infant sons, both by premature birth.

For three postwar years Edith Tiempo studied, along with her husband, on leave as chairman of the Silliman English department, at the University of Iowa Writers Workshop. From Paul Engle she learned objectivity. "Otherwise, people had somehow seemed so naked and vulnerable, it hurt at times just to look at them, let alone write about them."

At Iowa she finished the first draft of a novel, *The High Incline;* but she had come for another reason too: " . . . the gynecologist in Iowa City was sympathetic but surprised when I told him (my frankness disarmed him, I could see) that I got my scholarship not so much to earn the M.A. abroad as to try to have a baby." The Tiempos' first child was born at Silliman on their return; their second, during another extended visit to the United States while she took her doctorate at the

University of Denver (1958) and Edilberto, a Guggenheim recipient, published an American version of his novel, *Watch in the Night*.

Her poems have appeared in *Poetry, Western Review,* and *Span* (an Australian anthology), as well as in *Six Filipino Poets.* Her short stories have won two first prizes (1955 and 1959) in the annual *Philippines Free Press* contests, and two Palanca Memorial awards. With her writer-husband she has collaborated on textbooks only— three of them. "Once, before the war, we tried collaborating on a short story. Once . . . The story was entitled, 'Don't Break the Illusion,' and we heartily decided to endorse that idea thenceforward."

After their extensive experience at Iowa, the Tiempos set up a workshop of their own in Silliman, feeling however that they did not have to produce writers of all who took the course: "it's enough that it will produce perceptive readers." Nevertheless, recently under the auspices of the Asia Foundation and International P.E.N., they have arranged a special summer workshop which will subsidize ten young Philippine writers-in-residence and two guest writer-lecturers. The initial grant is for a three-year program.

THE CHAMBERS OF THE SEA

We have lingered in the chambers of the sea
By sea-girls wreathed with seaweed red and brown
Till human voices wake us and we drown.
                                   —T. S. ELIOT

CALL YOUR Tío Teban," Amalia nodded at her youngest son. This is very inconsiderate of Teban, went her hurried, flurried mind. "Tell him we are waiting lunch for him."

Tony flushed with importance. He slid off his chair and ran toward the bathroom where Tío Teban had haughtily locked himself in. The twins, Deena and Mario, were seated together on one side of the table, their identically turned-up noses were crinkled in a superior way. The twins had un-abashed eyes, very discomfiting to people because of the too-interested look in them. Their faces were quite alike, for all that one was a girl and the other a boy. Just now they broke out in suppressed grins at the thought of Tío Teban's grim and somewhat undignified retreat an hour before. Amalia and Miguel, and their oldest child Daniel remained grave. Tony's childish treble and his tapping on the bathroom door cut through the continuous background of freely-flowing water from the faucet beyond the door and the defiant *plop-plop* of Tío Teban's hands beating the soap and dirt out of his under-shirts and drawers and handkerchiefs. Whenever Tío Teban got indignant about something, he took to washing furiously his soiled undershirts and drawers and handkerchiefs. It seemed as though the sight of his intimate wear blowing fresh and white on the clothesline in the yard washed his soul clean of resentment, too.

"Tío Teban! Tío Teban!" Tony's knocks became frantic and his voice rose. The child sounded shrilly determined.

Pak! Pak! went the hands behind the door. The rhythm of the beating was broken. Then abruptly the silence was complete and almost weird. The faces at the table grew anxious.

"Get away!" The mean tight hiss of Tío Teban swished out suddenly. Tony jumped as from a lash. His face as he ran back to the table was screwed up in confusion and he blubbered on the edge of tears.

"Never mind," Amalia soothed her youngest. "Tío Teban did not mean to frighten you."

Thus it was minutes later when Miguel and Amalia had relaxed themselves and the children around the table.

Daniel observed, then, "It was Deena and Mario. Deena and Mario laughed when he slid coming up the back stairs with a pot of rice."

At this calm observation of his oldest brother, Tony looked at his parents expectantly. Deena and Mario were very studious with their food.

Miguel looked up at his oldest child, at Daniel's pimpled virtuous face. Sometimes Miguel's first-born irritated him, his voice, for one thing, was just starting to settle and it cracked and squeaked like an uncertain saw. Miguel put down his fork slowly. A frown crowded his brows together.

"Later, later," Amalia mumbled hastily. "Daniel!" she snapped, when the pimpled face stopped chewing to speak up once more. At his mother's level look Daniel shrugged and piously took up his spoon.

Often Tío Teban had threatened to himself to leave the

house and return to Bangan. The children drove him frantic. Even after five years he could not get used to them. Entrenched in his own room, he thought with satisfaction how the children might now be squirming with their guilt—for he had refused to eat his lunch. Directly after hanging out the wash he had gone to his room. And he was staying there. Amalia was a fool about her children. If they were his children he would know what to do with them. Those twins, Deena and Mario, they would feel the edge of his tongue as well as the edge of his belt. And that self-righteous Daniel!—he would put him in his place, conceited squirt! He thought with choking resentment of the way he had deteriorated in this house. He, with an M.A. in political science, washing underwear! It was those misbegotten brats. He was both powerless and indignant at how the twins crept up on him when he was most engrossed—sometimes at the siesta hour when he was writing his letters to his numerous far-away friends or to relatives in Bangan, sometimes at bedtime when he was reading Cervantes or Toynbee or Rizal—and suddenly how *that* peculiar feeling would hover in the air and ruffle his composure hard-won through the hours of reading, and he would look up from the page to see the two bland round faces staring from around the door. Four solemn eyes round and black and avid for something Tío Teban hastily refused to define even to himself. At first the little monsters even got into his room and made paper boats and planes out of the letters in his desk drawers, tearing around the room with them, shrieking back and forth and pommeling each other when they got excited. He kept a straight cold face throughout although inside he quaked with horror when their hands dived into the drawers for his letters. He remembered the time he saw Daniel reading one of his sheets which the twins had made into a paper boat. It was one of those he had failed to retrieve. The sly smirk on Daniel's face as he looked him shamelessly in the eyes and handed

him back the letter! Even until now he shook inside with in-
dignation. What right had that young lout to read what people
wrote him of their secret selves, their private feelings divulged
to him in complete confidence. What right had he to act
amused like somebody superior! And was he exempt from pain
and worry just because he was not a grown man yet? But
Tío Teban was triumphant about one thing. At least the twins
were more careful, since the time he had snatched the letters
from their hands and shaken them till their heads wobbled
on their necks. Now their vandalism was confined to the
doorway. It was true it was disconcerting to have their eyes
on him and his book for minutes at a time. It even occurred
to him they might just be wanting to romp with him—what
a thought!—but all the same he was glad he had frightened
them out of his room.

　　With all this Tío Teban did not think he would ever
go back to Bangan, even if his father asked him. And he knew
the old man would not. The old man could not forgive his
only son for turning out to be so like him in looks but quite
unlike him in his ways. His father had only a distant contempt
for what to him was his son's womanish disposition—his flower
garden of eighteen varieties of roses, his small framed water-
colors which he gave away to favorite relatives and friends, his
strolls along the countryside, his perpetual reading, reading
until he had to get a pair of glasses and never quite rid of that
forward bend of his head and the squint of his eyes as though
he were always in a dazed scrutiny of people and objects. Gradually as the old man grew physically less able he threw the
responsibility of overseeing the rice land on his son-in-law,
the huband of Tío Teban's younger sister Mína. Antero
should have been his father's son, Tío Teban thought in grim
amusement. They were so alike in their relentless preoccupa-
tion with fences and seedlings and ditches and patient sweating tenants.

How he had come to live with his Cousin Amalia's family he could tell to the last detail. It had been deliberate from the time he first thought of leaving Bangan to the day he moved into this room. It was a pleasant room overlooking the orange grove bordering the woods lot that had belonged to Miguel's father and to his father before him. Why have I come here, Tío Teban had thought to himself the first time he had taken possession of the room and looked out at the tops of the orange trees and at the woods beyond. Leaving my own father's land to live on another man's, with another man's family. But he had to get away from Bangan. His father's remote contempt was no longer to be met with a thick face. There was that odd speculative look, too, that lurked in his father's eyes whenever he looked at him. And his older sister Quirina, a widow, was embittered at him for allowing Antero to usurp his rightful place.

"And what happens when Father dies? Antero and his children will get the land. A family bearing an entirely different name will own the land! Even if my own son had lived I would not have allowed him to meddle with the land—no, not as long as there is still one of us with the name of Ferrer alive! Now there is Antero, with Father's eyes still wide open, to say nothing of you—although you'd rather poke at your flowers and your books—"

She made his engrossments sound indecent. It was oppressive. Unthinkable the way they expected him to canter around on a horse and bury himself in rice and rice and rice. All the same he could have stood it if he was sure it was only *that*—only their selfish desire to gain possession of his time, his life. But gradually he became aware of another kind of interest, even from his father—a surprised curiosity about him, a frank amazement, almost prying, on the part of Quirina. What made up his mind was Quirina's shameless question which even now he burned in embarrassment to recall. His

sister was gross to even mention it. And was it anybody's business if he kept himself to himself without putting his life in
the power of some snooping female creature forever prying
into his pockets and asking questions—exactly what he had
observed Mina to do with Antero, and what he had observed
other wives to do. How Antero, or for that matter, how any
man could stand it and had stood it since the fall of Adam,
he didn't know. This silent though shamelessly open wondering on their part about *that* and other things as well made him
feel he could not stay in Bangan any more. He felt violated
and exposed, and had also started to become suspicious of
everyone. For he could not help fearing that others looked
askance at him the way his family did.

It had been almost too easy, from the very beginning. He
had just announced he was going to Dumaguete to take up
graduate work at the university. And of course there was but
one place to stay, at Amalia's. He had been away from school
for five years but he had kept up with the study of history and
political science, and as a matter of fact had widened his read-
ings to include the humanities generally—philosophy, psy-
chology, the fine arts, literature. When he received his master's
degree after two years he had stayed on at Amalia's. By that
time neither he nor Miguel and Amalia made any bones about
it; they knew him and they knew his father—his studies had
been only a pretext for staying away from Bangan and they all
knew it.

Somehow as the months passed he found himself, to his
silent consternation, doing trivial chores in the house. It was
Amalia's fault, but by the time he realized what she was doing
to him it was too late; that was to say, without thinking anything of it he would go out to the yard with a basin of wrung-
out clothes and pin them up for her or she would ask him in a
hurried absent-minded way to go downstairs and fetch up the
pot of rice. And that was another thing; she had a gas stove

in the kitchen upstairs but she had a fetish that rice cooked over any other flame but that of a wood fire was not fit to eat. So Miguel had an open wood stove rigged up for her downstairs just for cooking the rice. Or she used to say, Teban, the diapers of Tony are in there and I have such a cold this morning and since you are there taking a bath, anyway, could you—

The first few times he was docile and that was the mistake. After that it was too late. Now he found himself washing his own underclothes as a matter of course, and bringing up the pot of rice. Amalia had no idea what it was to bring that huge pot upstairs on a wet day up those slippery steps. That was what happened this noon. He had to hold on to the pot of rice, hold it desperately aloft even when he lay sprawled on his back on the cement landing. The twins had seen him then and had straight-way gone running up to shout the humiliating incident all over the house.

Those two could most of the time do what they wanted with anybody, even with him. Especially when they got sick. At the hospital one time he looked into the two flushed faces and the fevered eyes, and going home he had sworn not to return to see them until they were better.

Nevertheless, he decided grimly, he was locking himself in this room until they came to say they were sorry.

When Amalia came to his door early the following morning he was awake but still in bed. Looking very prim, for she was dressed to go out, she led Tony by the hand straight to where he lay.

"I must ask you to look after him the whole morning, Teban," she said in her swift absent-minded fashion. "I have to pay the taxes and go downtown for some things after that." Her look went restlessly and unseeingly from one object to another in his room, and then out of the window, where it fastened intently on something there, and finally back to him.

"And that reminds me," she said before he could say anything, "the *Edward* leaves tomorrow for Manila."

She swept out of the room with the fat handbag tucked under her arm, leaving Tío Teban to decipher the last cryptic remark. Pulling off his pajamas he remembered how her look had darted out of the window and he decided she meant she must get the oranges plucked that day to be sent to her sister in Manila by the *Edward* in the morning. She had been reminding herself about it for days. He shaved, only a little disturbed by the scrutiny of the open-mouthed Tony. After watering the two ferns at his window he took his breakfast by himself in the kitchen. The other children were at school and Miguel had already gone to the bank. For a while he heard the tap of Amalia's heels downstairs and then he heard the gate shut as she went out. The house was quiet.

This was the time of the morning he could call all his own. He read, or he walked in the orchard or in the woods. Hemmed in there by ancient mangoes and guavas and tamarinds he sometimes forgot the sea was just nearby, and especially on a day of high winds there was something incongruous to him in the roar of the surf breaking through the walls of trees. Usually he walked across the woods lot and out on a path heading toward a part of the beach where a fisherman's shed leaned sideways in the sun. The shed was strung up inside with nets and traps to be mended. He often stopped in the shed to watch the divers out at sea setting up a fish trap or repairing the stakes of a corral that had been damaged by strong winds.

"Would you like us to go to the beach, Tony?"

"Now?"

"Yes." As the boy's face lighted up he added, "Only don't cry and say you are hungry or you want to swim or something. Remember now."

He had taken the twins to the beach a number of times

to watch the men come in from the sea. The bottom of their boats piled with gleaming *andohao* or *adlo*, the men swelled and swaggered a little as they came ashore and titillated the haggling market retailers with their catch. Or he and the twins would wander off one afternoon to a portion of the beach scattered over with salvage thrown up by the waves. One time they came upon a crowd staring fascinated at a whale flung up on the shore. The twins quickly squirmed through the crowd but he had to wait nearly fifteen minutes before he could come close enough to see the huge mammal. It was quite dead; perhaps wounded fatally by some fisherman's harpoon it had evaded capture but was soon washed ashore dead. It was the sea equivalent of carabao. Think of that dark, thick skin, he observed to himself, that compact body, more animal than fish in the effect of its tremendous weight.

When he and Tony reached the shed it was empty. All the men were out on the sea setting up a new fish corral. The boy wandered out of the shed after a while and started to build mounds on the sand, and the early morning sun glinted on his hair as he bent over his work. Out on the sea the naked men dived by turns from a *baroto*, and their skins, too, glinted in the sun. Their shouts came to Tío Teban, shouts full of glee and yet so far away. His look went beyond the men to the white cumulus clouds piled above the horizon, and then worked back over the whole stretch of undulating sea. Fishes and prawns and squids, he thought, lurked in that sea. Under the gently waving surface was active life. And the eyes of man could only steal brief glances at that life. And somehow, looking at the traps and the naked diving men he felt sad. There was a diver standing upright, straight and slim in the *baroto*. He dripped wet and glistened darkly in the sunlight. Tío Teban noticed the clean lines of his form, the hips that tapered to the quick legs, the flashing brown arms. Like a supplicant the diver raised his arms stiffly, flexed his knees and plunged into the sea. The sea rose around him, receiving him in a calyx of foam.

On the sand Tony had built three creditable mounds.

Coming home he and Tony took the longer way skirting the woods lot. Through his nonchalant enjoyment of the morning a mood of self-questioning sneaked in and would not be ignored. What am I doing here, playing nursemaid to a boy not even mine? What am I making out of my days—where are my garden and my painting? What had he done here but the creditable mound of a Master of Arts to be swept out at the wash of a wave! Since he arrived from Bangan he had not painted a single watercolor nor grown a single bloom. And a question even more disturbing—why am I not bothered by the loss of these occupations? What is wrong with me, anyway, that I should have betrayed myself into mean domestic involvements? In all these there was one thing that comforted him, though: he was still essentially untrammeled; with Miguel and Amalia he could never be forced into anything against his will. Ultimately, it was still true that he could involve himself or not as he pleased. Always as he pleased.

They were now in the orange grove. Beside him Tony tugged at his hand for attention.

"Tío Teban, Tío Teban! You will take me again to the beach, won't you?"

"I will see. That depends."

That afternoon as Miguel was leaving the house for the office he was met at the gate by the telecommunications messenger with a telegram. It was addressed to Esteban Ferrer and came from Bangan. Miguel signed for it. As the messenger rode off on his bicycle, Miguel turned the paper over in his hand.

"Teban!" he called out, suddenly realizing it was almost two o'clock and he must be off.

Tío Teban thrust an inquiring head out of the window. He hurried out when he saw what it was.

In his room Tío Teban sat staring at the opened piece of blue paper. It was from Antero. The old man was dead. His father.

Dead. . . . Quite without reason he remembered the day his father had stopped under the tamarind tree where Tío Teban had been sitting for an hour. Why he should think of that incident he could not understand. Perhaps because his father was dead and that was one of the times the two of them might have spoken, forgetting self and prejudice. He had been there an hour looking at the east corner of the rice field and trying to decide how to get the morning light not too harsh, and he was rapidly putting on the first large strokes of the watercolor as his father came up. He was hurrying, as the light on the east corner was quite what he wanted just then. He thought his father would pass him, and was uneasy when he stopped and looked at the picture. The old man tipped the front brim of his *balangot* hat a little over his eyes to shut out the glare as he leaned above the painting. For two or three minutes he stood like that, not saying anything, and all the time the painting grew swiftly under the sure, easy strokes of the brush. The old man straightened up then. He went silently apart and stood a few paces backward, still looking at him. The long eyes under white brows were deep and long-lashed, and just then had a puzzled squint.

"I have only now come from the *municipio*. They asked if I would lead the Red Cross drive."

Tío Teban laughed. "You should never have bought the arm for that man."

His father said quickly, "No, Teban. I told them I was too old. But I would ask you to do it."

A long line of yellow-gold streaked downward on the painting as his hand dropped to his side. "What?"

"Will you do it?"

"Of course not," he said irritably. "What did they say?"

"What do you think."

The painting was spoiled now. He rinsed his brushes and started putting them away. His father turned and walked off. As Teban folded up his chair he saw the old man's long figure pause on one end of the field to look at the east corner. . . .

Now his father was dead. Antero said the funeral was in a week's time, as soon as Tío Teban arrived. He laid the telegram on the table, put on his shoes and walked out of the house. He strayed through the orchard and out of the woods and was soon on the beach where he and Tony went that morning. It was close to four o'clock and the shadows of the coconuts were slanted all around on the sand. The men were not diving now and the sea was undisturbed by human voices. But the voices in Tío Teban were far from still. He could already hear Quirina's shrill tones demanding atrocious possibilities from him. Both his sisters would expect him to take over, now that their father was dead. Was that it after all?

He left the shed and walked along the shore toward a large bend. On that side of the beach were a few huts of deep-sea fishermen, and high up on the sand where some vines had partly covered the ground under the coconut trees, were five beached boats. Farther ahead he saw one boat that had come in. A group of people on the shore, about seven or eight fishermen and their wives, were looking at the catch laid out on the sand. A couple of dark things, whale or porpoise, may be, or some other sea monsters. They were each about four or five feet long.

As he stood over the creatures lying side by side he saw with horror that they were truly monsters of the deep. Strange, terrifying, half-human. Dark coarse hair sprouted from their heads and fell about their long horse-like faces. Slimy hair, grew on the spots where human hair would grow. Their bodies were a dark grey-brown, and the epithelium had a thick, rough, pore-ridden texture. Only the fin that formed the base of each figure was fish-like. Were they perhaps man and wife? Or twins? He pushed off the horrible thought. As the waves washed over them the long hair swayed and streamed out briefly and swayed again.

He realized with another shock that these were the mermaid and merman in the popular tales. But they must be beautiful and graceful in the deep! He remembered the straight young diver he had seen that morning. He was sure these creatures were lovely in their home. At the mouth of a cave a mother might nurse her young. She would lean there quietly while the lines of her form rippled and undulated with the waves. Her hair would stream softly around her face and her fin swish gently. Why could they not have been left to die in the sea? Who was to delight in this ugly nakedness?

At least Tío Teban knew one thing for himself as he turned and walked rapidly away.

FRANCISCO ARCELLANA [1916—]

Francisco Arcellana's father worked for the bureau of posts all his life—first as student operator, then as telegraph operator, then as chief operator, then as chief of telegraph construction and maintenance, and finally as submarine cable engineer. Franz' parents were Ilocano, the most migrant Philippine *provincianos,* so unyielding is the soil in rocky Ilocos. Jose Arcallana y Cabaneiro worked his way through Far Eastern College and studied by mail with ICS. When finally he topped a government *pensionado* examination for a fellowship in submarine cable engineering in London, he had to refuse. By then he had fathered seven children, from whom he refused to separate long.

Altogether there were twelve children, eventually; and three daughters who died young. Franz was the fourth eldest. In both primary and high school, in Manila's tough Tondo district, he graduated with honors, having been accelerated twice. It was in high school that he started to write. His first story appeared in the *Graphic* in 1932, just before he entered the University of the Philippines. In three years he had completed all his academic requirements but could not graduate for lack of credits in ROTC and physical education. At the same time, he served as contributing editor on the *Herald Mid-Week Magazine* and copy editor for *Acta Medica Philippina.* Briefly he joined, too, the staffs of the *Graphic* and *Woman's World.* Arcellana was enrolled in medical school when Jose Garcia Villa came home for his first visit in 1937. Although Villa advised him to stay in medicine because it was impossible to make an honest living by writing, Arcellana gave up his studies late in 1941, to marry and to write.

In December 1941, Arcellana's father left the government cutter *Bustamente,* which had been splicing cables fished from the ocean floor. "That was the last time I saw him healthy. He refused to work for the Japanese and without his work he was nothing: his health began to fail and in two years he was dead. I have always regarded him as a casualty of the war," Franz has written, adding a note about himself: "Very nearly didn't survive war; not sure that I did." During the Occupation at first Franz sold fruits and vegetables, brought several miles from Cavite by pushcart. Finally he entered the underground.

After the war he kept a small store for awhile. Then, quickly passing from one job to another, he worked for the *Evening News;* an advertising agency; as secretary to the president of Baguio Colleges; as correspondent and later bureau manager for International News Service; then as literary editor for the *Manila Chronicle.* Finally he joined the University of the Philippines as professor of English and its first public relations officer.

For his contribution as forthright faculty adviser to the campus newspaper during a religio-political crisis of national scope which was centered on the university, and also for special service during visitor William Faulkner's lecture at the University of the Philippines, Arcellana received the last Smith-Mundt "leader" grant awarded in 1955. After a tour of American campuses, he became a Rockefeller Foundation fellow in creative writing at the State University of Iowa, 1956-57, and afterward attended Breadloaf. He was accompanied by his wife, now a professor of political science at the University of the Philippines and formerly (1949) a Barbour scholar at the University of Michigan.

Fifty of Arcellana's over-a-hundred stories have been published, a number of them in Philippine anthologies. What at first strikes one as simple repetition becoming musical refrain, in Arcellana's stories, gradually builds bold momentum and the creative or destructive energy of a particle whirled in a cyclotron. The mechanical whine slowly becomes a function of things in motion, the tightening, narrowing circles of consciousness, like a metal noose inside the mind. He has won both Palanca and *Philippines Free Press* awards. In addition, the Art Association of the Philippines presented him with the first award ever given to an art critic.

DIVIDE BY TWO

God knows I hate the sight of violence.
But is it really violence I cannot stand?
Isn't it rather truth?

THEY have set down a line of adobe blocks, three blocks wide
and two blocks deep, across the lawn between their cottage and
ours," Belle said.

"Yes, I know," I said. I walked to the window and stood
there, looking at their cottage. The piano music from the cottage came strong and clear. "I was here this morning when he
brought those blocks home." I peeled off my shirt; it was soggy
with sweat. "He carried the blocks in the baggage compart-
ment of their car. It took him all of three trips. He had three
boys with him to help." I shook my shirt in the cooling air and
walked to my room. "And I know where he got those blocks,
too. There is a construction going on right now at engineering
school. They have a pile of adobe blocks there as high as the
Cheops. You can't miss it. You see it from the busline every
time." In my room, the strains of piano music didn't reach
sustainedly.

Belle had followed me into my room. "They have marked
off boundaries," she said. "They have defined limits."

I folded my shirt about the back of my armchair. "So they
have," I said. "So they have." My undershirt was wet, too. I
yanked it off.

"It is all as if they have put up a fence," Belle said.

"Fences make good neighbors," I said. I whipped the apple-green towel off the T-bar and rubbed myself briskly.

"It might as well be the great wall of China," Belle said.

"Well, no, not really," I said. "It is not as bad as that." I returned the towel to the crossbar. I looked around for a dry undershirt but did not find any. I went to the bedroom where my clothes closet was. Belle followed me. There was no light in the closet. The bulb hadn't been changed since it went bad shortly after we moved into the cottage. I fumbled in the dark feeling with my fingers. In the darkness in the closet the strains of the piano came steadily, strong and clear.

"She is no Turk but she keeps playing the Turkish March," Belle said.

I knew where my undershirts would be and it didn't take me long to find them with my hands. I pulled one out and was putting it on while I walked back to the *sala*.

"It is unkind, inconsiderate, not neighborly, not nice," Belle said.

I stopped beneath the light in the narrow passage from the bedroom to the *sala* between the book-closets and the bathroom, one arm through one armhole, half out of the *sandow* shirt the neck of which I held open with my hands. I looked at Belle. "Come again, Belle?" I asked.

Belle said again the denunciatory words.

I got my head through the neck opening and, jabbing my other arm through the other armhole, got into the shirt. I walked on to the *sala*. I didn't know how tired I was until I fell back on the lounging chair.

Belle picked up the footstool, brought it near my chair and sat down. "The least thing they could have done was to tell us first about it."

I felt very tired and shut my eyes and didn't say anything.

"Don't you think they owed it to us?" Belle asked. "Out

of regard for our feelings shouldn't they have asked us how we feel about a fence?"

The piano music threaded through the words like a leit-motif. "How is that again, Belle?" I asked.

"They have no regard for us," Belle said. "They don't care what we think. They don't think we feel. As far as they are concerned, we are not human."

The piano came jubilantly threading through the words.

"Is that right, Belle?" I asked.

"Don't you think they should at least have gone to us and said: Look here, you! We are putting up this boundary, see? You keep to your side of these markers and we will keep to ours, understand?" Belle asked.

"Do you really think that?" I asked.

"Yes, I do," Belle said. "Distinctly. Don't you?"

"I don't know," I said. "I haven't thought about it."

"Well, then," Belle said, "think about it. You can start thinking about it now."

I wondered why now the words came ringing clear to me. Then I felt and sensed that the piano had been stilled. Suddenly the night was silent; suddenly the air was still.

I rose from the lounging chair. I walked to the globe-traveler near the wall outlet, plugged the cord in and snapped the lid open. Belle followed me. I was playing the range disc for music when Belle leaned forward and snapped the lid shut.

"What's the matter, Belle?" I asked.

"There's nothing the matter," Belle said.

"Well, then, get off," I said. "Get off them and get off me."

Belle was silent for a moment. Then: "It is she," she said.

"What about her?" I asked.

"I don't think she likes me," Belle said.

"She doesn't like anyone," I said. "What makes you think so?"

"I have given her things," Belle said. "They don't seem to make an impression on her. I gave her cheese on her last birthday. She didn't even thank me."

"Why do you have to go around giving people things for?" I asked. "Maybe she doesn't like cheese. Maybe the cheese wasn't such a good idea."

"She doesn't like me," Belle said. "And she doesn't like anyone to like me. When he gave me flowers from her garden, I didn't think she liked that."

"Who would?" I asked. "Maybe the flowers wasn't such a good idea either."

"He was only being friendly as I was," Belle said.

"Oh, yes," I said.

"He was only being neighborly as I believe in being," Belle said.

"Sure, sure," I said.

"But she doesn't want to be and I don't think she believes in being," Belle said. "And I don't think she wants him to be either."

"Oh, well, Belle," I said. "I don't really know them. It is you they really know."

"Oh, you do, too," Belle said. "You ride with them too sometimes."

"I did that only once," I said. "I rode with them on the front seat. She tapped him on the thigh when she got off at Pavilion 2. That was the last time."

"Did that bother you?" Belle asked.

"Not that in itself," I said. "Only the demonstrativeness: as if to show that she is his and he is hers."

"What about the demonstrativeness of her puttering about her flower garden in very short shorts?" Belle asked.

"I don't like demonstrativeness," I said. "Moving here wasn't my idea."

"It was as much yours as it was mine," Belle said.

"When you visited this area for the first time to look at these cottages, did you have to ride with him in the car?" I asked.

"He was going to look at the cottages himself," Belle ssaid. "He was only being friendly."

"And the second time you looked at the cottages, was he looking at the cottages too—and the third time?" I asked.

"That was for our going to be neighbors," Belle said.

"There are forty cottages in this area," I said. "Why did we have to pick this one right up next to theirs?"

"It was as much your choice as it was mine," Belle said.

"So it was," I said. "So it can't be helped."

"No, it can't," Belle said.

"All right, then. Get off. Get off them and get off me," I said.

"But you must do something," Belle said.

"What about?" I asked.

"They didn't set the adobe markers right," Belle said. "They have been laid nearer our cottage than theirs. Their half of the lawn is bigger than ours."

"Is that right?" I asked. I walked to the window. It wasn't too dark to see the adobe markers gleaming in the ghostly light. I saw the flowers, too—the roses, the zinnias, the dahlias, the African daisies—swaying like specters in the night. Walking back to my chair, I looked up at the wall clock. It was getting on a quarter to nine. The clock began to chime just as I got to the lounging chair. I sat down and put my feet up on the stool.

"Their half of the lawn is bigger than ours," Belle said.

"Maybe they need all the lawn they can get so she can plant them all to flowers," I said.

"They haven't divided the lawn fairly," Belle said.

"You mean the halves are not equal? The halves are not halves?" I asked.

"What's the matter with you?" Belle said.

"What's the matter with him?" I asked. "Isn't he a doctor of mathematics or something? A fine doctor of mathematics he's turned out to be if he can't even divide by two!"

"What's eating you?" Belle asked.

"Maybe he should have brought a survey team with him and used a transit, a plumbline and a pole," I said. "Maybe he could divide by two then. Maybe he could even divide by ten."

"Don't tell me," Belle said. "Tell him. Tell them."

"For crying out loud," I said.

"Go ahead," Belle said. "Go over. Tell them off. Tell them where to get off."

"Get off, Belle," I said. "Get off them."

"If you won't, I shall," Belle said.

"Get off me," I said.

"If you don't, I shall," Belle said. "I shall right now." She started for the door.

"For crying out loud, Belle," I said. "I don't know them well enough to speak to them. I shall write them a note."

"All right," Belle said.

The portable typewriter was in its case under my bed. I set it up at the head of the dining table. When I pulled my hands away from lifting the case, they were covered with dust. I removed the lid but didn't take the machine off its base. The inside corners of the lid were spun with cobwebs. There were webs between the machine and the ridges of the base. I couldn't find any white paper anywhere so I decided to use one sheet from the legal size pad of ruled yellow paper.

I didn't date the note. I made it short and to the point. It was fascinating to watch the keys falling forward and then back leaving the black marks on the yellow sheet. As I typed I heard the opening bars of *Marriage of Figaro* from the high fidelity radio-phonograph next door.

("Mathematics and Mozart," I said. "Mozart and mathematics.")

I typed on my name but didn't sign it. When I saw that I had not quite filled half the sheet, I folded it once and tore it in half; I fed the clean half back to the machine and handed the other half to Belle. "There you are," I said. "Short and sweet: I hope he likes it."

Belle read the note. After she finished, she didn't say a word. "Is it all right?" I asked.

"Yes," Belle said. "Then send it off," I said.

"All right," Belle said. She called Nata and had the note delivered at once.

I didn't get to hear Mozart to the end that night. About halfway through the opera (that would be after Face I of the long-playing record), the player was snapped off. Then I saw him leave their cottage.

I sat up erect in my chair and watched his head bob up and down as he walked out to Finchshafen road. When he turned up the road and I knew where he was going, I stood up. I walked to the screen door and watched him walk up the concrete walk to the porch steps. He stopped at the foot of the stairs. I looked down through the wire screen at his upturned face.

"Yes?" I asked.

"Can I see you for a minute?" he asked.

"Me?" I asked

"Yes. You," he said.

"Won't you come up?" I asked.

"No," he said. "I'd much rather talk to you on the street."

"All right," I said. "If that's the way you feel about it."

I joined him at the foot of the porch steps. We walked down the cement walk together. As soon as we went past the shelter of the cottage, a blast of cold night air struck my face. I felt my left cheek twitching.

"Yes?" I asked. "What's on your mind?"

We walked down Finchshafen road. He didn't say anything for a long time. I looked at him. I waited. I had never spoken to him before. He considered a long time, long enough for me to be able to look back at the house to see if Belle was at the window watching.

When he spoke, his first words were: "Have you and Belle been fighting?" It was not only the words; it was also the way he said them: my left cheek was twitching so badly it was almost spastic. He had spoken so softly and in such a low-pitched voice I barely heard him. It was as if he didn't wish either his house or my house to hear; as if we were conspirators both and we were plotting a conspiracy together.

"Fighting?" I asked. "What about? What for? What are you talking about?" I sought his face for the guilt that could only be the mirror of the guilt in my own.

We stood on Finchshafen road halfway between our cottages; were we waiting to catch the guilt upon our faces which nonetheless we were mortally afraid to see? I stood on the upper slope of the road towards our house and he stood on the lower slope in the direction of his.

"Your note wasn't very friendly," he said. "It wasn't very neighborly."

"Why should it be?" I added. "It wasn't meant to be."

"Oh, so," he said. "It wasn't meant to be."

"You bet your life it wasn't," I said.

"Well, if that's the way you feel about it," he said.

"How else did you expect me to feel?" I asked.

"In that case then," he said, "you can appeal to authority and I shall not move the adobe blocks an inch."

"For Christ sake," I said. "Who is talking about authority? Who is talking about adobe blocks?"

"Don't raise your voice," he said.

"Why shouldn't I raise my voice?" I asked.

"Don't shout at me," he said.

"I shall shout at you if I please," I said.

It was a cool clear lovely night. The sky was clear and cool and full of stars. The sky and the stars seemed very far away but the air was clear and you could see all the way up to the sky and the stars and it seemed a long, long way. There was a very pale moon and a very cool wind and the wind was sweeping the pale moon and the white clouds before it all the way across the sky.

Across and up and down Finchshafen road in the cottages, people were coming out on to their porches to listen and to watch. I looked back at our house to see if Belle was there standing behind the window wirescreen and I looked at their house too.

"A plague on both our houses," I said.

Belle wasn't on the porch when I looked; I didn't hear her go down the porch steps, down the concrete walk, out to and down Finchshafen road.

"I shouldn't even be talking to you; this is pestilence," I said.

I didn't feel Belle around until I heard her voice rising shrill and clear above the snarl of our voices. She was standing beside me and before him and shouting in his face.

"For Christ sake, Belle," I said. "This is man's work."

Belle didn't hear me. She couldn't hear me. She was deaf, deaf with the fury that possessed her purely.

She had her face thrust outwards. She held her arms rigidly to her sides as if it were all she could do to keep them there, to keep them from rising and striking out. Her eyes— they never wavered, they never lifted from the face that they regarded—were flashing and her face was pale white. Her voice and her body both were shaking.

"For Christ sake, Belle," I said. "Let go. This is man's work."

She couldn't hear me.

Her voice rose clear and passionate, piercing and shrill in the inviolate night. I pulled at her arm to make her turn to me. I thrust my face savagely before her.

"For Christ sake, Belle," I said. "Get off. This is my fight and the adversary is mine."

Belle couldn't see me for the fury that possessed her purely.

I sought her face but couldn't look there long. Even as I turned away I had a fleeting glimpse of my declared adversary's face: the shock there was not more than the shock on mine.

"For Christ sake, Belle, let go. This is man's work. I have met the enemy and he is mine. Let go, get off. This is my fight —not yours. The enemy is mine," I said as I pulled at her and dragged her bodily away.

HERMEL A. NUYDA [1919–]

Hermel Nuyda is the son of Congressman Justino Nuyda, from Camalig, Albay. In order to practice law in the capital, Hermel Nuyda left the shadow of volcanic Mount Mayon, in Albay peninsula which extends southeast of Manila. After teaching social sciences for six years, he became an assistant to the Senate president and eventually a long-term technical assistant to the Senate Committee on Commerce and Industry. His duties have included drafting various economic control measures, the Philippine Government Reorganization Act of 1954, and especially laws implementing the revised trade agreement between the United States and the Republic of the Philippines. Under the new trade laws less protection is given to Philippine products through gradual suspension of American tariffs, but a wider latitude of crop-raising and manufacturing is encouraged, as well as greater flexibility in securing overseas markets.

When politics is not in season, Nuyda has published over twenty short stories. He has plans for a series of political novels, including one called *Fat of the Land,* whose appreciation of American aid has been influenced in part by his wife, Evelyn Rollins Suntay, an American. His brother, D'jahlma, is professor of cardiography at Marquette University.

PULSE OF THE LAND

THE AMERICAN was thirsty; very thirsty. The water jug had been emptied of its contents a mile back and, but for the assurance of his guide that they would find water in one of the huts scattered about the vicinity, he would have turned back and called it a day.

"You mean to tell me people actually live on this volcano?" he said, wiping the sweat off his forehead with the back of his hand. Although the morning was still early, already the sun had reddened his lean face, and his shirt was wet with sweat.

"Yes," the guide informed him. "People have been living on it for years." The guide was a short fellow and for every step the American took he took two. But there was power in his arms and legs, and he could speak English.

"But I understand this is an active volcano," the American said. "What happens to the people when it erupts?"

"That happens very seldom," the guide said, "and when it does they seek refuge in safer places. Then they come back after the eruption is over."

"Isn't that something!" the American said. "Well, tell me —how do they go about making a living?"

"They plant in the daytime," the guide explained, "and make charcoal at night. It is their fires you see at the foot of the mountain after dark."

The American shook his head. "What an odd way to live," he said.

"Have you stayed long in the country?" the guide asked in turn.

"Three months," the American answered. "Manila." This reminded him of the book he was writing about the country, of Manila and its populace. He smiled to himself. As he walked he thought of the pictures he had taken; the biting wit of the captions he had given them. That one about the market place, for instance: *"Native wares of all kinds, and one hundred odors for every one hundred yards."* Or that one about the street scene: *"And we can talk about the gals, and the smells, and the cartellas, and the smells, and the caribou carts, and the smells."* His was going to be some travel book! It was going to turn the country inside out, and the essence of it he would unfold by a few lines on the cover: *"If all the negatives I've shot in Manila were laid end to end, they would serve no lawful purpose. But, printed here, they'll serve to remind you that East is East and West is West, and I'll take North Overshoe, Nebraska."* He would be denounced; he could not help that. He had decided to tell the truth. *"Confused—not a trace of individuality—sadly wanting in sincerity and in clarity of purpose—a flax seed caught in the meeting of the winds—"* Such was his impression of the twenty-two million. Perhaps they would hate him for it, but it would not be his fault.

"Are you staying longer in the country?" the guide's voice broke into his reverie.

"Stay longer here?" he repeated. "No, no, I've stayed long enough. In fact I should be on my way back to the States, you know, but the fame of your Mayon Volcano altered my plans. I had to see the cone for myself."

The barking of dogs meant that they had come upon a dwelling. That meant water too.

When they reached the clearing where a hut squatted on the dry earth, two lean dogs bared their fangs at them so that they had to stop on the trail until a small boy (he could

not have been more than eight years old) backed off slowly
toward the hut, staring at them as he did, with timidity and
fright.

When the American grinned, the boy smiled back; and
his hands inched their way to cover his front which was un-
covered from the waist down. The boy stood thus for several
seconds: shoulders hunched, arms straight across the belly,
and the hands slipped in between the thin dark legs. Then he
ran up the low steps of the hut and almost immediately came
down again, this time followed by a young girl dressed in a
red chemise, a little taller than he was and, by her looks, no
doubt his sister.

The girl stared at the American in very much the same
manner as did her brother a moment before: shy, withdrawing.
She had long stringy hair, and her smile was pleasant; she kept
biting at her fingers as she looked at the strangers.

As the two children stood by their squalid hut: the boy
awkwardly shielding his nakedness with his hands, and the
girl, giggling, biting her fingers, the long stringy hair rubbing
against her scant red garment: the American thought they
made such splendid subjects for a candid shot! Without their
knowing it, he took their picture. The caption flashed in his
mind: *"The Slops of Mt. Mayon."*

The American told the guide to see if there was water in
the house and if they could be spared some. The guide talked
to the children in the dialect.

"May we have some water?" he inquired.

The small girl nodded and said: "I will get some." She
hurried up into the hut.

The two men walked to a bamboo bench. As the American straddled the bench, the little boy edged near him. The
American laughed and said: "Hello, boy, what's your name?"
The boy shook his head and, covering his cheeks with his
two hands, ran up into the hut. He disappeared for a brief

spell. Then slowly his head stuck out in the doorway, his big black eyes looking at the American excitedly. "Well, how do you like that!" the American exclaimed.

"They have not seen an American before," the guide explained.

"They're cute," the American observed as he looked at the little boy's face, at the same time peering into the interior of the hut which was almost bare except for a frail-looking bamboo stool, a crudely-fashioned weaving loom, a mat rolled up and laid against a corner, and a calendar with the picture of a saint nailed on the bamboo wall.

The girl came out with a black earthen bowl filled with water.

At first she made signs of giving it to the American, but on second thought, she turned to the guide and gave him the bowl instead. The guide handed the bowl to the American who took it, gave it a careful look, and before raising it to his lips, asked: "Think it's safe?"

"They drink it," the guide said.

The American saw the boy and the girl watching him with great interest. They were smiling at him as if their not doing so would offend him and make him decide not to drink the water. "Oh, well," he said, and raised the bowl to his lips.

The American gargled wiith his first gulp. He gargled with the second and the third. He gargled with half the contents of the bowl, the water he spat out forming a dark splotch on the dry earth. The next half he drank. The water was cool, sweetish, with a queer but pleasant smell. He liked it. He smiled at the girl and asked for more by holding up an index finger and nodding his head at the same time. The girl understood and returned his nod gleefully. She went into the hut once more, the boy running after her. "How white he is," she said, looking back as if to make sure the strangers had not decided to leave. "And big. How big!" exclaimed the boy.

The American drank half of the next bowl of water. The rest he offered to the guide. When the latter had finished drinking, the small boy suddenly jumped down the low steps and grabbed the bowl from him. Then with great excitement the boy faced the American, holding up his little index finger, his head nodding up and down, trying to ask if the tall white man wanted one more.

The American grinned and nodded back.

Proudly the boy went up the steps, laughing at his sister and sticking out the tip of his tongue at her as he passed by. When he came back, he walked very carefully, holding the bowl as if he were carrying the world in his hands. He pursed his lips, gave his sister a triumphant wink and, trembling, raised the bowl to the big white man.

For the third time the American took the black earthen bowl. But this time he did not drink. He stepped out into the yard and poured the water over his head, his face. After he finished he threw the rest of the water on the ground. Then he gave the bowl to the boy and sat on the bench once more.

"How come," he asked the guide, "these kids are alone in such a wild place?"

"They are used to it," the guide answered. "Their folks must be somewhere near, planting or looking for greens to eat." And to the girl, "Where are your parents?"

"In the *camote* patch," the girl replied. Then she walked straight to a jackfruit tree by the edge of the clearing, from which an empty bomb shell was hung. From the foot of the tree she took an iron rod with which she struck the shell five times. It made a sound clear as a church bell.

"That's one of our shells," the American observed. "How on earth did it ever get here?"

"Many of those were dropped on the towns," the guide explained, "before your soldiers came."

Shortly after the last impact of metal against metal, a

woman's voice came from way back of the clearing. A little later an old woman rushed into view. A strip of cloth was tied around her head and in her right hand was clutched a bolo smudged with fresh soil. When she saw the two men seated on the bench, she stopped and stared at them, her face tense and drawn. It was only after the children had talked to her that the tension on her face disappeared. She approached the two men and nodded politely to them.

"We came to ask for water," the guide said.

"We have water," the old woman answered and addressed the girl: "Go get the men water."

"They have already given us enough," the guide said.

"Are you sure? You must excuse these children if they have been rude. They are young and do not know much. Perhaps they did not even ask you to come up into the house?"

"That is all right," the guide assured her. "We are only resting for a while."

"I am glad it is all right. They are my grandchildren, you know, and there is only me to teach them what is right. Their father and mother died two years ago."

"The children have been good," the guide said.

The old woman looked at the American, and when she saw that he was looking at her, listening to her talk, she tried in the least noticeable way she could to rub the earth off her hands with her faded skirt. Then to the guide she said: "Where are you bound for?"

"He wants to go up the volcano," the guide replied, looking at the American.

"Why should he want to do that?" the woman asked. "There are no people living there."

"He is a visitor to our land," the guide explained. "And he wants to take pictures."

"Oh," the woman said. "Well, tell him that we are very

sorry it is only water we can give. But if he can wait, I can fry some *camotes* in a short time."

"What's she saying?" the American interrupted, conscious that he was the subject of their conversation.

"She says she is sorry the children did not ask you to come up into the house, and she is ashamed she can only offer water. But if you care to wait she could fry sweet potatoes."

"Oh no," the American objected, shaking his head. "Tell her not to do that. And thank her for me."

The guide conveyed the American's words.

"Well then," the woman said, "you must take some water with you. It is hot and you will be thirsty on the way." Then she picked up the empty water jug. "Is this for water?" she asked. The guide nodded. Without speaking further the woman went into the hut, taking each rung very slowly and with the same leading foot. She was gone for only a short time.

"Here," she said when she came back to the doorway. "It is full." The guide took the water jug.

The American stood up and thrust his hand into his pocket for some loose change, but as he did so, the woman shook her head and frowned. The American withdrew his hands slowly from the pocket and smiled his thanks instead, after which he bowed to her, nodded to the children, and walked out of the clearing. He looked back once and saw the three of them still looking at him; their lean dogs lapping the dark splotch formed by the water he had spat on the earth.

How far they had walked the American could not exactly tell. The guide said they had covered two miles from the hut. To him it seemed much more. But he did not care. The feeling inside him as he stood on the huge rock was well worth the cuts on his arms, the long uphill trek, the descent into the steep ravines and the arduous walk over their beds of rock and sand, the blistering heat of the noonday sun.

From where he stood, the peak of the volcano, although it had lost the smoothness of its contours, loomed before him like a tower in the sky: powerful in its ruggedness, immutable in its lordship over the land below—a sentinel keeping vigil over the brown and green of the plains, the blue of the distant mountain ranges, and the dull gray of the sea beyond them.

He breathed deeply of the cool air, feeling as big as the vastness of it all. Then he took his camera and set to work. He shot as many negatives from as many angles as suited his critical eye. Then he walked to where the guide was resting and said: "Nature has been most generous to your country. You should take pride in the beauty of your land."

"It is high noon," the guide remarked casually. "It is bad to let hunger pass."

They ate in silence.

Half an hour later the American decided it was time to go back.

"If you do not mind walking up a little more," the guide suggested, "There is a better way back."

"Lead on," the American said. "You're the guide."

They walked uphill for several minutes along the edge of a deep ravine until they came upon a trail that led to its bottom. This they followed. The trees were bigger and their foliage greener than those at the foot of the mountain. Around them they could hear the soft cooing of wild doves.

When they got to the bottom of the ravine, the American saw a group of people huddled on the other side of the ravine where the opposite cliff cast its shade. He could make out an old man sitting on a stone, some women squatting on the sand, and several children grouped in a circle playing with pebbles. Propped against the cliff, some pillowed on stones, were long bamboo tubes.

"What are all these people doing here?" the American asked the guide, wondering. "And what are the bamboos for?"

"The people are waiting for their turns," the guide explained. "The tubes are for fetching water."

"Water?" said the American, surprised. "How on earth could they get water from such a dry place? I don't see any sign of it anywhere."

"This place is called 'Tagdo.' In English it means 'drops.' It is the only place where folks for miles around can find water to drink. But go ahead," the guide suggested, "and take a look for yourself."

The American decided to do that. Curiously he walked toward the people who stared at him as he passed, smiled past them and looked for the source of the water.

What he saw startled him.

In the hard rock which was the base of the cliff was a very small well about six inches deep and a foot across. It was not a spring. Water did not come from under it but flowed into it over an inch-wide strip of banana leaf which was so arranged as to receive the weak flow of a very tiny stream formed by little drops of moisture. They came from the moss clinging to the rock and to the protruding roots of trees growing alongside the cliff. The American watched the tiny stream trickle over the banana leaf and flow into the well. He watched for a long time; saw the old man scoop the water up carefully with a coconut shell and pour it into his bamboo tube.

The American stood there, just watching, forgetting for the moment who he was, why he was there. "Twenty minutes," he said aloud to himself. "It would take twenty minutes to fill the well and four wells-full to fill the tube." Slowly he took his gaze off the well, and facing about, saw the people were watching him, smiling politely at him.

As he stared at them, searching into their brown faces for what he did not know, a small boy naked from the waist down broke out from the group of children and in a streak was at the well holding the coconut shell in his hand and twiddling the index finger of the other, his head nodding up and down, up and down. The American stared at him. He stared good and hard, and felt the blood creeping up his back, his shoulders, his face. Never before had he felt such dryness in his throat. There was no mistaking that ever-ready smile, those big black eyes, the eager nodding of the familiar head.

The American's white hand slowly found its way to the boy's hunched shoulder and, forgetting that the boy could not understand his language, blurted: "You mean you walk all that distance and get your water here too?"

Surprisingly the boy understood. He gave his biggest smile and nodded, his eyes gleaming with elation as he glanced about at the women, at his little friends, for his having been recognized and talked to by this tall white man. Then he pointed to a long-haired girl in red chemise hugging a bamboo tube twice her own length and smiling with her fingertips in her mouth.

As the American silently watched the scene before him, the guide approached him and softly asked: "Would you like to take a picture?"

GLOSSARY

Abah! — interjection of surprise or mild disgust.

adelante — a command to move forward.

adlo — Visayan term for scad fish.

adobo — fried chicken or pork, seasoned with vinegar and garlic.

Aling — title: Miss or Mrs.

andadasi — coarse, branched shrub in the Ilocos, often planted for medicinal properties or for ornamentation.

andohao — Visayan term for chub mackerel.

anito — transcendent power, usually benevolent; includes ancestral spirits.

anting-anting — talisman; charm for the wearer's protection.

antipara — goggles.

arrabal — suburbs.

arrais — Ilocano term for aromatic plant sometimes used for medicine.

balangot — hat made from thin strips of palm.

balaye — an in-law.

banca — long boat dug out of single log, with or without outrigger; propelled by oar.

barangay — Malayan term originally applied to one boatload of immigrants, family-size; now a village whose chief (*cabeza*) is equivalent to a *teniente del barrio*.

barong Tagalog — formal long-sleeved male shirt of sheer fabric, woven from pineapple or banana fiber, silk, etc.

baroto — dugout canoe with outrigger.

barrio — small unit of government, its officials appointed by the town or municipality to which constitutionally it is attached although from which it may be fifteen difficult miles distant.

batel — small, one-masted interisland cargo ship, carrying some passengers.

bolo — blade three feet long, used as weapon or farm implement.

buntal — tan, high crowned hat woven from dried palm leaves.

bunuan — wooden fish trap.

buri — species of palm whose material is woven into rough mats or hats.

buyo — leaf in which portions of betel nut and lime are rolled; the concoction is chewed like tobacco and its juices spat out.

Ca — Ilocano term of respect for elders.

cabonegro — large sugar palm, called "black rope" on account of its long leaves and trunk; it yields sugar, starch, alcohol, thatch, etc.

cacique — originally a Haitian term applied by the Spanish to *datus* or others of the economic-social aristocracy, in recognition of their continued support (as tax collectors, etc.) of the Spanish colonials.

calesa — semi-enclosed, horse-drawn vehicle for two passengers.

camachile — tree with long green and red, bean-shaped fruits which open when ripe.

camino real — royal highway; main road.

camisa — loose blouse.

camisa de chinos — thin, collarless shirt.

camote — sweet potato.

cara y cruz — game: heads or tails.

carretela — open horse-drawn vehicle for nine passengers, arranged on three benches.

cavan — large jute sack of rice.

champaca — hairy tree with fragrant yellow flowers used for garlands.

chichirika — reddish plant often placed as a border.

chupa — a small measure, one-third of a *ganta*, less than two per cent of a *cavan*.

constabulario — constabulary: national army for internal peace and order.

copra — dried coconut meat.

dalapang — unwieldy outriggerless *banca*.

dangla —aromatic shrub, in Ilocos, often used by *herbolarios* for medicinal purposes: for headaches; as antitoxin against poisonous bites, etc.

datu — ancient Malayan term for chieftain; current now only among Moslems.

duhat — black cherry.

dungon — timber tree widely used for pilings, bridges, wharves. Tannin from the bark is used to toughen fishnets; and the seeds are eaten with fish.

Ermita — a district in Manila famous for fine embroidery in Spanish times and now a fashionable shopping and residential area.

gangsa — brass gong used by northern mountain tribes and by Moros as musical accompaniment to folk dance.

ganta — one twenty-fifth of a *cavan* or large sack of rice.

gogo bark — yard-long strips of bark from *gogo* tree used for shampooing.

hangaray — Visayan term for shrub often found along swift streams; its roots are useful as an emetic.

hinagdong — small tree characteristic of second-growth forests. The wood is sometimes made into rope or into wooden shoes (*bakya*).

Hoy — equivalent to "Hey!"

indios — in Spanish times, natives of the Philippines as distinguished from Spaniards born in the Philippines and called Filipinos.

ipil-ipil — a hardwood tree.

Itay — Father.

jusi — sheer fabric made of banana fiber and woven, in the Visayan home industry, beneath nets so that wind cannot entangle threads.

kaingin — system of farming in which clearings are made by burning parts of the forest.

kaltang — wide-mouthed grouper, with sharp pointed teeth.

kangkong — succulent plant that grows in swamps; its tender tips are used as a vegetable.

lamparilla — kerosene lamp.

lapu-lapu — brightly colored sea bass or grouper, often found among coral reefs.

lauan — a hardwood; teak.

lechonada — feast in which pig is roasted on outdoor spit and is main course.

Mabuhay! — a cheer: "long life!"

macopa — spreading tree with clusters of red, bell-like fruit.

Manding — title of respect for elder sister.

mano a mano — blow for blow, when threshing rice with hand pestles.

Manong — elder brother; or title of respect for elder comrade.

maya — small brown rice-bird.

maya-maya — red snapper, a fish.

mestiza — originally the offspring of any *indio* and a foreigner, whether Spanish or Chinese.

municipio — municipality or town.

Naku! —interjection of surprise or disbelief; shortened form of "*Ina ko*": "Mother of mine!"

naman — interjection expressing objection; equivalent to "Enough of that!"

narra — the national hardwood tree.

nipa — palm used for walls and roof of bamboo houses.

nito — black pliant vine or scrambling fern that overgrows shrubs and trees. Parts are sometimes applied to venomous bites.

noroeste — nor'wester.

P.C. — Philippine Constabulary.

palay — unhusked rice grain.

palmabrava — hardwood palm often used for canes or pillars because of high polish; sometimes the leaves are sewn into a kind of rain cape.

pandan — plant with aromatic leaves.

papaya — fruit of plant that grows like coconut, with leaves on long stems at the top of a pulpy trunk.

parao — dugout with outrigger and sail.

pasacalye — musical prelude.

patadiong — wraparound skirt of native weave, reaching below knees.

pensionado — anyone supported by the government, but usually the recipient of a state award for study abroad.

piyapi — tree identifiable by its many air roots, found on the outer fringe of swamps; used for rice mortars or for smoking fish.

población — municipality, with self-elected officials.

rajita — swampland tree used for firewood.

Sakdal — Popular Front movement in the thirties, chiefly among tenant farmers.

samaral — black flat fish with white spots; a scavenger.

santol — tree with five-seeded fruit.

sawali — bamboo strips, often used for walls of house.

sentimiento — spreading sensitive plant, often a yard long; its leaflets fold when touched.

sinta — part of harness.

sinvergüenza — shameless.

sulambi — extension of a hut, often used as a sleeping area.

Susmariosep! — ejaculation of surprise; abbreviation of "Jesus, Mary, Joseph."

tamarind — tree with fruits resembling flat beans and which have a sweet-sour taste.

tampipi — luggage woven of palm leaves and composed of two sections which fit into each other like a box.

tangal — small tree found abundantly in mangrove swamps; the bark is used to stop hemorrhages and ulcers or is added to *tuba*.

Tatay — Father.

teniente del barrio — unpaid chief of barrio; appointed by municipal councilor.

Tía; Tío — Aunt; Uncle.

tienda — small retail store.

tuba — fermented juice gathered from coconut trees; the sap.

THE EDITOR

Leonard Casper was born in Fond du Lac, Wisconsin, in 1923. His three academic degrees are from the University of Wisconsin. An associate professor in creative writing and contemporary American literature at Boston College, Dr. Casper has been a member of the faculties of the University of Wisconsin and Cornell University. In the summer of 1962 he entered upon a Fulbright lectureship in Filipino-American Studies at Ateneo de Manila and the University of the Philippines, where he had taught in 1953-56.

Casper is editor of *Six Filipino Poets* (Manila, 1955) and co-editor with Thomas A. Gullason of *The World of Short Fiction: An International Collection* (1961). He is author of *Robert Penn Warren: The Dark and Bloody Ground* (1960) and *The Wayward Horizon: Essays on Modern Philippine Literature* (1961). From 1954-61 he served as contributing foreign editor of the Manila monthly *Panorama,* and was guest editor in 1960 for a Philippine number of *The Literary Review.* He has written articles on Philippine culture for the *American Oxford Encyclopedia,* and for *Antioch Review, Saturday Review, Journal of Asian Studies* and other periodicals.

Some thirty short stories and about forty poems by Leonard Casper have appeared in quarterlies in America and abroad, as well as in O'Henry and Foley anthologies.